Finding
FREEDOM

Finding FREEDOM

SHARON L. DEAN

Encircle Publications

Farmington, Maine U.S.A.

Editor: Cynthia Brackett-Vincent

Cover design by Deirdre Wait
Cover images © Getty Images

Published by:

Encircle Publications
PO Box 187
Farmington, ME 04938

info@encirclepub.com
http://encirclepub.com

For my Massachusetts Family.

Contents

Every day is a journey, and the journey itself is home.
—Matsuo Basho

Chapter 1
Saying Goodbye

Connie looked away from the hole to a field studded with the large yellow blossoms of balsamroot. Mountains rising in the distance held onto spring green, and behind her, a grove of pines sheltered a woodpecker tapping a rhythmic accompaniment to the burial.

Stuart's was a green burial. But it didn't feel green to Connie. The hole was dark, the earth piled beside it a mound of blackness. The linen shroud that wrapped him was too rough. She thought of the graveyard in Massachusetts where she imagined her parents lying comfortably in their silk-lined coffins. After forty years, she still considered herself an Easterner, unlike Stuart, who'd been a man of the West. He'd loved the tiny village of Green Springs with its mixture of hippies and young environmentalists and recluses who preferred wildlife to the frenetic lives of those who lived downhill in Ashland. Expensive, artsy, tourist infested, he'd described the town.

Two men lowered the shrouded body and stood aside. She reached for Molly's hand and led her to the pile of earth next to the grave. The men waited discreetly to fill the hole. Connie took a shovel from one of them, handed it to Molly, and took another.

They had old lady hands, wrinkled and veined and dotted with blemishes. But strong, Molly's from years at a piano, Connie's from years in her garden. They began to fill the hole. Molly managed only a few scoops before she relinquished her shovel to one of the men. Connie kept scooping and throwing, each shovelful a memory of the years she'd spent with Stuart. Their meeting in Green Springs when he helped her find her Uncle Charlie's wife and their daughter Molly. Their first lovemaking that washed away the hurt that had led her to Oregon. The way he pretended to love the novels she wrote and the way she pretended to like how he played the banjo.

The second man tried to take the shovel from her. She motioned him away. She'd shovel until the hole was as full as her life with Stuart had been. She kneeled on the grave when she finished, running her hands through the earth. She whispered lines from Emily Dickinson, "Death leaves Us homesick." She wanted, like Dickinson, to go through "former Places... seeking." Seeking what? A return to the world she grew up in, to the graves of her ancestors and to her sister who still lived? Forty years ago, she was sure she'd never return. Now she wasn't so sure.

She stood and took packets of wildflower seeds from her pocket, handing one to Molly. Together, they dropped the seeds onto the fertile earth. When they finished, they walked along the path that led through the trees to the funeral car. The two men would take them to the inn where she first met Stuart and where mourners would join her, trading memories and condolences.

She squeezed Molly's hand. "I need to go back."

"Don't leave me at the inn. People make me nervous. Except for you and Stuart. I liked him."

It was more than that. Molly was a recluse, not violent like someone with an antisocial disorder, but definitely eccentric. Only after Connie met the woman who was her first cousin did

Molly invite anyone who wasn't a piano student into her house. "That's not what I meant. I need to go back. To Massachusetts."

"Why? This is your home."

"I don't know. I've been dreaming about Freedom ever since Stuart got sick. Something happened when I saw the shroud being lowered into the ground. Something about ashes to ashes. The call of my history. Massachusetts is my home soil. My ancestry. I may not stay, but I need to make my peace."

"With Sarah?"

"I made peace with my sister years ago. It's something else. I don't know what. It feels like something in my DNA. Want to come with me? The last adventure for two old women."

Molly dropped her hand. "This is my home. The farthest I've been from Green Springs in eighty years is Ashland. I couldn't do it." Her anxiety was palpable.

Connie made the offer, knowing she'd be glad when Molly refused. She wanted a last adventure, unburdened with a reclusive cousin. She hadn't another novel to write, but she could write *Travels with Connie*, proof that an eighty-year-old woman had more than grief in her life. She had strength and courage and curiosity. Stuart would have laughed her on her way.

She woke covered in sweat from the kind of dream she'd been having since she buried Stuart a year ago. She was falling over a cliff on the Green Springs road. At the base of the cliff were the bodies of Charlie and her mother. Her mother rose from the ground and showed the scar on her stomach. A schizophrenic voice seemed to talk to her, telling her she needed to go home. The voice didn't say where home was, and she didn't know.

She got out of bed, showered off her sweat, and made some coffee before finishing the little packing she had left. She closed her last suitcase and walked through the house for a final check. Coffee pot and toaster unplugged, blinds drawn halfway to block the midday sun, and light timers set so it would look like someone was home. She went outside and up the stairs to the balcony where she saw that a raccoon had pooped on her roof again. She raised one leg to the railing, then the other so that she sat facing the flat portion of the roof. When she jumped, she made sure to bend her knees so she landed softly. She swept droppings onto a mini-shovel, rested the shovel on the railing while she climbed back onto the balcony, and picked up the shovel to throw the droppings into the bushes. The process she'd perfected reminded her of shoveling dirt into Stuart's grave.

She pushed away her sadness by turning to look at the mountains. A week shy of eighty years old and she could still hike them. She was still the same five-foot-four with the same sturdy build she'd had at forty. Long ago, she'd made peace with her hundred and forty pounds. Her hair might be gray, but its shortcut had none of the dryness typical of old age. Genetics that gave her a tendency for depression also blessed her with physical health. The genes of an elite athlete, her "23 & Me" DNA report said. She'd laughed when she got that report, but admitted to feeling proud.

Tim opened the door to the apartment and moved beside her. He was good-looking in the way Stuart had been when she first met him. He built sets for the Oregon Shakespeare Festival and was a perfect tenant. She called on him whenever she needed a fence repaired so deer wouldn't invade her backyard, or a rat removed from the trap along the grapevines, or a tree branch trimmed so it wouldn't touch the house. Ashland was a city, but deer owned the streets, and bears found their way into neighborhood trees.

"Having second thoughts?" He propped a canvas bag on the railing.

"Not yet. I'm remembering what it was like when I rented the apartment you're in. Forty years ago. Ruthie was as old as I am now."

"Want to tell me about her?"

"She knew everything about Ashland. She had the kind of deep history I have for Freedom."

"You can't repeat the past. Isn't that what Gatsby said?"

"I think it was Nick Carraway." She ran her hand along the railing as if it were traveling the roads that would take her back to Massachusetts and the decision she'd have to make.

He held the bag toward her so she could see the Siskiyou Mountain image on the front. "Oregon goodies to remind you to come back."

"If I don't, there'll be so much raccoon poop on my roof, I'll have to hire a backhoe. I just shoveled off another pile."

He turned away from the view of the mountains and leaned over the opposite railing to inspect the roof. "You climbed over the railing again? You should call me."

"I'm still agile enough. I'm not ready to declare myself old yet."

"I'll check every day. Keep all the wild creatures at bay."

She thought about the way he helped her keep depression at bay. "You've been a wonderful friend."

"Don't talk like I'm past tense."

"You'll never be past tense. Sit down a minute. Let me see what you put into this bag." She directed him to the patio chairs and table that she'd managed to put together herself when she ordered them from a catalog. With metal supports painted a light green and angled to hold mesh seats and glass for the tabletop, they looked like something out of a space-age movie.

He took the items out one at a time and set them on the table. White wine from Upper Five Vineyards and red from Irvine and Roberts. "I'm carrying a case to your car. Don't drink more than half a bottle a day." He took out the next present. "Put this rubber stopper in the bottle and use the white tube to suck out all the air. The wine will keep for days."

Instead of telling Tim that she never drank alone, she said, "Thank you. I'll need some when I pick up Hannah in Minnesota."

"Hannah?"

"My niece Lizzie's daughter. She's about to turn thirteen."

"You didn't tell me that, but I'm glad. You won't have to drive the whole way alone." He reached into the bag and handed her a framed photograph. "This will keep you company."

A mixture of grief and shock pushed into her body. The picture showed her and Stuart standing in the hollowed trunk of a tree in Lithia Park. The tree looked like a throne, but she and Stuart didn't look royal. It was taken two years ago, just after Stuart was diagnosed with the leukemia that killed him. He still looked healthy, but both of them looked old. Gray, wrinkled, not the way she thought of herself. She took off her glasses and wiped them on her T-shirt. "We had a good run."

"Are you running away?"

"I was running away when I came to Ashland. My mother had died. My partner had abandoned me. My writing felt paralyzed. And look what I found." She put her glasses back on and gestured toward the view of the mountains.

"So why are you leaving?"

"I don't know if I'm leaving. I just know that I need to take one last road trip to visit Freedom again."

"Why not fly?"

"Flying's not an adventure. At least not a good one." She ran her hand over the photo that would keep her company on her trip, maybe drive away the demon dreams.

"Remember to come back." He took out the last items. A bag of Oregon hazelnuts, a jar of Oregon marionberry jam, a T-shirt labeled Oregon Shakespeare Festival, a hat from Sunday Afternoons shaped like a baseball hat, its thin fabric mottled in the soft hues of a sunrise over a Siskiyou peak. Each item reminded her of the life she'd built, and each 'thank you' came with the deep breath she used to keep from crying.

She stood and thanked Tim again as she put everything into the bag. He pushed his chair back, stood beside her, and gave her the bag. "I'll get the wine and meet you downstairs."

"Meet me at my car. I just have one suitcase to close." She descended the stairs alone. When she went inside, she locked the back door, checked the front door lock again, and went into her bedroom where her suitcase lay open, a copy of *East Angels* resting on top of enough clothes to take her to Lizzie's before she needed to do laundry. She felt a little like its author, Constance Fenimore Woolson, a woman who fought her demons by writing. Everett had given her the novel Woolson had written about the Florida swamps. Their affair had begun when they were canoeing in a Florida swamp and had grown like lush cypress trees and silvery moss. She'd long ago forgiven him, but she hadn't forgotten him. He and Stuart would drive with her, memories to guide her to Freedom.

She put the book into the bag with the photograph of her and Stuart, closed the suitcase, and brought both out the side door to her driveway where Tim waited beside her car. She locked the door to her house and pressed the key fob to unlock her car. Tim opened the trunk and found a spot for the case of wine next to a suitcase and a plastic storage box.

He closed the trunk. "I don't like what I see here."

"What do you mean?" she said as she put her smaller suitcase and canvas bag into the backseat next to a cooler.

"Too much luggage. Too long away."

"At least I don't have boxes of books to hawk, like when I stopped to give readings on my last cross-country trip."

"You should have some. People might recognize you."

"Doesn't matter. This is a trip for *me*, not 'me, the writer.'"

"When it was 'you, the writer,' you weren't as famous. Didn't a friend come with you?"

"Eva. We drove my yellow Volkswagen. We called it The Yellow Sub after the Beatles' song."

"Got a name for this car?"

"It was one of the last Honda Fits. Boring white, I'm afraid, but it's all the dealer had and it's a good car."

"Maybe you can call it Last Chance."

"I like it. Last Chance for an old lady finding freedom."

He gave her a hug strong enough that it felt like it might be his last before she died. She refused to think that way.

Chapter 2
Antelope Remembered

She slowed at a pull-off on the side of the road to let a car pass. Oregon 66 was steep and curvy, wooded on one side and open to a vista of mountains on the other. She often stopped at this section to think of the uncle she'd never met. Last night's dream reminded her that he'd fled the kind of demons that could have invaded her if she hadn't channeled them into her novels. Twenty-one novels, a Pen New England award, a Pulitzer for *Twenty Years a Wanderer*, which opened with her favorite image of a little girl chasing a robin in a cemetery. Her fan base rebelled when she announced that *Forty Years Found* would be her last novel. It got good reviews, but she felt trapped by the thought of writing another. Her imagination had been sucked as dry as the soil in the West.

She eased her car back onto the road. A deer ran in front of it, followed by two young ones who'd just lost their white fawn spots. She felt like those young deer, finding her way into a new world but without a mother to guide her. "Last Chance," she whispered as she passed the resort at Green Springs where she first met Stuart. A line outside the restaurant signaled its popularity in July. If she went in to say goodbye to the owners, she knew she'd have to listen to a lecture about being careful. There'd be an undercurrent of what she'd heard for the last month. An old woman shouldn't drive alone across the United States.

A mile beyond the resort, she slowed at Molly's driveway. If she stopped there, she'd be tempted. A different choice. Become a recluse. Use music to avoid anxiety, meet the outside world only by giving piano lessons to children. A black pickup truck behind her beeped to tell her to move on. She let the truck pass and ignored the finger the scraggly-looking driver raised at her. The fog of anxiety she'd been feeling since she said goodbye morphed into anger at drivers who hovered at the edge of road rage. She was ready to enjoy her last train, to drive Last Chance to glory or defeat.

Further along 66, the fog of anxiety she'd been feeling drifted into the fog of smoke blowing from a fire east of Klamath Falls. Every year it was the same. Drought and fire. If she made it through the great midsection of the United States without meeting a tornado, she'd welcome the humidity of an Eastern summer.

The smoke cleared after she turned onto Route 97 out of Klamath. Her navigation app said she had almost four hours to get to Antelope. She passed cars and campers filled with laughing families headed to recreation spots. After the city of Bend, traffic thinned out along with the disappearing trees. When she took the exit onto 293, she could have been in a different country. *Wild, Wild Country*, Netflix called it in a documentary about Baghwan Shree Rajneesh and his commune. Forty years ago, she embraced the idea of living peacefully on sixty thousand acres of ranchland. The commune nicknamed the land 'The Big Muddy' for the tiny creek that dried up every summer, and the town of Antelope was renamed Rajneeshpuram. When plots surfaced of poison and voter fraud that involved bussing homeless from the South to vote in Oregon, she abandoned her idea of an escape into a commune. The Baghwan wanted the money he imagined she was making as a writer. Likely he would have welcomed sexual favors.

Still, she wanted to see what had happened to the little town of Antelope. She turned off 293 onto 218, hoping to find the town's café resurrected. Any tourists enticed by the documentary would stop there.

A few houses lined the road but no one was outside sitting on a porch in the midday heat. The school, still painted a soft green, baked in the sun. She found her way to The Antelope Cafe and Store, where she and her friend Eva first encountered Sadhana, the Baghwan's chief *sannyasin*. The café was still a garish turquoise, but it looked like it had been abandoned for years. A woman stood in its shadow. The town was so deserted, she wondered if the woman needed help. Connie stopped, got out of her car, and approached her. "Can I help?"

The woman looked like a folksinger. Her dark hair was braided, and her multi-colored dress rippled in the wind. A guitar case lay close to her sandaled feet. "I'm waiting for my brother. He drove into The Big Muddy to see what's left of it." The woman's voice was a husky alto.

"It's a long way in. You must have been here for hours."

"I'd rather stay here even if it takes him all afternoon. I went in last year. Found some Christian summer camp. Another cult."

"Were you there when it was Rajneeshpuram?"

"From age five to seven."

Connie wanted to hear more about the commune that had almost sucked her in. "What was it like?"

"It was all we knew."

"We?"

"My brother and me. A hundred or so other kids." She

looked over the horizon to where Rajneeshpuram had risen in an impossibly short time from a landscape that shouldn't have supported more than free-range cattle. "We ran free. The older kids watched the younger ones."

"It sounds like it would be a great childhood."

"Not so much. The older kids were more interested in collecting snakes or bugs and trapping them in boxes where they'd fight their own species. One day—I was about six—I smoked a cigarette and got terribly sick. After that, my mother took me to the fields with her. I learned to pick strawberries, beans, whatever crop was coming in before it turned frigid in winter."

"I was there in 1982. What people were building was amazing. Everyone working together, celebrating together. I guess everything turned rotten toward the end."

"It did. You're lucky you didn't stay. I learned to meditate, to pump myself into a frenzy like some whirling dervish in a Dynamic Meditation. Only when we got out did I learn to read and do simple math."

"I'm surprised. So many of the sannyasins were educated. I think they'd want to educate their children." She noticed a trail of ants following each other. They were like the sannyasins, following their leader.

"They were too busy working. My mother lasted two years before she left with me and my brother. I should say she escaped. They didn't like people to leave."

Connie remembered the man she'd met in Ashland. Deepak. He was heading for Rajneeshpuram. When she tried to find him there, she found only an undercurrent that he had been disappeared. "How did you get out?"

"It was a broiling hot day, kind of like this one. My mother begged a ride from a man who had come for one of our retreats. He drove us as far as Portland. I think she paid him with sex because she spent the night in his motel room. In the morning, she bought us bus tickets to Eugene, and we stayed with my father's parents until she found a job."

"Did your father join you?"

"He was a true believer. He stayed until the end. He's somewhere in India now. Unless he's dead like my mother. My brother and I never hear from him. Cults take away all sense of family. You're a cog in the wheel of the many. Another little body running without boundaries. Survival of the fittest until the community reins you in."

A vehicle appeared along the road. It looked like her old Yellow Sub until it got closer and she could see that it was a camper van painted in blended colors of a sunrise.

The woman picked up her guitar. "That's my brother, Harshad. He kept the name they gave him in Rajneeshpuram. I didn't. I'm Barbara. I've erased all reminders of the cult."

The man who got out of the car wore a full beard and hair that hung down to his shoulders. In a tie-dye shirt and red linen pants, he looked like he was still a sannyasin. He took the guitar from his sister and turned his eyes on Connie. They looked like the eyes of a madman. Blue and glazed over, as if he were seeing something that wasn't there.

"You harassing my sister?" he said in a voice that would have been incantatory if it hadn't sounded threatening.

"I stopped when I saw her standing here alone. How was The Big Muddy? I was there years ago. I met a man there named Harshad. I wonder if you're his son."

"Lots of men with that name. Rajneeshpuram is gone. With the wind." He motioned at the wind that was blowing over the open land. "If you were there, you weren't a kid like us."

She stepped further away from him. "I was about your age. I didn't stay."

13

"Neither did it." He lifted his head toward Rajneeshpuram. "If it had survived, I would have come back after our mother dragged us away." He turned his head toward Connie's car. "You travelling alone?"

"I am. I don't have much further to go today. I'm staying in Fossil." She wanted him to think she was expected somewhere.

"I'm on at five o'clock," Barbara said at the same time Harshad said, "You don't look like you're camping."

She had no idea what they were talking about. When she didn't respond, Barbara said, "There's a bluegrass festival all weekend. Best in the state."

"I didn't know that." She should have done more research. All she'd planned on was a visit to Antelope and an overnight stay in the closest town.

"Hope you got a reservation somewhere," said Harshad. "Woman like you traveling alone needs to be careful."

Connie felt his eyes on her body. He meant an old woman. She pressed her key fob and moved toward her car. "My partner plays a mean bluegrass banjo." She used the present tense as if it could protect her from men with mad eyes and the isolated road that lay before her as she crossed this stretch of Oregon range land.

Chapter 3

Bluegrass Memories

Barbara and Harshad's camper followed too closely behind her. Connie felt Last Chance swaying as much from her nerves as from the intense wind. When she reached the pinnacles of the Clarno Fossil beds, she put on her blinker and turned in, relieved when the van sped toward Fossil. One other car was parked and she could see a group along a path that led to the pinnacles she'd explored forty years ago.

She cut the ignition and got out. The sun blazed hot in the high dry air and the wind felt more like a furnace blast than the wind of the four elements. She opened the back door to get her sunhat. Stuart used to laugh at how the wide brim dwarfed her face. The photo of them together in the tree trunk stared at her from where she'd put it on top of Everett's gift of *East Angels*. She moved both of them to the front seat. Inanimate company was better than none.

Two children ran toward her. The youngest looked about five. She stopped running and looked open-mouthed at Connie. With a five-year-old's pronunciation, she announced, "Folsils are old like you."

The boy who must have been her older brother shushed her.

"That's not nice, Gladdy."

She laughed at the girl's innocence and the boy's attempt to quiet her. "She's right. I'm not quite as old as a fossil, but I can still climb to look at them. Did you find any?"

"We saw folsils and petrifried wood. That's wood that turned into stone. It takes a billion years to happen." The child rattled off her enthusiasm, oblivious of her mispronunciations.

"I hope I can find that petrified wood. Here come your parents. Make sure you drink water. It's a hot afternoon." She demonstrated by drinking from her water bottle as she started down the path. When she reached the couple she assumed were the children's parents, she smiled and said, "Cute kids. The little one told me about the folsils and the petrifried wood."

"She's a chatterer," said the mother. "Be careful up there. It's hot."

"I won't be long." She moved past them and looked up at the pinnacles. A cloud in the otherwise blue sky hovered over them, its shape like some mammoth that roamed a landscape that had once been filled with dense vegetation. The parched land formed by geologic time felt more hostile than any prehistoric mammal.

She followed the trail, stopping at signs that pointed out a fossilized nut or plant labeled in names she'd never remember. It didn't matter. She'd carry the feeling of the pinnacles into Fossil along with the memory of the time she stopped at Clarno with Eva. She turned onto the Arch Trail, drank more water, and forced herself to climb a little further so she could see the petrified wood the little girl was so excited about. She almost missed what looked more like a snake embedded into the rock than a piece of wood. Before she descended the path, she slowed her breath and drank again. She needed to be careful. It was a long way through the heat of the American West to Freedom.

When she reached the parking area, a black truck was just

pulling beside her car. It looked like the truck that had passed her in Green Springs. The man who got out put on a cowboy hat over shaggy hair the stone color of the pinnacles. His black T-shirt displayed a logo that looked like interlocking Qs. "You improve your driving?" He kicked a rock toward her car. His boots were pointed enough they could leave a dent if the rock didn't.

She stood as tall as her five feet four inches allowed and used the lowest register of her voice. "Do I know you?"

"I passed you at Green Springs. Can't miss old ladies who shouldn't have drivers' licenses." His voice battled with his dark eyes for which carried the most anger.

A red convertible with the top down pulled into the parking area next to Last Chance. Only the driver opened his door. Three other young people jumped over the sides. Connie pressed her key fob and got into her car. The veins in her hands pulsated when she turned on the ignition. She backed away. The four young people were talking to the man who was smiling at them. He took off his cowboy hat and lifted it upwards toward her as if it were his middle finger. She wanted to tell the young people to put up the convertible top and lock their car.

She steadied herself and her car in wind that was blowing across the high ranch land. The static on the radio competed with the sound of the wind. She turned it off and concentrated on the curves in the road.

Forty minutes later, her nerves had calmed and she drove into the town that welcomed her with a sign that announcing Wheeler County Bluegrass Festival. She cracked open her window and followed the sound to where she could see a stage erected in front of a brick courthouse with two turrets, one round and one square. It looked too big for a tiny town like Fossil. A sign in front explained why. It was the Wheeler County Circuit Court, surprising for what was the least populated county in Oregon.

Signs for parking led her to the Wheeler County Fairgrounds. Adjacent to the Fairgrounds, an RV site was filled with camper vans and tents. The multi-colored van that belonged to Barbara and Harshad was parked at the closest edge. She found a spot in the Fairgrounds for Last Chance and walked back along the road to the Festival. When she heard a vehicle coming toward her, she jumped to the edge of the road. The convertible she'd seen at Clarno. She relaxed when no black truck drove behind it.

In front of the courthouse, hundreds of people lounged on blankets or in chairs, listening to a group with two guitars, a fiddle, and a banjo. She recognized the song. "Red-Haired Mary," one of Stuart's favorites. Whenever he'd propose lying in the marriage bed like Mary and the song's narrator, she'd say she liked the rhythm they had. He liked the isolation of Green Springs and she liked the culture of Ashland. Their relationship survived for forty years because they each had their own space.

She concentrated on listening instead of on the sob she felt rising. When the song was over, she took off her sunglasses and used her fingers to wipe tears that were finding their way into the wrinkles of her face.

A young woman got up from a blanket and stood beside her. "It's not a sad song."

She put her glasses back on. "I know. It just made me think of a man who died recently. He played banjo."

The woman gestured to the blanket. "Sit with us. Barbara Comstock's up next. She's good."

"Thank you. I have a blanket in my car, but I didn't think to carry it here."

"Doesn't matter. There's plenty of room on ours." "Ours" were the young woman and a man Connie imagined was her husband or her boyfriend.

An announcer introduced Barbara Comstock as a woman who played a mean guitar, had a voice that could carry to the pinnacles, and was the winner of last year's Fossil song contest. When she climbed on stage, Connie recognized her as the woman she'd met in Antelope. She plugged her guitar into an amplifier and announced that she'd begin with the Fossil song she would have sung for today's contest if she had arrived on time.

The announcer leaned into the microphone. "Give it up now for Barbara Comstock and her never too late Fossil song."

Barbara began with a song that featured a geologist with a family of four kids searching for fossils at the Wheeler High School. Each of the kids found a fossil that Barbara pronounced with enough conviction that Connie wondered if she was a geologist. After each name, the geologist turned that child into an antelope. The song ended with the geologist adding her husband to the herd. She became a patriofelis, something the song identified as a cat-like animal similar to a panther. The panther then led the antelopes to Rajneeshpuram where they fossilized the Baghwan and all the sannyasins. The audience rose and cheered at the last lines. "*Oh give back my home/Where the antelope roam,/And intruders are turned into stone.*" Only Harshad didn't stand.

Barbara signaled the audience to sit and went into a half-dozen bluegrass songs with her powerful voice. She ended with "Last Train to Glory." Connie closed her eyes and imagined Stuart harmonizing with Barbara. Their voices would have blended and her guitar would have softened his banjo.

When Barbara finished, she set down her guitar and waved her arms to signal an end to the applause. "Thank you all. This is the Festival's dinner break. I hope you'll all support the fine people serving food and selling local crafts. Come on back at six o'clock for more great music."

19

Connie turned to the couple she'd been sitting with. "Thank you for sharing your blanket."

"You're welcome. Join us again at six o'clock," said the woman.

"I'm not staying, but let me buy you some dinner before I head to the Williams' Ranch."

"Not camping?" said the man in a crackling tone that sounded like he had a damaged voice box.

"No. I'm traveling across country to Massachusetts. "I've made reservations all along the way. I found the ranch online. Do you know how it is?"

"Nope. We're strictly campers. Mostly dry camping so we don't have to pay for hook-ups. Thanks for the food offer, but we bring our own. We're nomads." The more the man said, the more his voice cracked.

The woman took his hand and said, "Have a safe trip."

As they walked away, Connie could hear the man say, "Old woman like that shouldn't travel alone."

She stopped herself from shouting at him that she was enjoying the solitary travel. He had a choice. Get old or get dead. She wasn't dead yet and she chose to live the years she had left. Maybe she'd get revenge by putting him into her memoir as a vagabond with a damaged voice who thought life ended at fifty.

She walked around the Festival grounds, hoping to see Barbara and Harshad who must also be carrying their own food because they were nowhere in sight. She found a food tent and ordered a burger topped with blue cheese. In cattle country, the beef should be good and, if it wasn't, the blue cheese would mask the taste.

She found a place to sit by herself and observe. The hamburger was delicious. Even the bun was good and the French fries were crispy and not too greasy. Laughter and the sounds of small groups jamming filled her with such sadness she had to force herself to eat. She felt like an observer instead of a participator in the game of life. Her journey wouldn't bring her this kind of camaraderie, but it would keep her vitality alive.

When the announcer began to gather people for the next performance, she found a trash can and deposited what was left of her burger. As she walked back to her car, Barbara and Harshad came toward her. Harshad was moving his lips in some kind of silent conversation. He didn't stop when Barbara did.

"You were wonderful," said Connie. "I loved your Fossil song."

"Harshad didn't. That and his stop at The Big Muddy has set him off. I'm glad you enjoyed the song but I have to catch up with my brother. He's hearing voices again. Have a safe trip."

She was only a day into her journey and already she was tired of the "safe trip" mantra. She thought of her Uncle Charlie and the voices he heard. The trip was her safety net, a way of staving off the genetics that with one turn of the screw could have plunged her from depression to madness.

Chapter 4
Home on the Ranch

Harshad stood on top of a pinnacle, dressed in the red robe of a Rajneeshee. He cocked his head to the side, listening. A voice droned as if from the sky, its words unintelligible. A pointed cowboy boot appeared at the end of an impossibly long leg reaching down from a cloud. It hit Harshad like a bolt of lightning, jolting Connie awake.

She became conscious first of the cold sweat that had soaked her pajama top. She sat up and found the light and reached for her glasses on the table beside her bed. Her brain started to work along with her sharpened eyesight.

The room's décor announced cattle rancher. Wood floors with a carpet woven in a design of open range land. Wood bureau and nightstand, the drawers painted with images of cows. Photos on the wall of cattle grazing under a cloud-dotted sky and of cowboys posed in hats and boots beside horses ready for a roundup. The only break in the theme was a photo over the bureau of the Clarno pinnacles. It was easy to trace the origins of her dream.

She got out of the bed to change the top of her pajamas for a dry one and went into the bathroom across the hall. Whoever she was sharing it with had come in after she was asleep. She had fallen into bed exhausted and managed only a few pages of a novel by Mike Befeler that her publisher asked her to review. "Geezer lit" the publisher called it. The bathroom mirror reminded her she could have been one of geezers.

She crossed the hallway back into her room and found her cell phone. 2:15. Befeler's novel lay on the bed where she'd dropped it when her eyes closed. She straightened its cover, put it on top of her suitcase, and picked up the journal she'd bought for her trip. It was the size of a legal pad, filled with enough lined paper that she could write a novel. Its brown leather binding was designed with a pen loop where she'd inserted one of the fine point pens she liked to write with. Writing would help her process the day and push away the demon of another dream. She propped herself against pillows and began to write.

Travels with Connie

The Williams' Ranch where I'm staying is small, not what I think of as a ranch. But the land around it is vast. The owners, Callie and Brian, seem to love having travelers to share stories with. Callie's a big reader and recognized my name when I made my reservation. She showed me the shelf of books I'd written and had me autograph them even though they were dog-eared paperbacks. I told her there would be no more novels from me, but I'd plug the Williams' Ranch in my travelogue.

It's 2:00 a.m. and the dreams that started after Stuart died woke me again in the middle of the night. I wonder if this will be my writing time, a way to calm myself from my sadness and my fear of plunging into

the kind of depression my mother had. Or worse. A
family curse, mental illness.

I won't dwell. This is a journal about my travels,
about real landscapes not dream fugues. First day
done. Antelope a disappointment. The café is closed
but I met a brother and sister who'd been there as
children. Barbara and Harshad. She was glad to
escape, but he was still resentful at having to leave.
He has mad eyes and might be schizophrenic. That's
what Barbara suggested when I saw them again at
the Wheeler County Bluegrass Festival.

What a surprise. Little Fossil, Oregon, hosts a
bluegrass festival every year the first weekend in
July. Barbara was a solo musician.

She continued to write for a few minutes until her eyes started
to close. When she woke to the sun shining in her window and
the smell of coffee brewing, she looked at the last sentence she'd
written.

Harshad was more pitiful in his delusion than
another person I met. A scraggly looking man who
drove a pick-up truck. Eyes nearly as black and
furious as his truck. But enough of him. He's gone
and I'm writing comfortably in

Sleep had overcome her before she finished what was to be a
description of the Williams' Ranch. She grabbed her ditty bag
and opened the door to the hallway. A man was just coming out
of the bathroom. He smiled and said, "It's all yours. I'll see you
at breakfast."

She showered quickly, dressed in knee-length shorts and a

T-shirt with a logo of Crater Lake. The smell of bacon cooking drew her to the dining room where the man she'd seen coming out of the bathroom sat with two women and two men, all Black, all Connie's age, and all wearing shirts that announced them as The Old-Time Gospel Quartet.

"I'm Jordan," said the younger man. Younger, but more middle-aged than young and with a pale complexion that told Connie he wasn't part of the Quartet. He pointed to the empty spot at the table. "You traveling alone?"

"I am. I'm Connie."

"I'm Cedric," said one of the gospel singers in a voice that marked him as a base. "These here are Reggie, Olive, and Aretha, like Franklin the blues singer. You coming to our gospel show at eleven o'clock? We're first up on the open mic. Straight out of New Orleans."

"Long way from home," said Jordan, who seemed to be meeting the singers for the first time.

"Been doin' gigs all along the way. Olive here found this one, so we decided to stop on our way from Portland to Sandpoint. Looked like fun here."

"It is. You'll like it, Connie." Jordan swallowed some coffee.

She hated when people assumed what she'd like or not like. "I'm afraid I have a long drive today. I'm staying just outside of Sandpoint, Idaho."

"That's not too far. Maybe six hours," said Reggie, who was in the chair next to Connie.

Brian and Callie came in from the kitchen carrying steaming plates of bacon and scrambled eggs, a basket of muffins, and a bowl of fruit. "Never been there, but that's where Marilynne Robinson grew up," said Callie as she set down the platter of bacon and the basket of muffins. "We have all her books on the shelves in the sitting room. Along with Connie's. If she hasn't introduced herself, this is the writer Connie Lewis."

"I thought you looked familiar," said Jordan. "You on a book tour?"

"I'm done with book tours. If I write another book, it will be about this trip. *Travels with Connie.*"

"Where you traveling to?" Brian set the fruit in front of Connie and the eggs in front of Jordan.

"Massachusetts. To see my sister."

Jordan spoke through a mouthful of scrambled eggs. "That's a long way. Woman traveling alone. Be careful. Keep your car filled with gas and plenty of water in case you break down. Don't know about Idaho, but these eastern Oregon roads are pretty isolated. I travel them once a month."

"Jordan stays here every time." Callie stood behind Olive. She looked at Connie from across the table. "He's our traveling dentist. Makes the rounds so no one has to drive all the way to The Dalles just for a tooth cleaning."

Reggie loaded eggs on his plate. "This here place's so different from New Orleans where we're from. We could be on another planet. What y'all do when there's no bluegrass festival goin' on?"

Brian and Callie pulled two chairs over to the table and explained ranch life in a way that sounded like they'd rehearsed it for every guest who came through. Callie had grown up in Fossil, one of three children in a long line of Oregon ranchers. They'd all been sent to college, forced to live in a different kind of world before they chose whether or not to return to ranch life. Neither of her brothers came back, one choosing office space over open land, the other an FBI agent. Each in a different way tried to keep people like the insurrectionist Ammon Bundy or some Rajneesh-like cult from taking over land they'd been bound to for generations.

"Were you here when the Rajneeshees took over Antelope?" Connie remembered how the cultists had tried to poison the water supply in The Dalles. The people of Fossil must have feared the group that had almost recruited her.

Callie clutched the back of Olive's chair. "I was eight years old. A lot of ranchers have six or more kids. One day a couple of those red-shirted crazies came into town, stood on the steps of the courthouse and offered to buy us. They promised us education and a way to lead healthy, spiritual lives."

Olive reached behind her shoulder and touched Callie's hand. "I saw that documentary about the place. Looked like some of those snake-worshipping church services I grew up with in Mississippi. Gospel music without the discipline. Did anyone go?"

Callie pulled her hand away from Olive's. "Of course not. Until they kicked those crazies off the land, even the older kids couldn't go anywhere alone. We're lucky now. We've got bluegrass and peace and open spaces."

Connie looked at the four gospel singers. "Were you at the festival yesterday?" She didn't remember seeing any Black faces in this whitest section of Oregon.

"Just got in last night," said Cedric. "Why? You look like you have something to tell us."

"One of the singers—Barbara Comstock—she was at Rajneeshpuram when she was a kid. So was her brother." Connie didn't add, 'So was I.'

"She stayed here last year," said Brian who'd been listening quietly. "With a brother who spent all night talking to the animals. Not that there were any animals around."

Connie had heard enough about crazy cultists, so she changed the subject. "What about you, Brian? Did you grow up on a ranch?"

27

"Nope. Grew up in Tampa."

Connie thought of the years she'd lived in Florida with her mother, trying to build a writing career. "What a change Fossil must be for you."

Brian put his arm around his wife. "Callie's taught me how to love it. The sunsets go on forever and everyone minds their own business. It's the home I used to imagine when I got tired of Florida hurricanes and snowbirds from the North. Here the only time we get tourists is for the Bluegrass Festival."

Connie knew what he meant. Florida had never felt like home. Ashland or Freedom would be her last exit. She wasn't sure which.

The gospel singers stood up in unison as if they were about to harmonize "Peace in the Valley." "We'll be on our way," said Aretha. "Get ourselves all set up." She looked at Connie. "You should watch our show then follow us to Sandpoint. Not good to be traveling alone."

Connie pushed her chair back and stood next to Aretha, who was twice her size. With a smooth, full face she looked half her age even though they were both old-timers. She hated being cautioned about driving alone, but she liked gospel music and liked the idea of having someone to follow. "I'd like that. As long as you're leaving right after the show, so we can make it to Sandpoint by dinner time."

Jordan reached for one last muffin. "They'll keep you safe. You be careful when you're on your own. Keep that gas tank full. Here's to a safe trip." He raised his coffee cup to Connie as if to bless her journey.

Chapter 5

The Fisherman's Bar

She followed the Old-Time Gospel Quartet along Route 19 to Spokane and the interstates. They were easy to follow, slowing down to make sure she made every turn and keeping to seventy miles an hour. They were as reassuring as the gospel songs they sang. It was a welcome change from being warned to be careful. The last song the singers performed was "You're Home to Stay." She would like the sentiment if only she could decide if her home was in Ashland or Freedom.

In Idaho, the landscape changed into a road bordered by trees so tall they reminded her of the way the tip of the state looked on a map. It was nearing dinnertime when they stopped at a gas station outside of Sandpoint. Last Chance's small tank was almost empty. She waited for an attendant to come out of the station then realized what she hadn't planned for. Oregon was one of only two states where you couldn't pump your own gas. She didn't know how. She watched Cedric, but she couldn't follow what he was doing. When he finished, he came over to her. "Having a problem?"

She wanted to cry at her helplessness. "I've never pumped gas. I never used one of the self-serve stations that were popping up in

Florida before I moved West. I stuck with my favorite mechanic and the gas he always pumped for me. It's changing but in most of Oregon we aren't allowed to pump our own gas."

"I know. Reggie almost blew a gas cap when he found out. Adds more to the price. Give me your credit card and I'll do it for you."

She reached into the car for her purse and took out the card. "Just talk me through it. I need to learn."

He watched her as he gave careful instructions. "Open the tank lid and unscrew your gas cap."

She reached into her car to pop the cover. The cap was tight, but she managed to loosen it by using two hands. "Where do I put the cap?"

"There's a spot on the cover."

She found it and clicked in the cap.

"Now insert your credit card and take it out quickly. That will release the nozzle."

She took her credit card out of her purse, put it in backwards, tried again. It worked.

"Now look at the screen. What does it ask for?"

"My ZIP code." She pressed in 97520.

"Take the nozzle off its holder and press what grade of gas you want."

She lifted the nozzle, pressed regular, and managed to get it into the tank.

"Now you have to press the trigger."

The word sounded ominous. She pressed and heard the sound of gas going into the tank. She was still holding the trigger when the nozzle clicked off. She hooked it into its place and using two hands twisted the cover to the tank back on.

"Be sure you get it tight." He checked. "That'll do." He gave it another twist anyway and pushed the cover closed. The meter on the pump read thirty-five dollars and fourteen cents.

"I remember when gas was twenty-five cents a gallon."

"And I remember when we had to get it at colored only stations."

All she could think of to say was, "I'm sorry." She was in elementary school before she learned there were colored only drinking fountains and schools. She never thought to wonder why all the kids in her school, in her town even, were white. She imagined the servant Hannah in *Little Women* as Black like Aunt Jemima on the old syrup bottle. Only when she reached college did she realize that Hannah was Irish. Her past was her past. She couldn't change it and it was foolish to feel guilty about it. All she could do was be aware of all the ways racism, subtle and not so subtle, existed. She voted wisely and marched for equal rights. She supported the plays at Oregon Shakespeare Festival and how the theater selected ones that challenged audiences to think about racism and how stereotypes lingered in her own subconscious. Maybe if she lived in Boston like she had sixty years ago, she could do more than hang a Black Lives Matter sign in her yard and contribute money to social justice causes.

"Not your fault. At least you like the music my slave ancestors created." He looked back at the gas meter. "Press this button and you'll get a receipt. Your tank's pretty small, isn't it?"

"Eleven or twelve gallons. I'm not sure."

"Stop a lot. Keep it full."

"I'll be a pro by the time I get to Massachusetts. It smells, though."

"Come to the van. Use some of our hand sanitizer. It's laced with lavender and will take the smell away."

When they got to the van, Reggie, Aretha, and Olive stepped out. Aretha was the last to hug her. Her warm breasts felt protective. She pushed away the Mammy image. "Our concert's tomorrow. Stay an extra night. We can have dinner together."

She was tempted. "I wish I could but I've got a schedule."

"Not much of an adventure if you can't be spontaneous," said Aretha.

"Like Aretha is," said Olive.

Connie imagined that Olive had lived a quiet life but that Aretha had been a wild child. She'd like to have learned more about both of them, but it was too late. "I wanted to be sure I had places for most of my trip. The one I booked for tonight had plenty of openings, but rooms at Glacier National Park get reserved months in advance. I'm lucky I got one."

Cedric handed her the bottle of hand sanitizer he'd taken out of the van. "Keep this. Think of us every time you fill your gas tank."

"I will. And if you ever perform in Massachusetts let me know." Was she telling herself that she planned to stay in Freedom? "Wait a second." She went back to her car and fumbled in the storage compartment between the front seats for the bookmarks that described her last novel, the one she'd finally set in Oregon where she imagined a life for Molly that brought her out of her house, down the mountain to play for the Rogue Valley Symphony and to discover a love for something, someone, in addition to her music. Molly wouldn't have been like Aretha, even like Olive. She'd never have the adventure Connie imagined for her.

She wrote her email address at the bottom of the bookmarks, went back to the van, and handed them to the singers. "You've been wonderful. I feel like you're old friends."

"Old's the right word," said Olive. "We'll find copies of your books. They'll give us something good to read on the road."

Despite the awards she'd won, Connie still questioned the quality of her books. "I hope you'll like them. Thank you again." She returned to her car and drove it away from the gas pump where someone was impatiently waiting for the empty spot. She tensed when she saw that it was a black pick-up truck. She didn't wait to see to see if a man with scraggly hair the color of the Clarno pinnacles might be driving. Instead, she drove to the Walmart next to the gas station and stopped just long enough to turn on her phone navigation. The Five Trouts Resort was just twelve miles outside of Sandpoint on the northernmost shore of Lake Pend Oreille. She realized how hungry she was. A good meal and a good night's sleep would fuel her for tomorrow's drive to Glacier.

The Five Trouts Resort looked better online than it did in the flesh. It wasn't seedy, but it was more a 1950-style motel than a resort. Its clapboards had been recently painted a deep green to blend with the huge pines that shaded it. The color made it look more sinister than pastoral. She counted eight rooms, four on each side of a center lobby, all with no windows. But the doors were interesting, hand carved with images of Idaho's trees. Online photos had shown sliding doors at the back of the rooms with views of the lake.

Before she got out of Last Chance and grabbed her suitcase from the back seat, she touched the photo of Stuart and her in the Lithia Park tree stump. She walked to the motel's door and went inside to a deserted lobby. This wasn't a room with comfortable chairs and coffee for the guests. At the counter, a sign in front of a small round bell with a button on top said, "Please ring." "Please" was encouraging. She pressed the button. The ring was so soft someone would need bionic ears to hear it.

She was wrong. A young woman carrying a baby came through a door that must lead to living quarters that faced the lake. "I hope you weren't waiting long. I was nursing Amy." The woman's hair draped over the baby in a cascade of dark curls. Already the baby had hair that looked like it would match her mother's.

Connie was touched by the woman's youth and the way she cuddled Amy against her. "I have a reservation."

The woman switched the baby to her other shoulder and opened a guest book that sat on the counter. "You must be Constance Lewis. It's just you tonight. Thankfully. We got slammed this weekend even though the Fourth isn't until Tuesday. But I can't complain. My husband and I bought this resort a year ago. It's harder than we thought to rebuild a place that had a bad reputation." She handed Connie a key. "Room 1 on the left side of the lobby. Please let me know if you need anything."

"I'm sure it will be fine." She wondered about its bad reputation, but she liked the "please" again and all she needed was for it to be clean. "Is there a restaurant nearby? Nothing too fancy."

"The Fisherman's Bar. It's not on the lake, but it's where all the locals go. Drive a mile up the road and turn left. You can't miss it."

Connie wondered what locals there were. This wasn't Sandpoint. "Thanks. Go finish feeding that baby now. She's sweet."

The woman touched the baby's soft hair. "She is. Best thing that ever happened to me." There was a wistfulness in her voice that made Connie think this young woman's life had been difficult.

She left the lobby and unlocked the door to her room. It was shockingly coordinated. The bed's headboard was painted to look like water with swimming fish. The bedspread was light blue with fish that were identified in a darker script—catfish, whitefish, perch, pike, two kinds of bass, multiple kinds of trout. She wondered if all these kinds of fish could be caught in Lake Pend Oreille. Framed prints of men and women holding up their catch hung somewhat crookedly on the little wall space available. There was a nightstand but no bureau and only a tiny alcove that made a brave pretense at a closet. But the room was spotlessly clean and the view outside the sliding door made up for its kitsch.

She went into the tiny bathroom carrying her ditty bag. A shower curtain had the same kind of fish pattern as the bedspread. A shower could wait. She was hungry. As she set her ditty bag on the back of the toilet next to her glasses, she thought of Stuart who'd taught her to say "ditty bag" instead of "toiletry bag." Something he'd picked up in Vietnam, he'd told her. She took out her toothbrush and brushed the staleness out of her mouth. She took a facecloth off the rack next to the shower, hoping the dark blue wasn't chosen to hide stains. It smelled of lavender. She wet it with cold water and washed off the heat of the drive. She used the toilet, washed her hands, and put on her glasses so she could see to brush hair that was short enough she could have fluffed it with her fingers. At least she wasn't an old woman with beauty parlor blue hair that passed for white. Gray it was and gray it would stay.

She'd find a quiet table at The Fisherman's Bar, order dinner, and write in her journal. *Travels with Connie* would document a day filled with the kindness of gospel singers, a lesson in pumping gas, and an imagined life for a woman with a baby and a motel that needed resurrecting.

The Fisherman's Bar was one room decorated with trophy fish from Lake Pend Oreille. She ordered trout advertised as "today's fresh catch." She ate slowly, sipping on a glass of pinot gris and enjoying the buttery flavor infused into the fish. The few locals who were unwinding during the long tourist-filled Fourth of July weekend stopped at the booth, asking where she was traveling and cautioning her to keep her gas tank full and water in her car. When a couple talked about the peacefulness of POND-e-RAY after the tourists left, she learned how to pronounce the name.

When she paid the bill and got up to leave, a man at the bar twirled around in his seat and stopped her. He looked like an aging hippie or another escapee from Rajneeshpuram. His hair was gray and long, his beard full, his voice staticky. "I'm Gregory," he said. "I love your novels. Have another glass of whatever you're drinking." The man behind the bar who also served as waiter said, "I'm Austin. Drink's on the house."

He placed a glass on the counter and poured too much pinot gris into it. In the dim light of the bar, she could see that he was decades younger than Gregory, neat and clean-shaven with close-cropped red hair. "I'm Connie."

"Connie Lewis. Gregory here says you're a writer."

Gregory motioned her to sit on the stool next to him. "I heard you read once. In Boise when I was a student, thinking I could make it as a writer."

She accepted the stool and the glass of wine. "That was forty years ago." If he had been a traditional student, he must be about sixty now, younger than he looked.

"I've read all your books. You don't look like your photo."

"They airbrush me. Writers aren't supposed to be old. What about you? Have you become a writer?"

"Wrote one novel. After a hundred rejections, I gave it up, became a fisherman, and bought this restaurant. It's okay. I like it here. Quiet out on the water. I stay away from the beaches and the resorts and the places where there are too many motor boats going too fast. I caught that trout you ate. Cooked it, too."

She wondered how long he'd been watching her.

"We're closing up now, but stick around." Austin came out

from behind the bar, went to the door, and turned the open sign to closed. She looked at her watch. Just after nine. She'd already stayed longer than she'd planned. He came back and sat on the other side of her, and apologized in a way she'd heard too many times. "I'm not much of a reader, but Gregory says you're a good writer."

"Was. I'm retiring." She sipped some wine, getting ready to answer too many questions.

Instead she got a litany of stories they said she could turn into a novel. They told her about the compound of insurrectionists at the southern tip of the lake who wanted Idaho to secede from the Union and become a whites only state, about the local fisherman found bludgeoned to death and washed ashore on the lake, about the family whose eight kids were discovered locked in their house and wearing ragged T-shirts that read Kid One, Kid Two, on up to Kid Eight. Underneath the lake a Loch Ness Monster must lurk to cause such havoc.

"What about The Five Trouts Resort?"

Austin launched into a story about the man who'd owned the motel and how he'd stolen credit card numbers from all the guests. He sold the numbers to contacts he had all over the country. "Thought that would make it so they couldn't trace the fraud to him. He got caught when one credit card company noticed how many of his victims had stayed at The Lakeside Resort."

"The woman I saw changed the name?"

"Had to if she wanted to rebuild its reputation." Gregory slammed back a whiskey and followed it with a swig of beer on tap. "Boilermaker. Good for the stomach."

Connie wondered if a Boilermaker would settle hers. She'd had too much wine. "Is that why the couple was able to buy it? I only met the woman and her baby. She seemed determined to make it work." If she hadn't been drinking in a bar loaded with fish paraphernalia, she would have added something about the fish-laden décor.

"That's Nancy. She's not a couple. No one knows where that baby came from. Do they, Gregory." Austin bent in front of Connie to look at his friend.

Gregory drank down another shot of whiskey with a beer chaser. "Nancy's my granddaughter. Showed up one day with enough money to buy the motel. I help her out."

Gregory told the story as if he were plotting a novel. Nancy knew things that he'd never learned. Her grandmother never told him she was pregnant. He was going to be a writer, didn't need to be saddled with a wife and child. She'd take Nancy to the library in Boise and comb through new books and book reviews looking for his name. "I never found another woman to love. We could have married. I could have known my daughter. Nancy told me her mother and grandmother are both dead. That's why she decided to find me. She wants a sense of family for that baby of hers."

"Nancy never said anything about the baby's father?"

Gregory got up and stepped behind the bar to refill his mug. "Just like her grandmother who never told me she was pregnant." As he added more wine to Connie's glass, he said, "The baby came after she bought the motel. We haven't been able to get her to name the father."

Austin spun his stool in a circle, stopping it so he faced Connie. "I keep telling him that baby's father is a drug trafficker. Nancy's in witness protection until she can testify against him."

Gregory came out from behind the bar. He sat down facing Connie. "Austin's the one who should be a writer. The reality's more mundane. She's running from the baby's father. A shabby looking guy who shows up at our restaurant every couple of months in his dilapidated truck. When he does, we call her and say that Mason's here. She heads over to Austin's sister's house."

"Is she in danger?"

"We watch out for her." Austin picked up the glass of water he'd been drinking instead of alcohol. "He always leaves angry but peaceful."

"Nancy seems like a loving mother. She's gentle with that baby." Connie told herself that Nancy would be okay, she wouldn't be another victim along Lake Pend Oreille.

It was after ten when she refused another refill of her glass. "I've had too much. I'll regret it tomorrow." When she got off the bar stool she realized she was drunk.

"You can't leave yet." Gregory pulled a dollar bill out of his pocket. "Look at the ceiling."

She lifted her head and quickly lowered it to avoid vertigo. "There's money on the ceiling."

Gregory handed her a pen. "We have a tradition here. Anyone passing through signs a dollar bill and tacks it on the ceiling. We'll be able to tell all the locals that we chatted for two hours with a famous writer."

She looked at her watch. "Actually, I've been here almost five hours. No wonder I'm tired." She took the pen and signed the bill. "Travels with Connie" and initialed it CL.

Austin helped her onto the chair. She wobbled as she pushed the tack through the center of George Washington's face. The bill next to hers read "Keep on truckin', Mason." The name registered like a gutted fish. She needed Austin to steady her when she got off the chair.

The two men walked her to her car. "We should drive you home. You've had a lot to drink."

"Not my fault. It's only a mile."

"A mile and a half," said Austin. "Gregory had a lot, too.

Always does when he talks about Nancy. Give me your keys. I'll drive you and walk back. It's a nice night."

She started to argue but she knew she was too drunk to drive. Austin opened the passenger side door for her and got into the driver's seat. He pushed it way back for his long legs. When they reached The Five Trouts, he got out, opened her door, and gave her the keys. "Lock your door. Nancy's not dangerous, but there's something dangerous in her background. I'm not even sure she's Gregory's granddaughter, but it makes him feel better about losing that woman so many years ago."

"Thanks for the warning. I'll be fine. And thanks for the evening. Maybe I should call my book *Adventures with Connie*."

"We'll watch for it. Give The Fisherman's Bar a good scene."
He waited until she went into her room, then turned and walked away in the moonlight.

She locked the front door and opened the sliding one that faced the lake. The moon cast a line on the water that looked like a road beckoning her to follow it. A midnight swim would cool her off and sober her up.

She rummaged through the suitcase she'd set on the bed then remembered that her bathing suit was at the bottom of the large suitcase in her car. It didn't matter. No one would see her if she swam naked in the moonlight. She hadn't done that since she first met Stuart and he'd take her to a spot he knew at one of the mountain lakes. They'd only gone twice before someone saw them and she refused to go again.

One last swim for Stuart. She stripped off her clothes and went into the bathroom for a towel. The towel was small but it covered her body, hiding how wrinkled and hairless it was. She wondered why old women lost even their pubic hair. It didn't matter. Between the choice of getting old or getting dead, she chose getting old.

She stepped out the sliding door onto a deck that ran the length of the motel. No barriers would separate her from other guests if there had been any. This place should be packed for the extra-long Fourth of July holidays. Nancy had a tough job rebuilding its reputation. She climbed down the stairs and over an area of unkept grass until she reached a rocky beach. The water was cold from snow melt that kept the lake full even during this year of drought. She'd read that it was one of the five deepest lakes in the United States. It would take a bigger drought than this year's to dry it up.

She dropped the towel, waded in to her knees, then shallow dove. The cold on her head felt sobering. She was still a strong swimmer, but she knew she was too drunk to swim into the middle of the lake. She swam out a few yards then swam laps along the shoreline. Her muscle memory took over. Each lap was a memory of swimming lessons, of summer at Clearwater Beach in Florida where she took her mother to swim in the days she was becoming a writer. A lap triggered memories of Everett and canoeing in Florida swamps where they'd risk being attacked by an alligator if they swam. The memories were fresher than her body felt under the smooth water.

She took one last dive and swam to where the water was shallow enough for her to stand. She got out quickly, surprised at how winded the swim had made her. She wrapped the towel around her. As she walked toward her room, she saw a figure standing on the deck in front of what must be Nancy's apartment. Without her glasses, she couldn't tell if it was Nancy or someone else. When she got to the deck, the figure waved. It was a man with long hair, too thin to be Gregory. She went quickly into her room, locked the sliding door, and drew the curtains against a threat that had intruded onto her memorial dip in the lake.

Chapter 6
From Lake to River

She showered off the lake water and dried herself with the hand towel, avoiding the sand on the bath towel she'd wrapped herself in when she finished swimming. It was a silly idea to skinny dip at midnight, sillier to think no one would see her. She found her pajamas and felt better with her body covered. Her journal lay unopened on the bed. Morning would be time enough to decide whether or not to write about her swim and the man who'd seen her. It was an adventure she preferred to forget.

She checked the locks again and looked outside at the lake. The sky was clear, the lake lighted by a full moon and a billion stars. A man was just stepping naked into the water. She closed the curtain to block out his image and the realization that he could have come outside while she was swimming.

Her sleep was restless. Sometime in the night between dreams of her mother and her Uncle Charlie and dollar bills tacked to ceilings and a woman with a baby and a shadowy man, she heard a vehicle drive out of the parking area. It sounded like a truck. She fell back asleep, this time dreaming of scraggly-haired men in pick-ups.

The sound of a bird call, a high-pitched cry followed by a series of staccato notes, woke her. A bald eagle, maybe. When she researched Lake Pend Oreille, the sites mentioned that it was a haven for eagles. Her birder friends would love her to take photos, but she was anxious to leave. She wanted to get on the road so she'd arrive at Glacier National Park in time to enjoy the only fancy hotel she'd booked for her trip. The Lake McDonald Lodge would make up for a motel that was deserted even on Fourth of July weekend and bars where people left dollar bills on the ceiling. When she carried her suitcase to Last Chance, she felt as if someone were watching her. No faces peered from any of the windows and the only other car in front of the motel was an old Subaru that was there when she checked in. Nancy's, she assumed.

She dropped her journal on the front seat, planning to write in it while she ate breakfast. Nancy was in the lobby, sitting behind the counter and nursing Amy. She looked exhausted. Her eyes were red as if she'd been crying.

"Don't get up," she said when she dropped her key on the counter. "Amy looks too comfortable to disturb."

"She's a good baby. At least I have her."

"I enjoyed The Fisherman's Bar last night. I stayed too late talking with Gregory and Austin. Gregory said he's your grandfather."

Nancy shifted Amy to her other breast. "He's a good man."

"They both seemed nice. Accept their help."

Nancy jerked the baby, who started to cry. She calmed her and said, "I knew Gregory was the helping type."

Connie wondered at the reference to "Gregory" instead of to "Grandpa" or at least "my grandfather."

Nancy helped Amy settle into nursing again. "Go back there for breakfast. Tell them Mason was here. They'll find out. He won't come back."

SHARON L. DEAN

"I guess that's the man who saw me swimming. Is he Amy's father?"

"If he claims her, he'll have to pay child support. He's not interested and he's not welcome back."

"I guess you run The Five Trouts alone. No husband like the one you claimed yesterday."

"It's a line I've learned to use. Woman and baby alone are an easy mark. As easy as old women traveling alone." She stood up. "Baby needs changing. You be careful. Find your freedom. I exchanged mine for Amy," she said as she went through the door into her apartment.

As she drove to The Fisherman's Bar, Connie went over their conversation. A lie about a husband helping her run the motel. A baby whose father was a threat. A grandfather Nancy called by his first name. If he was her grandfather. She suspected there was more to Nancy's story than she'd ever learn. How did a single mother with no kin have enough money to buy a motel and run it on her own? She remembered Austin's speculation about witness protection. The idea wasn't that far-fetched.

The bar was more crowded for breakfast than it had been for dinner. One booth held a group of men who were exchanging stories about how many fish they'd caught at dawn. A family with three kids were discussing whether to swim or to rent a pontoon boat. The kids voted for swimming. It sounded like the dad just wanted to leave them all and go fishing. She chose a booth in front of a group of women her age who sounded like they gathered regularly for morning coffee.

A solitary man sulked in a booth beside hers. She recognized him as the man who'd passed her at Green Springs and at the Clarno Fossil Beds. She remembered the black pick-up truck from when she was learning to pump gas and the man at Nancy's last night. It felt like he was following her. She wanted to confront him, but even in a public restaurant she was afraid to. She relaxed when Austin put a menu in front of her. He turned to the man. "You're not welcome here, Mason. Nancy called this morning and said you were there last night. Stay out of her life."

"I could tell you a thing or two about her. And her so-called grandfather. How do you think she found him?"

"It doesn't matter. She's here now, she's working hard, and we like her and her baby. Stay away. Go back to wherever you came from. You won't be served in this restaurant again."

Mason slid out of his booth so fast he nearly knocked Austin over. He stopped in front of Connie. "Enjoy your swim last night? You looked okay in the moonlight. For an old lady." When he walked from the aisle to the door, he exaggerated the sound of his boots. He turned the handle on the screen door then kicked it open.

"He'll not be back," said Austin. "What can I get you? Trout and eggs are always good."

Her stomach recoiled at the thought of fish for breakfast after a night of too much drinking.

"Just coffee and an English muffin."

"Feeling the effects of the wine?"

"I'm afraid I am. A glass of water will help." She needed to flush out her system, even though she'd regret how many times she had to stop to find a restroom. "I tried to swim off the wine last night."

"And Mason saw you? That wasn't a smart idea."

She wondered if he meant swimming while drunk or swimming where Mason could see her. "I know. But it was a beautiful night. I don't think Mason was there long. I saw him go into the water and a little later I heard a truck drive away."

"Did you see Nancy this morning? Was she okay?"

"She looked tired but seemed to be in control. She said Mason wouldn't come back unless he wanted to pay child support. I guess he's Amy's father."

"That's the story. I'll get you your coffee." He left her to wonder at what he meant. Why a story?

While she waited, she opened her journal and began to write.

> *I could spin yesterday into a novel. I stayed on Lake Pend Oreille—locals pronounce it POND e RAY—in a motel being resurrected by a young woman, Nancy, who claimed to have a husband who ran it with her. I ate dinner at a place called The Fisherman's Bar and discovered that it's all a lie. Nancy claims the bar owner, Gregory, is her grandfather. The waiter, Austin, isn't sure about that. But the two of them have taken to protecting Nancy and her baby. The guy in the black truck showed up at the motel last night. Turns out his name is Mason and he might be the baby's father. Whoever he is, Nancy doesn't want him around.*

She stopped writing when Austin returned. "Writing about us?" he said as he put coffee and water on the table.

"Sort of."

"Make it fiction. Nancy doesn't need the publicity." He left her to wait on a middle-aged couple who'd just come in holding hands. When she imagined them as lovers escaping the boredom of their marriages, she realized she'd have to concentrate to make *Travels with Connie* non-fiction. If she followed Austin's caution to fictionalize Nancy, she'd end up writing another novel. That might please her fans, but it would suck her dry.

While she waited for her English muffin, she alternated between sips of water and sips of coffee. She listened to the coffee klatch women in the booth behind hers. They were talking about Nancy. Their voices blended into a thread of speculations.

–I've seen that guy who just left. At The Five Trouts.

–He's the baby's father.

–Must have been a rape then. She's quite beautiful and he's a creep.

–Too scruffy for her.

–She's not making money from that motel. There are never any cars in front of it.

–Stan told me she paid cash.

–Maybe she's one of those people Thaddeus siphoned money from before he got caught for that credit card fraud and sent to jail.

–And she's hiding it. In a bank or under a mattress?

–Mattress. She even uses cash at the grocery store.

–I heard that Gregory's her grandfather.

–Not what I heard. I heard she's having an affair with Austin.

The women stopped their speculations when Austin came down the aisle with Connie's English muffin. "This should settle your stomach," he said as he put the muffin and a little packet of jelly in front of her. He glanced at the booth of women and mouthed the word "gossips."

She smiled and lifted her coffee cup toward him. He refilled it with the pot he was holding then moved to the booth of women. "More coffee for any of you?"

They answered "please," "just a tad," "none for me."

When he left, he raised the coffee pot toward Connie. The women changed their conversation to a discussion of their grandchildren. Alisha was going back to U of Idaho in the fall. Liam was taking a gap year. Kate had found her dream job with the FBI. She stopped listening when they got to George who'd decided to go to art school in Rhode Island. It sounded like all of the young people wanted to discover a world beyond Lake Pend Oreille.

She opened her journal and wrote again.

> *The secrets of The Five Trouts will stay hidden in the deepest part of this deep lake. Whoever Nancy is, whatever her relationship to Gregory and Austin and Mason, the man I keep seeing in his black truck, wherever she got her money, I'll remember her as a young mother doing her best to raise a baby she obviously loves.*

She closed her journal and went to the one bathroom that served for both women and men. Austin and Gregory had a sense of humor. A photograph about the toilet illustrated how to put a roll of toilet paper on its holder. A "no" on the illustration of rolled under. A "yes" on the rolled over illustration. An X on the one propped on the holder. She used the toilet, already regretting the coffee and water she'd drunk. When she went to the counter to pay, Austin was waiting on a lone customer who'd chosen the bar over a booth. "Don't leave yet," he said as he gave her the bill. "Gregory will want to say goodbye."

She took enough money out of her wallet to pay the bill and leave a substantial tip. As she left it on the counter, she thought of Nancy and how she paid for everything in cash.

Gregory appeared holding a copy of *Twenty Years a Wanderer*, the novel she'd written forty years ago when she first moved to Oregon. It was a first edition, at this point in her career worth well over the cover price. He handed her the book and a pen. "It was the first novel of yours I bought. After that time I heard you speak in Boise."

"That was before I wrote it. But I remember that journey well. Books are more valuable with nothing personal. Only an author's name. I'll just write Constance Lewis."

"Please make it personal. It will mean more to me that way."

She thought a moment, then signed it "To Gregory and the welcome of The Fisherman's Bar. Connie Lewis, July 2, 2023." She pushed the book across the counter to him. "I'm glad I found you. You've been wonderful. If I ever get *Travels with Connie* written, I'll give your restaurant a great review." She looked at Austin. "No mention of Nancy and The Five Trouts. Some things should remain a mystery."

Gregory covered her hand with his. "You take care, now. When you finish that book, will you send me a copy?"

"I will." She left them both at the counter and went out the door to Last Chance, feeling as if she were leaving old friends.

More old friends greeted her when she got into her car and turned on a rebroadcast of The Old-Time Gospel Singers' performance in Sandpoint. Their voices accompanied her until she lost the radio signal when she crossed into Montana. In Libby, she followed signs to the Kootenai River Visitor Center. There'd be a bathroom where she could empty herself of the coffee and water she'd had at breakfast. There might even be something interesting about Libby. This was an adventure, not a race.

The Visitor Center was a small building with an arched roof and a poster on the side with a picture of a woman in a cowboy hat welcoming visitors to Big Sky Country. Behind it, an area of inviting green grass held a few picnic tables, all empty in the mid-morning sun.

When she went inside, a heavy-set woman stood up from where she was sitting behind a counter and said, "Welcome to Libby, gateway to the Kootenai River." She pronounced it KOOT-nee.

"First a restroom, then you can tell me about it."

"Right over there." The woman pointed to a door clearly marked for women.

Connie managed a thank you, used the restroom, then returned ready to hear what Libby and the Kootenai River had to offer. The woman was still standing. Her name tag identified her as Cora.

"You staying long?" she said. "Lots to see here. We've got plenty of cricks and the big river. In a couple of weeks, we'll have Scottish games and in August, a bluegrass festival."

"Unfortunately, I'm just passing through. I'm looking for something I can do for just a couple of hours."

"Heritage Museum's interesting. It will tell you all about mining and logging. Even a little about the Kootenai Indians and how they fought the government in 1974 and got back some of their land. Not much, but they have enough of a voice now to fight for the environment."

Connie wondered if the woman had Kootenai heritage. "I bet it's interesting, but I'd like to do something outdoors. Are there hiking trails?"

"Ever see that movie *The River Wild*? Filmed right here at Kootenai Falls."

She'd watched it years ago in Ashland with Stuart. Parts had also been filmed on Oregon's Rogue River and they'd tried to identify where. They liked the movie. Great acting as always by Meryl Streep. Kevin Bacon was one of the bad guys who try to murder a family on a rafting trip. Those were the only names of performers she remembered, but she remembered comparing it to *Deliverance*. She'd seen that movie alone in Boston long before she met Stuart. The only actors whose names she remembered in *Deliverance* were Jon Voight and Burt Reynolds, but the movie still haunted her with its scenes of male rape and murder and its ending where a bloated hand rises from the water. The stereotype of the sadistic mountain men would be criticized in the twenty-first century the way it hadn't been in the twentieth. When Stuart talked about it, he focused on the scene with the "Dueling Banjos." She was still terrified that an innocent adventure could turn so deadly.

Cora pointed to a brochure about the hike. "It's just a mile and a half round trip. You'll see rapids and cliffs and huge evergreen trees. Only scary part is the swinging bridge over the river. You look like you can handle that."

"Will there be people on the trail?"

"It's July Fourth weekend. There'll be too many."

"That's okay. I don't mind a crowd." She did, but she felt uneasy after remembering horror movies. "Is it hard to find?"

"Easy-peasy. Just go back out on Route 2 and you'll see the sign."

The moment she pulled into the parking area to Kootenai Falls, she knew this would not be a solitary hike. There were at least a dozen cars with room for a few more. She got out and started along a trail that was marked with a stone cairn. A dirt path wound along the river. People sat picnicking on boulders or stood at vistas looking down at the rapids and across at trees growing out of stone cliffs on the other side. The shoes on many identified them as tourists, not hikers. She never understood why someone would walk a wooded trail wearing flip-flops.

She came to a bridge encased with metal fencing that spanned long-ago abandoned railroad tracks. After she crossed it, she followed the trail that descended steadily as it followed the river. She stopped to do what all the tourists were doing. Take pictures with her phone's camera. She turned on her video when she saw two kayakers negotiating the rapids. They wore helmets and paddled with enough skill that she assumed they would make it down the steepest part of the falls without capsizing. On the other side of the river, a man who was fishing reminded her of Gregory.

She slowed down at a metal staircase to catch her breath and stop a cough that she blamed on an allergy to something in the unfamiliar landscape. The staircase led to the swinging bridge advertised in the brochure. Several people stood at the top of the staircase watching others brave enough to cross the bridge that swung in a way that justified its name. The kayakers navigated beneath it and disappeared into the rapids.

When the bridge had cleared of people, she descended the staircase and stepped onto it. She'd never liked the feeling of swings or even rocking chairs. Her queasy stomach reminded her that she was still a little hungover. She hurried across and followed the path to the base of the falls. Three young people had plunged into a pool in front of them. Their squeals told her the water was as cold as in Lake Pend Oreille.

A wave of grief surprised her. She watched people enjoying themselves. They were all in groups of two or three or a half-dozen. She was the only one alone. Grief ebbed and flowed in ways as natural as the flowing of the river. She wasn't in denial. Her adventure was a way of coping, but it was still an adventure.

She turned back, stopping only when a couple with binoculars pointed her to the bald eagle they were watching. When it flew out of the tree where it was nesting, she continued back to the parking lot where she stopped to use an outhouse. It smelled, pieces of toilet paper littered the floor, and the dispenser with hand sanitizer was empty. She held her breath as she used it. When she came outside, the air started her cough again. A small stand labeled Trail Head Grill had a line in front of it and a sign that announced its specialty, huckleberry ice cream. The grief she'd been feeling about losing Stuart changed to sadness for the way tourism invaded a place that had once been sacred to the Kootenai tribe. She feared that Glacier National Park would be even worse.

Chapter 7
From Mansion to Resort

She wanted to drive slowly from Kootenai to Kalispell. Route 2 was lined with trees and views of mountains in the distance. But too many people drove Montana style, fast on the hills and curves. When she researched her trip, she'd learned that this was called the most dangerous road in America. She wished other drivers heeded the warnings. Several times she pulled to the side to let cars pass. When she came to a chain of lakes, she hoped she'd find a town that catered to tourists and supported a gas station. She saw none. Last Chance was nearly empty when she reached the outskirts of Kalispell. She found a gas station and followed the directions Cedric taught her. Gas cap off, credit card, regular gasoline, insert hose and pull the trigger.

Finished, she doused her hands with the lavender sanitizer and thought of the Gospel Singers and their music.

She started her car and parked it away from the pumps then went into the station that also served as convenience store. When she came out of the bathroom, she stopped at a freezer holding an array of ice cream treats. She opened it to choose something when a voice behind her said, "'Less you're in a hurry, get ice cream at Sweet Peaks. Best in Montana."

She turned to the voice and saw a double of the old Marlboro Man advertisement. In her head she was thirty years old ready to start a flirtation. "Tell me how to get there and I'm all in for the real thing."

"Just turn left onto South Main. It's in a brick building that was once a gas station. The pumps are still in the parking lot. Try the huckleberry."

"Thanks, but I might pass on the huckleberry. If you tell me your name, I'll tell them you sent me."

"Stuart. They'll know me."

She murmured "thank you" again and left the convenience store thinking of her first attraction to her Stuart. He'd never been as good-looking as this Montana cowboy.

At Sweet Peaks, she parked next to an overhang to a single gas pump. They were both clean and painted blue. She walked around a staircase to the roof garden and found the front of the building. The booths inside were taken by people escaping the heat of the afternoon. Shelves and tables displayed T-shirts, mugs, jars of huckleberry jam, and other Montana goods. She picked up a brochure on one of the shelves that described Kalispell's attractions. The sign above the ice cream cases listed huckleberry ice cream first in bold letters. Huckleberries always reminded her of Thoreau, who Emerson called "the captain of a huckleberry party" and of Twain's *Huckleberry Finn*. She never thought of it with ice cream, but she'd add the Montana flavor to her associations.

While she waited in a line long enough that it indicated the ice cream must be good, she glanced through the brochure. She had plenty of time to do something before she drove the last thirty miles to Glacier. The brochure described the Northwest Montana Historical Museum, the collection of Western paintings in the Hockaday Museum of Art, the twenty-six room

Conrad Mansion, and a half-dozen parks along Flathead Lake.

She eavesdropped on an older couple in front of her who were talking about the mansion. "We missed the docent tour but we can try a self-guided one at two o'clock," the woman said. "We need to do something besides driving and looking at scenery."

The woman was right. The scenery of Idaho and Montana was eye candy. The Conrad Mansion might be an interesting change. She could walk through it on her own then burn off some energy on one of the trails along Flathead Lake. She'd still arrive at Glacier in time for dinner.

The couple left with large cones of huckleberry ice cream, still discussing if they should tour the mansion. She looked at the list of flavors one more time and ordered a small Coffee Traders Espresso in a sugar cone.

"My favorite," said the young man who took her money. He was as good-looking as the Montana cowboy at the gas station's convenience store. "Here you go," he said as he handed her the cone. "Best ice cream from the best state in the country."

"That's what Stuart told me. He sent me here from the gas station."

"One of our most loyal customers. We both love Montana and Sweet Peaks."

"Guess you'll never leave the state," she said, paraphrasing Brad Pitt's line in *A River Runs Through It*.

"Why would anyone?"

"If it's all like this, I understand why you love Montana. Thanks for the scoop. I think you made it a little bigger than normal."

"Always want to treat travelers well."

She pushed the ice cream into her cone with her tongue. It exploded with flavor as good as a morning cup of coffee. She left the shop and meandered through Kalispell's downtown, passing shops for crafts and clothing and the Kalispell Brewing Company. All the buildings were the kind of block style she associated with the West, though she wondered why the flat roofs didn't collapse under the snow.

When she got into her car and turned on her navigation system, it told her to go south toward 4th Street. She'd be fine if she knew which way was south or where 4th Street was. Someone should teach navigation systems to begin by saying left or right instead of north, south, east, west. She guessed and the system quickly told her to take a left onto 4th, then left again onto 3rd. Unlike the businesses, the houses on these streets all had peaked roofs. They wouldn't collapse under the Montana snow. She could live in a neighborhood like this, but she'd been a Bay Stater, a Floridian, an Oregonian. Beautiful as this state was, she wouldn't end her life as an outsider looking for new friends.

She took one more left and turned into the parking lot of the Conrad Mansion, surprised that there was only one car in it. When she got out, she saw why. The couple she'd seen at Sweet Peaks were walking toward her, waving a brochure. "Closed Mondays," said the man. "All you'll get is one of these brochures. They're next to the door. Who'd want to live in a place like this anyway?" He opened his car door and threw the brochure into the back seat. "Let's get out of here," he said to the woman, as if they were escaping the scene of a murder.

The mansion looked like a good setting for one. It was enormous enough to hide murderers or illicit lovers or ghosts of the Conrad family. With its brown shingles and multiple gables, it reminded her of The House of the Seven Gables. Strange, because that house was on a postage-sized piece of land on a narrow street in Salem instead of on manicured grounds like those surrounding this mansion. The brochure told her it was built in 1892. Western forests and two hundred years after the house in Salem made a difference in architectural possibilities.

She walked along the pathway to the entrance, wondering what secrets it might hold. No one was in sight, so she took a brochure and sat on the steps to read through it. The pictures showed an opulent interior with massive, ornate furniture, far different from the dark, rustic interior she remembered when she toured The House of the Seven Gables as a kid. Charles Conrad had been a river trader along the Missouri River while the builder of the Salem house had been a ship-merchant for trade in the Atlantic Ocean. She remembered the secret staircase in the House where the family would hide in case of an Indian attack.

From what she read about Charles Conrad, he wouldn't fear the Blackfeet. He'd married Sings-in-the-Middle and lived with her until she returned to her tribe. The brochure gave only the model-citizen account of Charles. He'd founded Kalispell along with his second wife who brought what they considered high culture to the region. But he also was raised on a plantation in Virginia and fought with Mosby's Rangers on the Confederate side during the Civil War. How many Native Americans and immigrants did he exploit to build this statement of his worth? She couldn't help imagining a novel about some dark ancestral history like the one Hawthorne imagined for the House of the Seven Gables.

She put the brochure back into its holder. There'd be no novel set in Kalispell, Montana. She wanted to clear her mind of thoughts about social hierarchies achieved on the backs of the tired masses. She went back to her car and drove the short distance to Flathead Lake and walked on a trail open to everyone.

After a drive thinking about the gap between the rich and the poor, she felt guilty checking in to the Lake McDonald Lodge.

The brochure for the Conrad Mansion said they were both designed by the same architect, but the lodge had none of the mansion's elegance. It was what its name suggested. A lodge that looked like a chalet that could have been in the Swiss Alps. Its brown clapboards were softened with white trim and a white chimney. Cabins beside the lodge mirrored the design.

She parked Last Chance next to a green Subaru then touched the photo of herself and Stuart on the seat beside her. "You should be with me, but you'd never pay what I did for what's labeled the value room. I had to remind myself that I'm a wealthy, best-selling author. I'm not a rich-bitch like Sarah. I earned my money." As she got out of the car and took her suitcase from the back seat, she told herself to stop criticizing the sister she'd long ago stopped resenting.

She noticed the license plate on the Subaru. *The Spirit of America* was written across the bottom. The Massachusetts' motto was better than New Hampshire's *Live Free Or Die*. She caught up to the man who was a few yards ahead of her. He slowed when he heard her roller bag on the pavement. "Just checking in?" he said.

"I am. I noticed your license plate. Are you from Massachusetts?"

"I hear the 'ah.' If you're not from Massachusetts, you're from New England."

People still noticed the accent she thought she'd lost. "Born and raised in Freedom, Massachusetts."

He glanced around the parking area. "Looks like you're traveling alone."

"I've been living in Oregon for forty years. I'm taking a last road trip to see if I want to move back to Freedom."

He stopped in front of the steps to the lodge. "I'll get that." He pushed down the handle to her suitcase and picked it up before she could object. "You don't look like this will be a last trip."

She liked that this man didn't suggest she was old. He looked well into his sixties, but he was good-looking in an older man sort of way. Gray hair that was thick and wavy, a thin body that still looked muscular despite the tell-tale loose skin on his triceps. "Not my last trip," she said. "Just my last long road trip. I'm calling it Travels with Connie."

"I like that." He opened the door into the lobby. When he pulled her suitcase handle out, and gave it to her, their hands touched. He wore no ring on a hand that showed remnants of paint around his fingernails.

They both stopped inside a lobby that announced the rustic elegance of an historic lodge. The ceiling stretched three stories high and along the walls taxidermied eagles and deer and elk heads stared down at them. Oblong chandeliers embossed with some kind of nature designs she couldn't make out cast a dim light onto an interior made darker because her transition lenses were still affected by the sun outside. Everything was wood and beams. Even the cushions on the wood-framed furniture were upholstered in shades of tan and brown with geometric designs that showed a hint of red. The room seemed designed to keep out the summer heat. A fireplace with a stone façade signaled that the lobby would warm visitors in the winter.

"Nice architecture, but I could do without the dead animals and that painting." The man pointed to a painting of teepees in an Indian village. "It's a good thing it's hung high up so I won't have to look at the brushstrokes."

"It reminds me of how lodges like this were built on the backs of Native Americans and immigrants."

"So people like us can spend four-hundred dollars a night on a room." He walked toward the check-in desk that stood discreetly at the back of the lobby.

She followed him, wondering if his sarcasm was directed at

her. She heard him say, "Jackson Armstrong" as he registered. The name explained the paint around his fingernails. Jackson Armstrong was as mysterious as Thomas Pynchon. His paintings of iconic places like Niagara Falls and Mount Rainier sold for hundreds of thousands of dollars. His subjects were always of bodies of water or high places distorted in a style somewhere between Salvador Dali's and Vincent Van Gogh's. He was notoriously reclusive, never giving interviews, never having gallery openings. Because he stayed invisible, people speculated that he hated humanity and only felt comfortable in nature, that he had Tourette's and couldn't control his outbursts, that he had been born with a face like The Elephant Man's. She looked at his back and dismissed the speculations. He was well-spoken and if he hated people, he'd been friendly enough to her.

He moved aside so she could register. If he recognized her name, he didn't acknowledge it. When she finished, he said, "Your room's across from mine. I'll carry your suitcase."

"I can get it."

"Independent, aren't you."

"I am and it's not heavy." To prove her strength, she lifted her bag and carried it to the staircase. When she reached the third floor hallway, she choked back a cough and disguised that she felt winded.

He followed her with his pack over his shoulder and stopped while she unlocked her door. "Nice to have a real key instead of one of those electronic ones."

"Everything authentic." She nudged the door open and said, "It was nice to meet you."

"How about we meet for dinner? We can talk about Massachusetts. Seven o'clock. I'll make a reservation for two."

She thought about the last night with Gregory and Austin. This trip wasn't turning out to be lonely. "I'd like that."

"I'll knock on your door when I'm ready."

She pushed open her door. "I haven't been back to Massachusetts since my brother-in-law died five years ago. It will be good to hear how it's changed."

"I'll give you all the gruesome details." He opened the door across the hall from hers. He'd paid the exorbitant price she couldn't bring herself to pay for a view of the lake. She could get plenty of viewing when she walked around the grounds.

She closed her door, wondering why he said "gruesome."

Her room was exactly as advertised. A twin bed with a tan spread, no carpeting and only a wooden chair. The sink was in the bedroom and a shelf substituted for a nightstand. The bathroom was tiny with only a shower and toilet, but at least it wasn't a shared one.

She put her suitcase at the end of the bed and opened the blinds and the window to let in some fresh air. She found her journal and put one of the bed pillows on the chair. Dinner was an hour away. Time enough to record her thoughts about the Montana landscape, the threatening rivers captured in movies, the ubiquitous huckleberry ice cream, her increasing discomfort with the social hierarchies that hit the West as soon as it was settled and were as bad in the East. She wrote:

> But it's an adventure, and I'm about to have another one at dinner with Jackson Armstrong. He's a famous painter, a recluse, a man who'll be safe enough in the crowded dining room of the Lake McDonald Lodge. Too many people have been recognizing me. Maybe I'll learn something about how he hides away so successfully.

The Fireside Dining Room carried through the theme of a

rustic lodge with enough touch of elegance to justify the prices on the menu. The windows showed a view of the lake. Connie and Jackson both chose a steak that was cut, the menu said, from cattle on a Montana ranch. They talked about Freedom. She complained that it had grown into a suburban bedroom community with cookie-cutter houses, good schools, and low crime rates. He said he was from a neighboring town that was the same.

"Which one? Westford? Dunstable?"

"Westford."

"I water skied on Lake Nabnasset as a teenager," she told him. "We used a beach in front of a sandpit a friend's family owned. Last time I was there, I visited it. It had been developed, but no one seemed to live in the fancy houses. It was a beautiful Sunday afternoon and there wasn't a kid in sight or a barbecue happening. The cottages on the lake were all turned into fancy year-round homes. Except for one little cottage near the old sand pit. I asked my sister who lives there, but she didn't know. She prefers something more upscale."

He paused a moment, then said, "I live there. There might be no partying in those houses where there was—What did you call it? A sand pit?—but there's plenty of partying on the lake. Everyone has a water-ski boat, a pontoon party boat, and a jet ski."

"Like all the lakes in New England. At least there are still a few hidden ones in Oregon. Not that there are many lakes. It's more river country. What about you? Do you have parties of your own?" She wanted to ease into a question about how he kept his identity secret.

"I keep to myself. Enough talk about Westford and Freedom. Tell me more about why you left the East and why you're going back."

She told him about leaving to live with her mother in Florida and trying to become a writer, about driving across the country forty years ago to escape the memory of her mother's death and a broken relationship.

A waiter interrupted her narrative to clear their plates and ask about dessert. Jackson ordered a dish of huckleberry ice cream. She passed on dessert and asked for a cup of coffee.

"It will keep you awake," he said.

"I'll read a book and drift off into sleep after about five pages."

He confessed that he recognized her name, but he'd never read one of her books. She told him that she'd given up writing fiction and that part of the reason for her trip was to write a travel narrative she was calling *Travels with Connie*.

"An echo of Steinbeck's *Travels with Charley?*"

"It is and it's funny because I've never read that book. I'm guessing Charley was his dog."

"A poodle. And Steinbeck didn't much like what he was seeing. Is the same happening for you?"

"I don't know yet. This is only my third stop. I've met interesting people. Like you." She confessed that she knew who he was, but had only seen photos of his paintings. When the dessert came, she used her coffee cup and he used his spoonful of ice cream to toast their superficial knowledge of each other's work. They agreed to stay mysterious strangers away from the prying eyes of the media.

"Mystery sells paintings," he said. "You should keep your route a secret. You'll sell more copies of *Travels with Connie* if you do. Promise you won't mention my name."

She promised before she asked, "Why so reclusive?"

"Like I said, it sells more paintings."

She imagined there was more to the story but she didn't ask. She thought of Nancy and the idea of witness protection.

Maybe he knew something about the theft of paintings at Boston's Isabella Stewart Gardner Museum. Maybe he was one of the thieves, but the stolen paintings were far from his style. Whatever his story, she'd enjoyed the evening.

When the waiter presented the bill, they split it with no argument then climbed the stairs together to the third floor.

"Thank you for a lovely evening," she said as she put her key in the lock.

"Are you staying another night?"

"I am."

"Then we should drive the Going-to-the-Sun Road together. No reason to go alone. Did you make a reservation?"

"I didn't know I needed one."

"All the more reason to come with me. Wear some hiking shoes. Can you handle a long hike?"

"I'm almost eighty years old, but I can still do a dozen miles. As long as we're not bouldering." She wanted him to know her age, to know that she wasn't a target for a one-night stand.

"So you'll join me?"

When she hesitated, he said, "Don't worry about being alone with a strange man. The place will be loaded with tourists. I'll order us a picnic and meet you in the lobby at eight o'clock. I never eat breakfast."

"Okay, then, she said. But I'll have breakfast first. I never skip it."

As she opened her door, he said, "I would have guessed sixty."

Chapter 8
Going to the Sun

A black truck nearly pushed Last Chance over the cliff at Green Springs. A man with scraggly hair threw a woman over a swinging bridge into rapids. The strains of a gospel chorus drifted into the sky and formed a cloud that turned into a ceiling made from dollar bills.

She woke to the cries of a baby in the room next to hers. Her phone said 4:17. She analyzed her dream the way she'd analyzed the ones she'd been having ever since Stuart died. These were easy, all generated by worry over Nancy and her baby and the man called Mason. She willed herself back to sleep and woke, dreamless, when her alarm sounded at six-thirty. She dressed quickly and went to her car to get her backpack and hiking shoes and the layers of clothing for Glacier's changeable weather. If Jackson didn't show up after she ate breakfast, she'd spend the day as she planned. Alone with nature and a spirit of independence.

A thin cold mist lined the Going-to-the-Sun Road. Within the first two miles she saw that if she had driven alone, she wouldn't have been alone. A couple of red tour buses had already started and dozens of cars were creeping along the road. They passed bicyclists riding in groups or solo. She felt sorry for them until the sky cleared and many of them stopped to catch their breath and look at the view.

"These mountains remind me of Franconia Notch," she said to Jackson, who'd been quiet as he concentrated to avoid forcing a cyclist over a steep drop off that dwarfed the ones on the Green Springs road.

"I haven't been to New Hampshire since the Old Man fell off the mountain." He glanced at her and almost hit a guardrail.

She stopped herself from saying something about Montana drivers. "I used to love going there as a kid. My sister and I always had a competition to see who could spot the Old Man first."

"Forget the nostalgia. It's not like New Hampshire after this curve."

He negotiated a hairpin curve that opened to a view that changed from the forested peaks of the White Mountains to the snow-covered pinnacles of the Rockies. Trees grew impossibly in some of the cliffs and avalanche floes still held snow. The mist and the clouds created rainbow after rainbow. A tunnel through the mountain made her nervous the way tunnels always did. She held her breath until they came through the other side.

"Can we pull over to one of the view spots?" she asked.

"Too many people. We need to get to Logan's Pass before all the parking spots are taken." She didn't like his refusal, but she remained quiet. They reached a sign announcing Logan Pass and The Continental Divide that reminded her of a song about the great divide and the rivers changing directions. She vowed to notice which one flowed west to the Pacific and which east to the Mississippi River.

A Visitor Center loomed at the end of a parking lot that was only half-full. They could have stopped on the road up.

The building was something Frank Lloyd Wright could have designed. It was built of stone and timber and was tucked against the glacial rocks. The roofs were slanted enough to withstand the hundred feet of snow that often fell in the winter. When Jackson parked his car beside a black pick-up truck, she sucked in her breath then let it out when she saw that it was newer and in better condition than the one Mason drove.

"No need to get out here," he said. "We'll keep driving, down the other end of the road to the Iceberg Lake Trailhead. We need to start before there are too many people on it."

She resisted his instruction. "I'd like to see inside. I also need to use the restroom."

"I'll wait here, then. Don't take forever."

She left him standing in the wind next to his car, rationalizing that he was dictatorial because he was afraid he'd be recognized. Inside, a huge fireplace with a copper dome formed the centerpiece of the room. A group of cyclists they'd seen on the road stood in front of it, though it had no fire. They looked like college students and wore cycling jackets that said Bike and Build. She approached them and asked, "What does Bike and Build mean?"

One of the cyclists who must have been growing his hair and his beard for as long as they were riding answered. "We're biking across the country and connecting with Habitat for Humanity every five hundred miles or so. People house us and feed us and we spend a week building."

"Sounds tough."

"It is, but we love it," said a young woman who still wore her bike helmet. "We started in Portland, Maine, and we'll finish in Portland, Oregon. Everybody needs a house."

"A home, not a house," said the young man. "I've been telling Rebecca that every day since we started."

"And I've been telling Tony that home isn't a place, it's the people." Rebecca gestured to the rest of the group who were snapping photos of each other in front of the fireplace.

"Looks like you have both house and home on this trip. Good luck for the rest of your journey." She thought about their debate as she found the ladies room. Maybe neither was right. Maybe home was the journey, not the destination.

When she finished in the ladies room and walked back through the parking lot, she was still thinking about her journey. Jackson was waiting beside his car. He was an interesting interlude, but she was beginning to resent how he directed her without asking her.

"Ready?" he said.

"I am. I talked with some cyclists inside. They're biking from Maine to Oregon and stopping to help build houses with Habitat for Humanity along the way."

"Do-gooders. Just what the world needs."

She got into the car, unsure if he was being serious or sarcastic. On the drive to the trailhead, she decided serious because he was quiet again, careful to avoid cyclists on the road.

He turned at the Swiftcurrent Motor Inn. It displayed a No Vacancy sign despite what looked like a hundred cabins. There were more rooms in a single-story motel with a long porch in front and immaculate white pillars and railing.

"If there are no parking spaces at the trailhead, we'll have to park here." He swung the car to the right and followed the road a few hundred yards to an open parking space. "Good. The trail shouldn't be too crowded yet."

They got out of the car and he handed her the backpack she'd brought. She barely had time to get it on and buckled before he started walking. As soon as they got a half-mile along the trail, she relaxed. The altitude and his fast pace challenged her, but she managed to keep up by concentrating on the landscape instead of her heavy breathing. Yellow lilies and deep pink flowers she couldn't identify lined much of the trail. In the distance she could see bighorn sheep and mountain goats on the sides of the cliffs.

A solitary hiker came at them from the opposite direction. He stopped and said, "Careful up ahead. There's a grizzly with her cubs. A group of hikers are watching it. They've got a guide with a whistle and bear spray so you'll be okay unless they've left and the grizzly hasn't. It's worth the risk. The lake is extraordinary today."

Jackson continued forward without asking her if she'd rather turn around. She would have said no, but she wished he'd asked. The trail wasn't as crowded as the one at Kootenai Falls, but they still passed several groups, some even with young children. An empty six-pack of beer and a crumpled bag of potato chips next to a boulder at the side of the trail nearly destroyed her sense of beauty. The lake restored it. High cliffs enclosed water the color of emeralds. It reflected clouds that seemed to float between a few islands of ice that remained after the summer heat.

Jackson found a spot at the edge of the lake where a cluster of boulders provided shelter from the wind. "Take off your pack and sit there," he said. "I'm going to sketch you."

"I'd rather you didn't." She didn't want to be reminded that she looked like an old woman.

"Please. I'd like to remember our interlude."

"Since you put it that way, okay."

He sketched long enough that her back started to hurt. She ignored it and listened to the sounds around her. Birds, the wind, a piece of ice breaking, the voices of the myriad hikers who began to arrive. When he finished, he closed his sketchbook and took out the picnic box he'd ordered at the McDonald Lodge.

"Do I get to see it?" she asked as he handed her a box.

"Not until I turn it into a painting."

"I'll be gone by then."

"I'll paint it when we get back." He sat beside her, opened the picnic box, and unwrapped a sandwich that smelled like salami. She would have chosen something different if he had asked, but she accepted the salami sandwich he gave her. They ignored the other hikers around them, and talked about mountains they'd climbed, lakes they'd swum, and animals they'd spotted. She began to like him again. Nature had taken away his arrogance.

It was almost nine o'clock when she settled onto the bed in her room and began to write in her journal.

> *Jackson Armstrong seems to have tired of me. I drove with him on the Going-to-the-Sun Road and then we hiked what he said was the best hike in Glacier. I never did learn how he knows the park so well, but he was right about the hike. Except for the bit of litter we saw. I can handle tourists, but I get furious when I see that someone has trashed nature. Anyway, about Jackson. When we got back to the lodge he said he wouldn't be going to dinner, so I sat alone, ordered a Caesar salad, and read some of A River Runs Through It. It seems an appropriate choice for the long drive through Montana.*

She was about to describe the Bike and Build cyclists and how they made her think about why she was traveling and what she meant by home. A knock on her door stopped her. She got off the bed and opened the latch. Jackson stood there with a glass of champagne in his hand. "Come to my room. There'll be fireworks for the Fourth of July. We can watch from the balcony."

"I asked at dinner. This lodge doesn't set off fireworks."

"We might be able to see the ones from Whitefish. Besides, it's a beautiful night. We can pretend the stars are sparkles in the sky."

He sounded poetic and she would be happy to see the lake from a room with a view. "Just let me get a sweater." She found the one sweater she'd packed in her small suitcase, slipped her arms into it, and opened the door. He'd left the one to his room open. When she followed him inside, he closed it. She wanted to say that he could leave it open but decided that would make her look like she thought he had more than fireworks in mind.

They went onto the balcony where they could see children running along the lake shore waving sparklers. There were no fireworks, but the moon and the stars and the lights from boats on the lake were enough. "Do you stay here often?" she said. "You seem to know everything about Glacier."

"I come once or twice a year."

"It's a long drive from Massachusetts."

"Confession," he said. "I've never been to Massachusetts. The car's a rental. When you said Westford, I agreed. I live on a tiny lake in Minnesota."

"You lied." She started off the balcony.

"Don't go. I didn't intend to. When you asked me about my license plate, I thought you looked interesting so I let you think that. It was easy to fake the little cottage on a lake. It sounds like the one I call home. Besides, you are interesting."

She put the glass of champagne he'd refilled onto the bureau. "That's not an excuse. Are you even Jackson Armstrong?"

"I am. Here's what I was doing at dinnertime." He turned on a light next to an easel where he'd transformed the sketch of her into a painting. She cringed at what she saw. It showed her sitting among rocks that bled into Iceberg Lake. Her hair was emerald and she wore a dress as white as the ice floes. The lines of her body were distorted and the wrinkles on her face were as grooved as the lines on the cliffs that seemed to reach down for her.

"Like it?" He put his arm around her and pulled her to him. She pushed him away. "It's terrifying."

"Just like old age. I knew you'd be a good subject when I saw you in the parking lot." He put his arm around her again. "You've proven to be feistier than I expected."

She twisted out of his arm.

"Relax. A little sex will liven up *Travels with Connie*."

"I'm not interested." She backed away toward the door, afraid that he'd come after her.

He didn't move. "Too bad," he said. "I usually find someone who is when I come here. They always consent. I'm not a rapist. Of course, I always choose younger women and they never know who I am. Eighty-year-old novelist and sixty-year-old painter. Sex might be tame, but it will be something to write about."

"Pig," she yelled as she reached the door. She opened it, and ran across the hallway, glad that she hadn't locked her door. She slammed it and locked it, already knowing what she'd do. In *Travels with Connie*, she'd make her pen as poisonous as his paintbrush.

Chapter 9
Lights Out in Glendive

She woke several times in a cold sweat caused by dream she couldn't remember. Toward morning a hand like the one at the end of *Deliverance* pulled her, naked, under an ice island. Jackson's face came at her through the water, his lips pursed like a fish ready to bite. She woke for the last time, gasping, pushing away the bed covers as if they were ice floes. Slowly she became aware of her tiny room where light was just peeking through the line of windows. She pulled the covers around her, but they weren't comforting. Jackson Armstrong had spoiled what was supposed to be the most spectacular part of her journey.

She got up and dressed without showering. When she closed her suitcase and stepped into the hallway, she looked at Jackson's door. The hallway was cold and she felt like the painting Jackson had created, her face distorted and the hand that rolled her suitcase wrinkled like an old crone's. Defiantly, she picked up the suitcase and carried it down the staircase without holding the banister. She checked out with a desk clerk who must have gotten up hours early to apply make-up and style her hair into just the right jagged edges.

"No breakfast?" the clerk asked in a voice that sounded too

cheerful for the early morning.

"Not today." She pulled up the handle to her suitcase.

"Wait. I'll get someone to help you with that," said the clerk.

"I'm fine." She realized how she must look. An elderly woman, the wrinkles of her face free of disguising make-up, her hair barely combed. She pushed the handle of her suitcase back in and picked it up to defy the image of age before she went through the front door. The McDonald Lodge could keep its overpriced breakfast.

She found a drive-thru Burger King in Browning. Her breakfast sandwich wasn't good, but at least the coffee was hot.

The landscape in Eastern Montana overwhelmed her as much as the memory of Jackson Armstrong. She should have seen the signs. The way he let her do most of the talking about Massachusetts, the way he knew so much about Glacier National Park, the way he commanded instead of consulted her.

She put Last Chance on cruise control and focused on the road instead of her encounter. It took her beyond the buttes near Glacier to the high flat plains of ranch land. She'd visited Eastern Oregon enough that the vast space wasn't a surprise. Still, it felt foreign. Even boring. She was traveling exactly the way she had wanted to avoid. A long, straight road with nothing to break the monotony except the cloud formations that she couldn't appreciate from the car. This wasn't the Montana of mountains and rivers and movies.

After nearly five hours of mesmerized driving, she began to worry about gas. The tank was almost empty when she came to a sign that pointed her to food and fuel. She drove into a town with a gas station, a feed supply store, and a church with rows of chairs set up in front of it. Despite the chairs, the town seemed deserted. She recited the steps as she got out of Last Chance and stood in front of the pumps. Unscrew gas cap, card in and out, select regular, nozzle into the tank, pull the trigger. When she took the nozzle out of her tank, it hadn't fully emptied and gas sprayed onto her hands and arms. She put the nozzle back onto the pump and went to find a restroom in the station. The door was locked, the station as empty as the street.

She went back to the car and found the water jug she'd been cautioned to always carry in the back seat. She splashed water onto her arms and hands, wiped them with a paper towel, then rubbed on the lavender hand sanitizer and thought of the Old-Time Gospel Singers. Instead of getting back onto Route 2, she followed the main street, hoping to find some place to use a restroom. The center of town had a couple of houses, a grocery store, and a bar with a casino. Everything looked worn out. If this was a prosperous town, it didn't show. A building labeled Café was on a corner. A blinking light flashed Open, so she parked in front of it. Behind it, she saw what looked like a school.

A bell jingled when she went into the café. The room held four empty booths and a line of empty stools along a counter. Not a good sign, but she was committed. A woman stood behind the counter. As if she could read her mind, the woman pointed her to the restroom. It was clean and after using the toilet, she soaped her hands and arms to get rid of the gas smell.

When she came out and sat on a swivel stool at the counter, the woman said, "I told my husband we needed to stay open. Travelers always come by at this time of day." The woman was gaunt with blond hair styled in the kind of beehive that was popular in the 1950s. "I'm Hazel. It's just me and Tina over at the grocery."

"Is it always this quiet?"

"I get a good breakfast and lunch crowd when ranchers come in to buy what they need at the grange. I don't open at night. Anyone who comes to town goes to the bar. No one will be anywhere today except at the funeral."

"That must be why there are chairs in front of the church."

"Dumb kids. One dead and three taken off to the hospital in Glasgow. What are you ordering?"

Connie looked at the menu board on the wall behind the counter. Everything looked heavy and grease-laden. "Grilled cheese. Water to drink. What happened to the kids?"

"What happens every couple of years. Joy riding on the ranch roads. Going nowhere special. Just passing time after working the ranches all day. Most times kids get hurt but not killed. Real bad this time. Todd Edwards was going off to college in New York City. Used to come in and talk about how he needed to get out of Montana. Now he's dead. Don't know why these kids all think it's greener pastures in some crowded city. Eleven kids graduated from the high school this year. All wanting to leave to see the world. Most come back."

Connie thought of how Callie explained that her parents sent her to college so she could decide if she wanted to live the life of a rancher in Fossil. She knew that she had done what these teenagers wanted to do. Explored America. Deciding now where to live. And where to die.

The phone rang. Hazel set a grilled cheese sandwich with a tiny slice of pickle in front of Connie and answered it. "That sounds bad. What about Clyde and Marlyss? ...Check in after the funeral. Tell me how Todd's parents are holding up." Hazel hung up and wiped her eyes with her apron.

"Are those other kids going to be okay?"

"Two are on their way home from the hospital. Getting here in time for the funeral. Stephie's not so good. She was Todd's girlfriend. Bad enough that he was leaving for college. Now he's dead and it looks like she'll be paralyzed." Hazel cleared the plate. "Where you headed?"

"Home to Massachusetts. She surprised herself with the word "home.""

"One of those Easterners wanting to come out here and buy up land. They soon find out that the federal government owns most of it. Too many people taking away our freedoms." She picked up a knife and sliced into a roll of salami. The knife strokes were angry.

Connie reached into her purse for her wallet. "I'm just passing through. I won't be looking to settle here."

Hazel stopped slicing. "That'll be nine dollars. We've got no meals tax so I keep it simple. Just the dollar amount."

Connie left eleven dollars on the counter for a sandwich made with thin white bread and processed cheese. "How far is it to Fort Peck?"

"About an hour. Stopping at the dam, are you? That's what all the tourists do."

"Is it worth the stop?"

"I wouldn't know. I've never been there. Drive safe."

"I will." Connie left, another wish for her safety mingling with thoughts of the boy who'd died because of Montana drivers' love for speed and teenagers longing for freedom.

Outside, a few pick-up trucks and SUVs drove passed the café. Rancher's vehicles. She wondered what those teenagers had been riding in when they crashed. Was life any safer for teenagers here than in a city? Boredom or bedlam. Either way, people lived and died in places as different as the vast landscapes of the world.

She drove past the church. Except for the landscape, the scene could have been anywhere. People consoling each other with hugs and hand-holding. She reached across her seat and touched the photo of her and Stuart in the hollow of a tree. Was the outpouring of grief she saw in front of the church any deeper than hers when she stood with Molly while he was lowered into the earth?

She watched the scene recede in her rearview mirror and drove back onto Route 2 until she reached a sign that directed her south to Fort Peck. When she parked at the dam, she understood its magnitude. The late afternoon sun bounced off the twin towers of the dam's power control buildings. Under the concrete pillars that supported the spillway, the Missouri River flowed into the artificial lake created by the dam. She got out of Last Chance and took a few photos. The massive construction interested her less than the view of the water it controlled. Nature might be tamed but it wasn't defeated.

When she went inside to look at the displays, she couldn't process the technical information about the dam's length, its height, the number of kilowatts of power it generated, the length and depth of the artificial reservoir it created. She was a writer, not an engineer.

The visitors around her were predictable. The men studied the engineering detail, the women looked at photos of the families who settled in the area while the dam was being built or brought the children to the floor below to look at the dinosaur exhibit. The site had been chosen to control floods and provide irrigation. She wondered if it had really been necessary or if Roosevelt used the dam as a way to provide jobs. Those families who found work in Montana were grateful to a president who was leading them out of the Depression.

She stayed long enough to stretch her legs and to appreciate what engineers had achieved a hundred years ago. Maybe their ingenuity could figure out how to solve the water problems of the twenty-first century.

She spent the last of her drive thinking about how environment shapes people's views of the world. Engineers wanted to control it. Even American Indians wanted to control the fires that plagued the West. Stuart had preferred living in the hills above Ashland despite the danger of fire while she needed the culture of the town. She thought of the people she'd been meeting. Harshad had been shaped by the lifestyle of Rajneeshpuram so much that he longed to go back even as Barbara rebelled against it. Callie chose the isolated life of an Oregon rancher and the woman at the café couldn't understand why anyone would want to leave Montana. The world was different for young people now. Television, movies, social media. Kids grew up knowing there was more to the world than their postage stamp of soil. Even regional accents were disappearing.

There'd been no universal media when Cedric, Aretha, Reggie and Olive were growing up. When she was a kid, she hadn't known about the hostile environments that had been their heritage. She thought of Nancy. What environment had prompted her to get involved with a man like Mason? Was she like Gregory, trying to find a home on the waters of Lake Pend Oreille?

She turned her attention to the thunderclouds she could see in her rearview mirror. Montana was Big Sky country. Storms announced themselves. As she got closer to Glendive, she felt like she was driving away from a sword shooting lightning bolts. She found her way to the chain hotel where she'd reserved a room, parked under the overhang to the lobby, and went inside to register.

The receptionist looked like she was a high school cheerleader, small with an animated face. "I'm sorry. The only room we have left has been reserved," she was telling a man who wanted a room.

The man leaned on the counter toward her. "Unreserve it. There's a fuckin' storm outside."

The receptionist backed away. "I can't do that."

"Can't or won't? Whoever reserved it probably ain't comin'." A tattoo of a snake pulsed along the side of his neck.

"Last month I gave away a room and had to turn down a family with two little kids who reserved it." She reached for the desk phone, ready to call for help.

"Fuck it, then. I'll sleep in the back of my truck." The man slammed out of the hotel into the storm.

Connie approached the counter. "I'm Connie Lewis. I have a reservation for that last room."

"I'm glad you made it. That man was scary. People like him used to come through all the time. Oil workers from the Bakken fields in North Dakota driving two hundred miles to get a break from the trailer camps they were living in. Most were nice, though. Just wanted to get away from the fields. Not many come now since jobs dried up during Covid. A man tried to talk me into giving away a reservation last night. He was creepy. Scraggly gray hair and a T-shirt with Qs on it that looked like it hadn't been washed for weeks. I felt bad after I gave him the room, but at least the person who reserved it didn't show up."

Connie tensed at the description. "Do you remember his name?"

"I don't." The young woman slid Connie's credit card and a key across the desk. "Room nineteen. To your right. There's a parking space in front of it. Better get settled before the power goes out. It always does in a storm like this. If you need to eat, The Homestead is just down the street. Take a left and you'll find it. They've got a generator."

"Thanks." She went back outside, glad of the overhang. The rain was coming down sideways. The only truck she saw was black, but much bigger than a pick-up. The man who wanted a room would be comfortable enough sleeping in its cab.

She found Room 19 and ran through the rain to get inside. Her suitcase could wait until the storm passed. The receptionist was right. As soon as she got inside, the power went out. It wasn't even six o'clock in the middle of July, but there was barely enough natural light for her to find the bed. She lay down and counted the seconds between the lightning flashes she could see outside the window and the thunder that followed. Gradually, the lightening stopped and the thunder became more distant. The storm passed but the power didn't return. She could have fallen asleep, but she knew she'd wake hungry in the middle of the night so she got up and went to her car to find her way to the restaurant the receptionist mentioned.

The Homestead was lighted and its parking lot was full. When she went inside, she saw that most people were eating family style. Plates of food, half-eaten, filled round tables set for eight or ten. A woman holding a baby in a pink onesie stood up when she saw her looking around. "We've got an empty seat. Always happy to welcome strangers caught in a storm."

She accepted the invitation. She didn't have much choice and meeting locals the way she had at The Fisherman's Bar could be interesting, help her forget the encounter at the hotel and the receptionist's description of a man who could be Mason.

"I'm Agatha." The woman pointed around the table. "Polly. Tom. My daughter Trixie. Her husband Joe. Joey. He's five. My husband Clyde."

"And the baby? Are you her grandmother?" Connie hoped she'd guessed right. The woman could be still young enough to have a child.

"Baby belongs to Nora. She's working in the kitchen. This here's Connie." Agatha held the baby against her shoulder.

"That's my name."

"Want to hold her?" Agatha moved the baby away from her shoulder and held her toward Connie.

Connie took the baby and held her so her head wouldn't wobble. She patted her dark wisps of hair and studied her face.

Her eyes were wide open and she looked like she was about to cry. Connie moved the baby to her chest. She smelled of powder and nuzzled at her neck. It felt good.

A woman approached the table carrying a glass of water. "All the tables tonight ordered family style. Best we can do when the power's out. I can fix you a plate of pot roast or a chicken casserole that comes with a side of corn."

Connie looked at the nearly empty containers of food on the table. A casserole dish with chicken mixed with a creamed soup, a huge pot with the remains of a roast, a smaller bowl with the last remnants of corn that came from a can. No salad or anything green but at least pot roast had carrots in it. "Pot roast."

The waitress looked down on Connie then quickly turned away. For a moment, Connie thought she was Nancy. She had the same youthful body structure and facial features, though unlike Nancy, she wore glasses. Her hair was cut short. If she grew it long, it might curl like Nancy's, but it was blond instead of dark. Connie pulled the baby away from her chest and murmured "Amy."

"I'll take her." As Agatha took the baby and settled her, she said, "Maybe you had a baby named Amy?"

"No children. Just a niece who's in her fifties. I'm picking up her daughter in Minnesota and driving her to Massachusetts to see her grandmother."

"Sounds like you're a long way from home." Clyde started a conversation that lasted through the plate of pot roast a different waitress put in front of her. Five-year-old Joey kept them entertained with questions about mountains and trees and what kind of big machines she'd seen. His favorite word seemed to be "gigantic." He talked like a savant about trucks and tractors and bulldozers and graders and excavators that weren't the same as backhoes.

They were finished eating and counting out money for the meal when the lights came on. The waitress who looked like Nancy returned to the table. Agatha handed her the baby. "Here's your mommy." When Nora took her and the baby tried to root, Connie felt a tinge of regret. Her books were her babies. None ever loved her back.

She tousled Joey's hair as she got up from the table. "I'll watch for backhoes and excavators on the rest of my trip. I promise I won't mix them up." Outside, the air smelled fresh after the rain. No black pick-up truck passed her on her way to the hotel. When she took her suitcase out of the back seat, she noticed the case of wine. She hadn't uncorked a bottle in the five days she'd been on the road, so she opened the trunk and chose a red because it didn't need to be chilled.

She set the bottle and her suitcase on the ground in front of her room while she fumbled for the key. A loud, choking cough startled her. She turned and saw that it came from the truck where the man who'd wanted a room was sleeping. She unlocked the door, grabbed her things, and locked the door behind her. Joey's litany about trucks and Nora's resemblance to Nancy had unnerved her.

She changed into pajamas, opened the wine, and settled herself with her journal on an upholstered chair generic to chain hotels. The wine was a smooth pinot noir from Irvine and Roberts. She sipped it slowly as she wrote in her journal, concentrating on the people and land of Montana. Ready for sleep, she wrote a last line.

After this, one more night alone in a motel room. Seeing this family at dinner made me ready to see Lizzie and Hannah. Even Sarah. I'm tired of talking to strangers and a photograph in the passenger seat of my car.

Chapter 10

Invaded Landscapes

The waitress named Nora was standing next to Last Chance with a sling wrapped over her shoulders and around her baby. An enormous duffel bag, a diaper bag, and a car seat lay on the ground.

Nora held a coffee cup from Starbucks in her free hand. She pointed her cup to another one next to a paper bag on the roof of the car. "I brought coffee and croissants. Please, take us with you. I know you recognized me last night."

"I recognize you now that you're not wearing glasses. You're Nancy."

"And this is Amy."

"How did you find me? How did you get here with all these things? Why should I take you with me?"

"One question at a time. I have to get some place where Mason won't find me. It wasn't hard to find your car. Second hotel parking lot I looked in. I hid my things under it and drove back to The Homestead. Mason will think I'm still in Glendive."

"How did he know you were in Pend Oreille?"

"I was at the lake for over a year and thought I was safe. Someone who knows me came into The Fisherman's Bar one night. He must have told Mason. Gregory and Austin watched out for me, but after the night you were there I knew I had to leave."

That sounded plausible, but it didn't explain Montana. "How did he find you here?"

"I figured that out last night. He came into the restaurant when we were closing and asked Ronnie if a woman with a baby left her cell phone."

"Ronnie?"

"The owner. He does some of the cooking. He said he'd ask in the kitchen. He told me a man wearing a T-shirt with a bunch of Qs on it was looking for me.

"That doesn't explain how he found you."

"Ronnie said anyone who knew my number could trace me through a service called Spyic. Mason must have seen my phone the night he found me in Pend Oreille. I gave Ronnie my phone and he told Mason I left it on one of the tables. Amy and I have been staying at Ronnie's."

Nancy's story sounded as fishy as the name of The Fisherman's Bar. "You were in Pend Oreille three days ago. How did you get here and get a job so fast? And an owner who took you in with no questions asked?"

"I left Pend Oreille when you did. Drove ten hours to Glasgow, Montana, so I could get far away from Mason. I checked into a cheap motel, and cut and dyed my hair. When I reached Glendive, I saw a Help Wanted sign in the window of The Homestead. It wasn't hard to talk myself into a job. Ronnie even offered me a room until I got settled. I told him a story about an abusive husband. Not much of a lie except that Mason's not my husband."

"What about your car? Doesn't Mason know what it looks like?"

"I left my car in front of The Homestead and walked here. It won't take Mason long to figure out I'm gone. Please, take us with you." She put her coffee on the roof of Last Chance and shifted Amy to her other shoulder.

"Why don't you go to the police? They'll find a shelter for you."

"I don't need a shelter. I just need a place where he can't find us. Please. You can leave us wherever you're going."

"I'm going to Massachusetts." Connie didn't trust someone who appeared mysteriously in Pend Oreille, bought a motel with cash, and found a grandfather who might not be her grandfather. Taking Nancy and Amy wouldn't be a journey to freedom. "He could find us both. You need to contact the police."

"Please. He won't find us right away. You can leave us some place in a couple of days."

Connie studied Nancy and her baby who was snuggled against her shoulder. Whatever her mother was, Amy was innocent. The worst Nancy or Nora or whatever her name was would do was steal her car. The only things in it that she cared about were the copy of *East Angels* and the photo of her and Stuart. She hesitated another minute. When Amy whimpered, she gave in. "Okay, then. Put the car seat in back."

Nancy unwrapped Amy and gave her to Connie while she secured the car seat. The baby smelled warm and delicious in the cool morning air. When she handed her back, Nancy said, "I named her Connie after you."

"Is her name really Amy?"

"I'll tell you the whole story when we're driving." She strapped the baby in while Connie opened the trunk of the car and made room for her duffel bag. Nancy put the diaper bag next to Amy and got into the back seat.

"You can sit in front," Connie said.

"I will. Just let me settle her. She'll sleep."

She wondered why Nancy didn't say the baby's name. As soon as she started Last Chance, she saw that the fuel gauge registered close to empty. She found the closest gas station and decided to test Nancy. "I'm uncomfortable pumping gas. Will you use your credit card and do it? I'll give you cash."

Nancy kissed Amy on the cheek and got out of the car. "Can I use your card? Mine's at the bottom of my duffel bag."

She remembered all the talk at The Fishermen's Bar about her paying for everything with cash. She was sure Nancy was lying. "My ZIP code's 97520."

Nancy took the card and filled the gas tank like a pro. Wherever she was from, it wasn't self-serve-only Oregon. Amy had stayed asleep, so Nancy got into the front. Connie took back her credit card and handed her the lavender hand sanitizer.

As they drove out of Glendive, they passed the high school. It displayed a huge sign showing its mascot, The Red Devils. The logo was oval with a black and white border and the words Red Devils painted red with a three-pronged spear going through them. If it was originally a reference to Native Americans, the logo showed no trace of it.

"When we get out of Montana, can we stop in a mall so I can buy a new cell phone?"

"We can stop in Dickinson. It's a college town. You'll be able to find something there."

"You've done your research."

"I have. First stop I want to make is at the Theodore Roosevelt National Park. Do you feel comfortable with that?"

"No problem. Mason will think I'm still in Glendive. I'm good for an hour carrying the baby in her sling."

Connie noticed "the baby." Not "my baby." Not "Amy."

When they crossed into North Dakota, buttes rose against a cloudless sky. They followed a sign into the Theodore Roosevelt

National Park. It wasn't as famous as Mount Rushmore with the carvings of Roosevelt and three other presidents. Washington. Jefferson. Lincoln. All governing during times even more fraught than the present when a former president was lobbying to be added to the row of monuments. Connie preferred the natural landscape of this North Dakota park.

She parked next to a giant van and wondered how much nature people who used these actually saw. Vans with bathrooms, kitchens, television sets. They might as well stay home and save the gas money. She'd been stopping more than she wanted to fill Last Chance's gas tank, but at least she got good mileage and prices were lower than a year ago. Then, again, maybe a van permanently parked somewhere would be an option for Nancy and Amy.

Nancy opened the door. "I'll meet you in the Visitor Center. I need to change the baby."

Connie followed her into a Visitor Center that looked like all the others she'd seen. Someone at a counter giving out information and collecting entry fees. T-shirts and magnets and coffee mugs for sale. Photos of the most famous views hung along the walls. A case with artifacts found in the park stood in the center of the room. She imagined the area when the native peoples lived in an environment without needing camper vans with running water and gas-powered stoves.

She found the restroom and watched as Nancy changed Amy. She was a good mother. She was whispering something about making her all clean and fresh. Amy's eyes were tracking her mother and her mouth was almost a smile. Watching her, Connie realized that she was only three or four months old. If Nancy had owned The Five Trouts for over a year, she bought it before Amy was born, maybe even before she was pregnant. Maybe she wasn't running from Mason because he was the baby's father. But if not Mason, who?

She went into one of the stalls, planning how to open a conversation about where and when Amy had been born. When she came out of the stall, Nancy said, "Will you watch her while I pee?"

"Of course."

Nancy carried the diaper bag into the stall. Connie stood in front of Amy, her hands resting on the baby's stomach even though she was too young to roll over and off the counter. "Who's your daddy? You'll have dark hair. Wavy like your mommy's." Amy found her fingers and put them into her mouth. Connie took them away and lifted her up, nuzzling their faces. She'd never wanted a child of her own. Lizzie had been enough and she'd had plenty of babysitting time before her sister took Lizzie to Europe and she took their mother to Florida.

"Let me carry her awhile," she said when Nancy came out of the toilet stall.

Nancy unzipped the diaper, quickly stuffed in the blanket she used under the baby, and zipped the bag closed. "She'll get heavy."

"A load I'll treasure. When we get on the trail, I'll give her to you. I'm pretty good on my feet, but I need to remind myself that I'm about to turn eighty."

"Really?" Nancy sounded shocked. "If I live that long, I hope I'm in as good shape as you are."

"If?"

"Forget it. What should we do first? Find one of the trails or look in that cabin outside the Visitor Center."

"That was Roosevelt's cabin. I learned about it when I researched the park. It was called the Maltese Cross when he bought it, so he kept the name."

"What's the Maltese Cross?" Nancy shouldered the diaper bag, clutching the bottom as if it were as precious as Amy.

"It's a medieval symbol of knighthood. It looks like four arrowheads connecting in the middle. I have no idea why the name for the cabin. Maybe Roosevelt liked how it dignified him. It's also a symbol of protection the way he wanted to protect the wilderness."

"I could use a bit of that protection."

"From Mason? What's with those Q's on his T-shirt?"

"Ever heard of Q-Anon? He's a follower. Thinks there's a cabal of pedophiles in Congress run by the Democrats."

"They're crazy. You need to get away from Mason. Amy needs a home. I'll help you make a plan."

"That doesn't concern you. Can I have your keys? I'll leave the diaper bag and get the baby sling."

Connie held Amy tight with her left arm while she fished the car key out of her pocket. She started to give it to Nancy then changed her mind. She pressed the key fob. "Lock it when you finish. I'll meet you at the cabin." She put the key back into her pocket and shifted Amy, who'd started to squirm.

As she walked with Amy to the cabin, she whispered the story. "Roosevelt was a good president. He wanted to preserve all this beautiful land." She stopped talking to a baby who couldn't understand her and looked over the gray buttes tinged with shades of greens and reds made by geologic deposits eons ago. She thought of Roosevelt, who promoted conservation at the same time that he was a hunter who indiscriminately killed buffalo. The piece of land preserved in his name was now invaded with camper vans and mountain bikers who tore up the trails open to them in the park.

Nancy joined her inside. They walked quickly through the three rooms. Living room with a coal stove, the rocking chair Roosevelt liked to sit in, and the desk he liked to write on when he wasn't too busy hunting. Bedroom with bureau and mirror and a rifle standing behind his trunk. Kitchen with a large cookstove. She learned that ranch hands bunked in the attic. She assumed they cooked for him. Roosevelt's ability to rough it only went so far.

Nancy held her arms out for Amy. "Let's go outside. I'm feeling trapped in here."

Connie held Amy close before releasing her. She needed to help Nancy so Amy wouldn't be raised by a mother on the run. She gave Nancy the baby and followed her outside.

"Can I have your keys again? I should nurse the baby before we hike."

This time Connie let her keep the keys. "I'm going into the Visitor Center to find a trail map. How long should we plan to hike?"

"Not too long. It's getting too hot for the baby."

Connie would have liked a long hike, but Nancy was right. The sun was already strong. She went inside to ask about trails. A park ranger was standing next to a photo of what was labeled "mushroom rocks." The group of rocks on pedestals did look like mushrooms. "Is it a long hike to these rocks?" she said.

When the ranger looked at her, she realized he was seeing an old woman. "Probably longer than you want. The best short hike is the Wind Canyon Trail. A bit steep, but only half a mile."

She felt compelled to defend her fitness. "Not a problem. We have a baby with us. A long hike will get too hot for her."

"Just drive part way along the scenic loop. There's a parking lot at the trailhead." He pointed to a shelf of teddy bears. "We sell lots of these bears in honor of Teddy Roosevelt if you want something to occupy the baby."

Even park rangers had turned into marketers, but Connie liked the idea. She read the sign next to the display of bears and discovered that Roosevelt earned the name when he was hunting in Mississippi. He refused to kill a bear that was tied to a tree.

Not that he was opposed to killing bears, just that to kill one tied would be unsportsmanlike. She'd get money from her purse that she left in the car and buy a small one. She'd have to tell Nancy to remove the glasses and the rough riders shirt when Amy was big enough to pull them off.

When she got back to her car, Nancy was sitting in the front seat with the door open still nursing Amy.

"I'm getting money for something in the gift shop. Need anything?"

"No. Amy's almost finished so we can get on with this hike."

She took her credit card out of her purse. She had plenty of cash but she liked the airline miles she could earn by using her card. When she entered the Visitor Center again, she smiled at the ranger and held up her credit card. "You talked me into it."

She paid and carried the bear unwrapped back to the car where Nancy was strapping Amy into her seat. Nancy accepted the bear Connie held out to her. "You're too good to us." She rested the bear in the car seat next to Amy who paid no attention.

"When she's old enough to hang onto it, take off the clothes so she doesn't put something she can choke on in her mouth."

"Of course. Give her another month and she'll know how to cuddle it. I'll tell her that the nice woman who gave us a ride bought it for her."

Connie felt a moment's relief that she wasn't going to have to help Nancy forever. She adjusted the bear next to Amy. She'd miss her.

They drove in silence to the parking area for Wind Canyon Trailhead. When they got out of the car, Nancy wrapped Amy in the sling so she was facing forward. Her eyes were wide open and she moved her head around as if she were appreciating the scenery. The Little Missouri River lay below them and grasses that were still green in early summer blanketed the canyon.

The trail was short, but the altitude challenged her breathing. Except for the number of people taking an easy hike, Wind Canyon had been a good choice. Amy stayed wide-eyed until they returned to the car. Nancy put her into her car seat and her eyes closed. Connie wondered what babies who had no language dreamed. Maybe Amy was seeing images of the sun-dappled buttes and the winding river. Maybe she was seeing the teddy bear she hadn't yet reached for.

They drove out of the park and along Route 94. They had only gone a couple of miles when Nancy said, "Can we stop so I can buy a phone?"

"Let's skip Dickinson and wait until Bismarck. There's a little town I found online called Hebron. It's known as The Brick City. We can find a place to buy sandwiches and eat in a park." Connie knew that the drive through North Dakota after the Theodore Roosevelt Park would be along a boring interstate, so she'd researched a place to stop that wouldn't dump her into a city. Hebron looked perfect. Online it boasted its school, its library, its museum, and its history of brickmaking. All this in a town of fewer than a thousand.

"Okay, but then I really need to buy a phone."

"Do you have people to call? Someone I can take you to?"

"I have no one. Except for the baby."

"Are you ready to tell me your story?"

"I'll tell you when we're having a picnic. Right now, I need to rest a bit. I didn't sleep last night."

Connie glanced at her. She'd already closed her eyes.

The park in Hebron was tiny, but it was right on Main Street near where they bought lunch. It offered shade under a maple tree, green grass, and quiet. Amy lay on a blanket watching the sunlight flicker through the leaves while Connie and Nancy ate tabouleh salads garnished with spring greens and sugar snap peas. They were both glad to eat something that tasted fresh from the earth. Hebron had been a good choice.

When Amy started to whimper, Nancy picked her up to nurse her.

Connie tried an opening to get Nancy to tell her story. "You take good care of her. You said you bought The Five Trouts a year ago. Were you pregnant then?"

"I didn't find that out until I already bought the place. The baby complicated things, but I managed. Gregory and Austin helped me. Gregory's not my grandfather, by the way."

"I didn't think so. How did you manage to convince him that he was."

"It's easy. All you have to do is listen to people. Let them fill in the gaps."

It was easy. Jackson Armstrong had duped Connie into believing he lived in Westford. "They would have helped you anyway."

"They're good people. When I told them I was pregnant and had no insurance, they found me a midwife. By the time the baby was born, I'd earned enough to pay her. Childbirth is a natural thing. My daughter was born on my bed in The Five Trouts. On April Fool's Day." She shifted Amy to her other breast. "We fooled them, didn't we, Sweet Cheeks?"

"Fooled who?"

"Gregory. Austin. The midwife. The whole town, actually."

"Why do you never say Amy?"

"If I'm going to have to run again from Mason, she'll need different names. Our real names are on the birth certificate. At least I could do that much for her."

"What are your real names?"

95

Nancy pulled Amy from her breast. "Why would I tell you?" Amy must have sensed her mother's anxiety because she started to cry.

"I'll take her." Connie reached for the baby and swayed with her so she stopped crying. "You're not Nancy. Not Nora. Amy's not Amy or Connie. How can you get away with changing identities?"

"I had sources. You can get passports, birth certificates, financial records, but I settled on just a driver's license and a social security card. I had a half dozen made, all with different names, all with photos of me with different glasses, different hair color, different hair style. I knew I might need them. This baby has created complications, but she's the best thing I have."

Amy's hand touched Connie's neck. She wanted to take care of her the way Nancy was. "Why are you running?"

"You met Mason."

"Is he Amy's father?"

"That's what Gregory and Austin think." Nancy avoided answering the question.

"It doesn't matter. He's a threat and I'm helping you get away. I suppose you thought you'd be safe at The Five Trouts forever. Where did you get the cash to buy it? How do you manage without a credit card?"

Nancy reached into the diaper bag for a clean diaper and baby wipe and quickly zipped the bag again. "I had savings," she said as she changed Amy. "When I had to leave Lake Pend Oreille, it wasn't hard to find a job. It won't be hard to find another one. People like to help a woman alone with a baby." She got off the blanket and picked up Amy and the diaper bag. "Let's go. I want to get to Bismarck so I can buy that cell phone. I've got enough cash from last night's tips. We had plenty of customers because the power went out."

The drive through North Dakota had seemed interminable. This was farming territory. Fields of sunflowers that hadn't yet blossomed followed by fields of wheat and soybeans. The farms were huge industrial complexes with power lines crisscrossing the landscape. Mass production rivaled tourism for a blight on the environment. The only break they had was in Bismarck, where Nancy used cash to buy her cell phone. She used Connie's credit card to pump gas. When Connie asked again how she had so much cash, Nancy said that she closed The Five Trouts bank account before she left. Connie suspected that she never had a bank account.

Nancy fell asleep for the rest of the drive, leaving Connie to watch the open spaces of North Dakota. In the silence, she thought about the legacy Amy would inherit. An earth dying under climate change, a mother raising her alone, an unknown father.

Only when they reached another chain motel that she'd booked in Detroit Lakes, Minnesota, did she begin to feel better. The motel was on a lake and it had a restaurant attached so they wouldn't have to get back into the car to find a place to eat. Connie paid for the room she'd reserved. There were no others available, but there were two queen beds in the room so they ordered a crib brought in for Amy.

When they took their luggage out of the car, Nancy insisted on bringing in the car seat. She set it on the floor in the room and put Amy in facing outwards so she could look around.

"Want to swim?" said Connie. "Amy might like to feel the water."

"I should feed her again. You go. We'll come down later."

Connie put on her bathing suit, grabbed a towel, and left Nancy and Amy alone in the room. She needed exercise. She tested the water then walked into the lake and did a shallow dive. As she swam back and forth a dozen times, she went over what Nancy had told her. She'd explained how she'd convinced Gregory that he was her grandfather, but she hadn't explained how she found the motel or had enough money saved to buy it. She hadn't explained why Mason was following her or if he was Amy's father or what her sources were for her fake documents. Maybe she really had been put into witness protection and was supposed to testify against Mason for some crime. But if that were the case, why wasn't Mason in jail and why did Nancy have to escape on her own? She gave up thinking. She didn't know where Nancy had come from or where she planned to go. The only thing she knew was that Nancy loved Amy and took good care of her.

She got out of the water and lay on a lounge to rest after a swim she used to be able to do without losing her breath. She dozed and woke chilled when the sun had moved away from where she was lying. She went back into the room, wondering why Nancy hadn't brought Amy outside for some fresh air.

When she opened the door, she saw why. The car seat was gone. So were the diaper bag and Nancy's duffel bag. Connie's wallet lay next to her purse on the bureau. A note lay beside it.

You've been good to us, but we have to leave. If I
ever find you again, I'll return the money I took.

The note was as empty of a signature as Connie's wallet.

Chapter 11
A Story to Tell

Goosebumps erupted on her skin. She wrapped the towel around her and opened the curtains. Nancy had taken her money but not her car.

She called the front desk. "Did my roommate order a taxi?"

The receptionist sounded like she'd had a long day and was ready to go home. "No one ordered a taxi. Maybe your friend called an Uber." She hung up before Connie could ask if she'd seen Nancy leave.

Using Uber would explain why Nancy wanted a phone. Until it didn't. Connie had no account and Nancy would need a credit card to open one. She checked her wallet. Her credit card was still there.

She stepped out of her wet bathing suit, toweled off, and slipped into a pair of jeans and a T-shirt. A hot shower would feel good, but she needed to find Nancy. She picked up her phone that was charging on the nightstand. The last call was to Lizzie. She found the phone number for Detroit Lakes police then changed her mind. Nancy was resourceful. Whatever reason she had for leaving, she'd protect her baby.

The phone showed 6:22. Gregory and Austin would be busy at

The Fisherman's Bar. She found the phone number and pressed the call button.

"Fisherman's Bar."

She recognized the voice. "Austin. This is Connie Lewis. I've seen Nancy."

"Seen her? Where? She bolted."

"She was in Montana working at a restaurant. Her hair was short and dyed blond and she was wearing glasses. She'd changed her name. This morning she was standing at my car asking for help to get away from Mason. I drove her and Amy through North Dakota and now she's disappeared along with the little money I had in my wallet. What's going on?"

"Is the baby okay?"

"She's fine."

Austin's voice was drowned out by the laughter of what sounded like a full table at The Fisherman's Bar. "We're slammed right now. I'll call you back in an hour. There's a story to tell."

She distracted herself from the wait by going into the hotel restaurant and ordering the quickest thing on the menu, macaroni and cheese with a side salad. The cheese was the orange Wisconsin cheddar. She never understood why it was dyed orange, but she'd read that the dye was from a some kind of natural seed. Her New England roots kicked in. Mac and cheese should be white. Maybe it was her memories or maybe the color or maybe her impatience to hear what Austin and Gregory knew about Nancy. Whatever it was, the meal tasted as flat as the grilled cheese sandwich she'd had in the little town where the teenagers died.

She finished, put the meal charge on her room tab and went back just as her cell phone rang.

She pressed the green call button and blurted out, "What's the story? I'm worried about Nancy and the baby."

Austin asked what he had before. "Is the baby okay?"

"She's fine. Nancy wouldn't even let me change her diaper. She's a protective mother."

"I worry about Amy more than Nancy."

"Don't." Connie wondered if she should do the same until she remembered how Nancy nursed Amy.

Gregory took the phone and started to tell the story. He kept detouring into how Nancy had betrayed him. Finally Austin took the phone from him.

"We called the police when we found out that Nancy was missing. It only took a day before they traced her real name through the baby's birth certificate. Naomi Bagshaw. She was a runaway at age sixteen. Apparently her father was abusive, though her mother denies it. Her mother's name is Amy, by the way. Nancy got caught in the surge of Oregon's pot growing. Her baby's name is Alice, father unknown. That's when the Feds got involved?"

"The Feds?"

Gregory yelled into the speaker. "She's a liar and a thief. You're well rid of her."

"Easy Gregory." Austin turned off the speaker and held the phone close to his mouth. "Nancy stole money from an illegal marijuana grow in Oregon."

"Where in Oregon?" If it was close to Ashland, that would explain why Mason passed her in Green Springs.

"Central Point."

"That's close to where I live. Lots of illegal grows that are sucking up all our water."

Austin continued. "This one was a snake pit. Illegals living in squalid conditions and working fifteen hour days, all too scared to complain. When the police raided, Nancy took hundreds of thousands of dollars from the safe and drove away in a car she'd parked at the edge of the grow. Apparently she and Mason had been planning this for a long time. She bolted on him."

"Maybe she wanted to help," Connie rationalized. If Nancy wanted to help, she wouldn't have stolen money. Her head spun explanations. Nancy feared the police would take her baby from her. She needed to escape Mason and protect Amy.

Gregory turned the speaker on and spat out his words. "Don't be naïve. The growers traded marijuana for tools and snowmobiles and dirt bikes. They could sell those legally and put money they couldn't deposit from illegal pot sales into the bank. Nancy knew the schedule. According to Mason, the bank run was scheduled for the next day."

"Why isn't Mason in jail?"

Austin spoke more calmly than Gregory. "He's missing. The owner of the grow is in jail, charged with human trafficking, illegal sales of marijuana, illegal use of the mail, and bank fraud. The police, the FBI, the postal service are all involved. They'll find them both."

She wasn't so sure. "Nancy told me she had access to fake documents. I thought maybe she was in witness protection. Something to do with Mason."

"Naïve again," said Gregory. "The grow site had access to documents for the illegals. She knew how to use the system. She and Mason planned this together. How'd she get to wherever you are?"

"She said she needed to escape Mason again so she drove until she found a job in Glendive, Montana. She saw me when I stopped at a restaurant. She was waitressing."

"If nothing else, she's resourceful," said Gregory. "Probably traded sex for a job."

"It doesn't matter. Mason found her again and she's bolted."

"You need to call the police."

She paused before she answered. "She has enough documents and enough money to hold her until she finds a job. And find a safe place for herself and Amy away from Mason."

Gregory yelled into the phone. "She's a thief, Connie. She knew how those people were living. That sweet mother image is all a façade. She deserves to be arrested."

"What about her baby? If Mason's the father, he could claim Amy."

Through the speaker phone, Connie listened to Gregory and Austin arguing.

"Leave her be," said Austin. "Let that baby have a life. Mason's not the father."

She heard Gregory slam a glass on the counter before he said, "You've been saying that for days. She puts on a good show. Maybe you should take the baby."

Austin spoke softly. "I'm a single man. Forty years old. All I know is fishing. What kind of father would I be?"

One of them turned off the speaker phone so all Connie could hear was mumbling between them until Austin picked up the phone. "I convinced him. Whatever Nancy is, she was escaping an illegal marijuana grow. Not just illegal. People were living in a barn with no running water and only porta-potties that hadn't been emptied in weeks. It's a good thing she didn't get pregnant while she was there. Don't worry about her. She knows how to take care of herself." He said something to Gregory that sounded like "Forget it now," then said to her, "Let us know if you find her." He ended the call.

She debated with herself. Should she listen to Gregory and call the police or listen to Austin and let Nancy find a life for herself and her baby. She remembered how Nancy knew to undress the teddy bear when Amy got old enough to pull off a button. Maybe she was naïve like Gregory said, but she pushed away her doubts and chose Austin's way. She wouldn't call the police and let them take Amy away from Nancy. At least not yet. The only thing she could do now was drive around Detroit Lakes, find a taxi company, a bus line, a car dealership.

She went outside to Last Chance. A note lay secured beneath the windshield wiper.

> *Don't try to find us. We'll be okay. I won't let anything happen to my daughter.*

No name for the baby. No signature. No thank you.

She put the note in her purse, got into Last Chance, and typed Detroit Lakes Bus Terminal into her map application before she noticed that the teddy bear was lying in the back seat. Was Nancy discarding her gift or was she leaving a gift so Connie would remember them? "I'll call you Amy," she said over the voice giving her directions.

The app led her to the bus terminal on Highway 10. She whispered "Stay safe" to the bear and went inside.

A few people were sitting on benches under a sign displaying arrival and departure times. She described Nancy and Amy to each one. A young mother holding a baby said, "I would have noticed. I've been here for two hours waiting for a transfer bus to Fargo." An older man with a bald head that made him look like an aging Yul Brenner overheard them and said, "Try the Amtrak station. It's on this street."

She thanked him. Before she went outside to her car, she stopped at the ATM in the station to replace the money Nancy had stolen. When she got into Last Chance, she talked to the teddy bear. "Don't worry. We'll find her." She followed her navigation system to the Amtrack station. It might once have been busy, but now it was nothing more than a whistle stop.

A schedule posted on the door indicated trains leaving only at 12:05 P.M. before she and Nancy had arrived in Detroit Lakes and at 3:15 A.M. If she didn't find Nancy and the baby, she'd set an alarm and come back, though it seemed like a weird time for a train stop at an isolated station.

She drove around Detroit Lakes until she found a motel chain similar to the one she was in. In the lobby, she realized she didn't know a last name for any of Nancy's aliases, so she simply asked if a woman with short blond hair and a baby had checked in. A receptionist with piercing blue eyes pushed a blond curl away from his forehead. "I just came on duty, so even if I could give out that information, I wouldn't know. You can call her. If she's here, she can call the desk and ask me to give you her room number."

She cursed herself for not insisting on getting a number when Nancy bought the phone. "Thanks anyway." She tried three more hotels and gave up. Every receptionist said they couldn't give out information about guests. Every one of them was tall, blond, and blue-eyed. This was Minnesota at its most Scandinavian.

She drove around Detroit Lakes for another hour, admiring the high school with its sign Home of the Lakers, its Carnegie Library, two of its numerous golf courses, and its waterfront along the lake. At nine o'clock, she realized she was hungry and found a pizza place still open. She ordered a take-out pepperoni pizza and took it back to her room where she wrote in her journal. She recorded what she remembered of the day. Nancy's fake IDs, her fear of Mason, her pleas to get a cell phone, her stealing. She stopped and read over what she'd written. Her handwriting was wobbly, like the writing of an old woman. She flexed her fingers and continued.

I'm eighty years old. I shouldn't be so gullible.
First Jackson Armstrong, now Nancy, Nora, Naomi,

whatever her name is. I can't imagine her at a marijuana grow as squalid as Gregory and Austin say it was. Why didn't she report it? Why did she take the money without Mason? Maybe she wanted to escape before she gave birth.

She crossed out the line.

She wasn't pregnant when she left. She's protective of Amy. Wouldn't even let me change her diaper.

She stopped, then added:

She wasn't protective of Amy. She was protective of the diaper bag. It was filled with money she was hiding at The Five Trouts.

She stopped writing again and went over the conversation she had with Austin and Gregory.

Austin is Amy's father.

She closed the journal, set her alarm for 2:30 and went to bed.

The alarm woke her from a dream that was the worst she'd had since Stuart died. It had been unreeling in slow motion. A young woman who looked like Nancy was staring at a rerun of *Days of Wine and Roses,* drinking steadily from a bottle of gin on the nightstand, laughing with a man next to her who looked like Mason. The woman was running her fingers through his not quite clean hair. At first she cut the gin with ice and tonic water.

When the ice was gone, she drank it warm until the tonic water disappeared. After that, she took swigs from the bottle until she passed out on the man's shoulder. Slowly he moved her aside, opened the curtains to survey a parking lot and a Holiday Inn sign. He pulled on his clothes, turned to look at the woman, picked her up and carried her out the door. The scene shifted to a black truck parked on a cliff above a lake with murky water filled with algae. The man took a baby out of the truck bed, walked to the edge of the cliff and dropped the infant in. When the alarm went off, the baby's arm was slowly sinking beneath the water.

She shook off the dream and went into the bathroom to splash cold water on her face. It wasn't a dream, it was a nightmare like the ones that had started when Stuart died. They were getting worse. She needed to stop sleeping in strange hotel beds. Maybe they'd stop when she had Hannah with her for the last part of her journey.

She dressed quickly and went outside into air that was still warm and humid. She drove out of the hotel parking lot and turned right. As soon as she made a second turn, she realized she had no idea how to get to the station again. The street was so deserted she could have stopped in the middle, but she pulled to the curb. Her navigation system was the only noise that broke the silence. The voice directed her around a few more streets back to the one where she'd stopped. "Frontage Road," the voice said. She obeyed its directions onto North Shore Drive then quickly onto Route 10 and into what served as the Amtrak parking lot. Her phone said 3:06. The station had a waiting room, but no ticket counter, no kiosk for purchasing a ticket. Unless she could pay in cash on the train, Nancy would have to order a ticket online, but she had no credit card to do that.

She sat on a bench where she'd be able to see Nancy if she appeared. She knew it was unlikely, but she waited anyway. The train whistle blew in the distance, announcing its arrival. Still no Nancy, no anyone. A lone man exited, the train doors closed, and it pulled away at 3:15, as punctual as a Swiss train.

The man approached her. He was tall, thin, and under the station light so pale she thought he might be albino. The white shirt he wore and the glow of the light made him look like an apparition. "You waiting for someone? The train only gives you two minutes so if you're not at the door, you're out of luck." His voice was as wispy as his appearance.

She pretended to look at her phone for a message. "She missed the train. She'll be on the next one."

"Noon. Too bad you had to stay up for this crazy hour. You going anywhere near the Radisson? If you are, you could save me calling an Uber."

"Sorry, no." She'd had enough of strangers. As she left the station, she felt his eyes following her. She got into Last Chance and locked the doors. The teddy bear in the back seat seemed to whisper "Stranger Danger."

She talked to the copy of *East Angels* Everett had given her so long ago. "I trusted too many strangers the way I trusted you. Jackson and Nancy betrayed me more than you did. I long ago forgave you." She glanced at the photo of her and Stuart. "It was a good break-up. I found you."

She thought about the name she'd given her car. Was this her Last Chance? So many people around her were dead or dying. But she still felt young despite how winded she'd been in the high altitudes and a stomach that was starting to rebel against bad restaurant food. She wondered if she'd feel young again when she was driving to Massachusetts with an almost teenager. It had been years since she'd been around girls that young. She wouldn't have the same connection with Hannah that she'd had with Lizzie when she was twelve.

She found her hotel and her room. In the bathroom, the haggard face of a stranger startled her. She was a woman traveling alone, trying to reinvent herself. Lizzie and Hannah wouldn't know that today was her birthday. Eighty wasn't a number to celebrate. She vowed to sleep late and not arrive in St. Paul until dinner time. A day alone would help her get ready for the company of family instead of strangers who weren't what they seemed. She crawled into bed and drifted into a sleep filled with images of empty trains and albino men.

Chapter 12

Perhem Pride

Her pledge to sleep late hadn't worked. She woke with the sun and tossed in bed for an hour before she gave up and got dressed. As she checked out of the hotel, she asked one more time about a woman with a baby. The receptionist hadn't seen anyone like Nancy and Amy.

She felt too jittery to eat breakfast so she drove around Detroit Lakes one more time, past the empty train station and the bus station where a few people were going inside to wait for the next bus to wherever Nancy might have gone. The only way she'd find her would be for Nancy to call.

She focused on the road instead of her stomach that was unsettled from her day of searching. She turned on the radio but could find nothing except a religious station and one that ran through the price of corn and wheat. Minnesota land was fertile, kept moist by the state's ten thousand lakes. The season should be a good one if summer didn't bring drought or floods or a bug infestation. She concentrated on its beauty instead of the toll of industrial farming on the environment.

A half hour beyond Detroit Lakes, she turned into a town called Perhem and found a café. Only one table was left. The accents with long o's filling the room told her the other diners were from the Midwest. Most wore T-shirts and tank tops that marked them as tourists getting ready for a day on a lake. She opened the menu and found the café's signature breakfast. Walleye, eggs, home fries, biscuits. It made her think of The Fisherman's Bar where Gregory and Austin would be busy serving breakfast. If she called them now, they wouldn't be able to talk.

A waitress stopped at her table carrying a coffee pot. "What'll you have?"

"Some of that coffee, please. And the Sunrise Breakfast."

"How do you want your eggs?"

"Over easy."

"Bacon or sausage?"

"Bacon."

"White, wheat, rye toast, or biscuit?"

"Wheat toast."

"Juice or home fries? They cost extra."

"No, thank you. Just some water."

Their conversation was as clipped as ones captured in jokes about taciturn New Englanders. She felt comfortable until a man stopped behind the waitress and put his hand on her waist. "See you tomorrow, Debbie."

The waitress pulled away from him. "You touch me again and I'll call the police."

Connie watched the man go out the door. The back of his T-shirt showed a single Q outlined in black. She told the waitress what she'd told Nancy. "If he keeps bothering you, you should call the police."

"Won't need to. He'll leave with the other Q people camped out at Big Pine Lake. They'll head to Minneapolis and start some kind of demonstration. They're all crazy." She poured coffee and left to place the order.

Connie listened to the conversation of four women behind her the way she'd listened in The Fisherman's Bar. The talk could happen in any small town in America. Whose child or grandchild was going to what school. Whose zinnias had started to bloom. Recipe ideas for the zucchini they'd soon be overloaded with. One woman suggested stealth offerings on people's porches and another suggested a contest for who could grow the biggest zucchini. When they launched into gossip about people they knew, they said nothing about a woman with a baby who'd come to town and paid for everything in cash. Wherever Nancy was, Connie hoped she wasn't in Perhem near more Q-Anons.

After the waitress returned with her breakfast, Connie took out her cell phone to see if she could find something to do so she wouldn't arrive in St. Paul until late afternoon. The Perhem website revealed a town proud of itself. It rose with the railroad and the logging industry and had managed to stay vibrant despite fewer than three thousand residents. A place to live, work, and play in the center of lake country. Besides gift shops and golf courses, resorts and campgrounds, it boasted a history museum, a veteran's museum, and an international turtle competition.

The waitress appeared again. "Finished?"

"I am. Tell me about this turtle competition."

"Too bad it's Friday. You could see one for yourself. Every Wednesday morning people come out and race turtles."

"Race how?"

"Not what you think of as a race. The turtles all go into the center of a circle. Whichever turtle crosses the ring first wins."

"Why international?"

"People come from all over the world during our Turtle Fest in June. Mostly just locals and summer people after that. Don't know if it will last much longer. The animal rights people are complaining. They're as crazy as Q-Anon."

"Do you think the town mistreats the turtles?"

"They're native to the area. The town collects some and rents them out for the summer. We adopt them and feed them well. They race on brick pavement and we splash them with water so they stay wet and the bricks stay cool. At the end of the summer, we release them back into the wild."

Connie wasn't surprised about protests. Any animal released into an area it didn't come from was likely to die. She managed to say, "It sounds interesting. Like you said, 'it's too bad it's Friday.' Can you recommend a hiking trail?"

She gave Connie a you're-an-old-lady look. "Lots of easy trails. What are you looking for?"

"Maybe something around one of the lakes."

"Go to Maplewood State Park. It has lakes and ponds and miles of trails to choose from. It's about a half-hour, just off Route 10."

"Thank you. It sounds lovely." Connie left money for the bill and the tip and went outside. She looked around nervously, half expecting to see Mason in his Q T-shirt. She was glad the waitress hadn't recommended Big Pine Lake.

If Minnesota was the land of ten thousand lakes, Maplewood Park was the land of ten thousand people. Beaches were as packed in the early morning as ones she remembered in Florida when snowbirds invaded in winter. Paddle boats and kayaks dotted the water on the biggest lake. The smaller ones were edged with camper vans and tents. She'd driven around the labyrinthine roads until she saw a place to park. She'd hiked the Grass Lake Trail, stepping aside too often to avoid cyclists and horseback riders. As much as she longed for the quiet she knew with Stuart at Green Springs, she was glad to see people outdoors.

After an hour and a half, she drove back to Perhem, hoping that its history museum was cooler and less crowded. She parked in an empty lot and studied the outside of the building. It was stone with a cupola that looked like it had once been a church.

Inside, she was greeted by a blast of cool air and a lone volunteer. She stopped herself when she noticed that the woman was elderly. Today was her eightieth birthday. She suspected they were contemporaries, but this woman had hair rinsed with whatever salons used to make the hair more blue than gray. "Blue hairs," she and her friends used to call them. The woman wore bright red lipstick and glasses with rhinestones edging the black frames. She must have been farsighted because the lenses magnified her blue eyes. A badge on her white blouse identified her as Engla, a name as old-fashioned as her appearance.

"Welcome." Engla pointed to a guest book. "Sign yourself in. We like to know where our visitors come from."

Connie signed her name and paused before she wrote down Freedom, Massachusetts.

Engla looked at the book. "Long way from home. What brings you to Perhem?"

"I've been living in Oregon. I'm driving home to Freedom." She surprised herself again when she said "home."

Engla studied her then looked back at the book. "Connie Lewis. I know who you are. I've read all your books."

Connie felt the momentary fear of what would come next. A comment about a good book but not to my taste or a bland I liked it.

She relaxed when Engla continued. "I read that you stopped with the last one. Too bad. I liked that one. *Forty Years Found.* You always make me feel like I'm in the places you write about. Never been out of the Midwest myself. My favorite was *Twenty Years a Wanderer.* All about that little girl who chases a robin around a cemetery. If you like cemeteries, Perhem has three. One's right here on First Avenue. St. Stan's. It's a Catholic one."

Finally, Engla stopped and gave Connie a chance to respond. She was sincere when she said, "You're the kind of reader I imagine when I write."

"You should write another one. They help me through Minnesota's winters."

"I'm planning to write a kind of travelogue about this trip I'm taking. It won't be ready this winter, but maybe the next one. I'll write a section about Perhem. It seems like a nice town."

"The best."

"I'll include something about this building. Was it once the Catholic church?"

"Episcopal. Got lots of Catholics in town, though. Used to be a crossroads for the clergy. I'm not a Catholic myself. Minnesota Lutheran. What about you?"

Connie wasn't going to tell a church-goer about her transition into atheism, so she said. "I do like cemeteries, but first I'd like to look through your museum."

"It's all about Otter Tail County, not just Perhem. We go way back to the railroads. Not as far back as Massachusetts, but far enough. Built up as a logging town. Now we've got tourists. Year round even."

"I noticed."

"They're all out on the lakes now. It's just me and you in here. I'll walk you around. Explain the exhibits." Engla stood up and reached for a cane that hung from a coat rack behind her. Her commentary was non-stop. She didn't converse, she talked, giving Connie no chance to ask a question.

At a case showing artifacts from the railroad, Engla expounded on how Josiah Perhem settled the area. He was president of the Northern Pacific Railroad and seized on the location where he helped to build the logging industry. Connie thought about the man at the Amtrack station in Detroit Lakes and wished that Engla would become as ghostlike.

"The logging display is one of our most interesting." Engla pointed her cane to a series of photos along the wall. "These photos show how the logs were cut and hauled to the Otter Tail River. I like the memorabilia from the logging camps best." She pointed her cane again to items displayed on the floor and along the wall. Axes and saws, spiked boots, woolen socks, and woolen underwear. Connie imagined the smell of wet wool. "This is my favorite. Imagine cooking a stew in that pot. They served eighty men who needed five thousand calories a day. Imagine how much bacon they ate. Hard work logging. Imagine how much energy a lumberjack used."

Not as much as the energy from your mouth, Connie thought.

"Too bad logging died when the amount of white pine became scarce. But Perhem knew how to survive."

Connie thought about the controversy over its turtle races. Perhem might have to change its marketing to emphasize the lakes.

"Here's our school exhibit. Do you remember these wooden desks? We didn't have ink in the ink wells when I was a kid, but we still lifted the desk top and put our books inside. Flippy Rochen used to flip the tops closed so they pinched our fingers. How he got his nickname. He was mean. Used to kill frogs just for fun. I wonder what happened to him. Did you have a bully like that in your school? Teachers watch out for bullying these days."

Engla talked so much no one would have a chance to bully her. "Do you quilt?" she said.

Connie started to say that her pen was her needle, but Engla didn't wait for an answer.

"Lots of ladies in Perhem still quilt. We've only got two quilts here in the museum. This one's a log cabin quilt. It uses small strips that can be pieced to together to form blocks or any other kind of geometric pattern. This other one's my favorite, though. Just a patchwork that Velma Adams, 1875 to 1926, made from her husband's shirts. He had lots of them. See how she alternated his white ones with blue ones and pinstripes. I wonder if it gave her comfort, all this sewing."

Connie thought of Stuart's shirts. The flannel ones he wore in winter would make a quilt, but she'd given them all away.

"Right here's the film clips we have from the 1920s." Engla used her cane to press a button just as a young couple came inside. "Guess you'll have to watch it alone. It's good. Got lots of postcards you're allowed to look through." She pointed the cane to a table with several photo books lying open on it, then walked to greet the newcomers.

Connie stayed long enough in front of the film projection to see a clip of a woman posing in a black bathing suit cinched at the waist, high on the neck, and boy cut at her upper thigh. She waved at the camera and dove off a dock into a lake. The film reminded her of the joy of growing up with a circle of friends. Since she became a writer, she let herself become isolated. Not that she didn't have friends, but she no longer gathered with a group to laugh. With Stuart gone, she was letting herself become old and crotchety. Engla was tiring, but at least she had enthusiasm. She walked by the desk where Engla was saying, "Sign our guest book. We like to know where our visitors come from."

If the museum had a wall map with little pins to mark locations, Connie would have taken one out and left it on Engla's chair. Something Flippy Rochen would have done. When she got outside and into her car, she spoke out loud to the teddy bear. "That was an ordeal. I'm glad you can't talk. Let's get some lunch and find a quiet spot in a park to eat." She stopped herself then spoke again. "I'm as bad as Engla. Talking where no one can answer."

She drove to the café she'd gone to in the morning and ordered a take-out Cobb salad. The waitress named Debbie took her order. She was more talkative than she'd been in the morning. "How was Maplewood?"

"Crowded. I didn't stay long. I just came from the history museum."

"I hope Engla wasn't there."

"She was. She knows a lot about Perhem."

"She doesn't converse, she just babbles." Debbie put the salad container into a paper bag.

"Thanks," Connie said as she took it. "Can you direct me to a park I can walk to?"

"Go to the right, walk past some of the shops and you'll get to Turtle Race Park. You'll see why we love our turtle races."

She took the bag from Debbie and opened the door just as the man with the Q T-shirt entered. He bumped against her and said, "Watch out, lady."

"You as well. Stay away from Debbie."

He bumped her again, harder this time. She looked back into the restaurant. Debbie had disappeared, she hoped to avoid him.

She passed several shops that displayed stuffed turtles in the window. After she ate, she could buy one to keep the teddy bear company.

When she reached Turtle Race Park, she found that it wasn't a park where she could wander tree-lined paths. Its focus was a giant sculpture of a turtle painted in the colors of a Rubik's cube. A circle formed with gray brick was surrounded with grass. An inner circle where the races began lay within the larger circle that had a diameter that looked about fifty feet. The race ended when a turtle crossed the circle's circumference. Water sprayed on the turtles during the race would catch in the grass. She'd like to be sprayed herself. It was hot, which explained why only one group of women were sitting at a shaded bench. They looked like they were on their lunch break. She found a spot under a tree and sat on the grass. As soon as she opened her salad, yellow jackets found it.

A woman in a light cotton dress came over to her. "I see you found the yellow jacket tree. All us locals know not to go near it. We've been trying all summer to get the town to spray them. Can't use pesticides, they tell us. Mosquitoes are even worse but not at midday."

"Isn't Minnesota the mosquito capital of the United States?"

"Beats me, but we've sure got a lot of them. We're headed back to work." She gestured to the bench where two other women were packing up their lunches. "Use our bench. It's shady there."

"Thank you. I'm just going to eat this salad, stop in one of the shops to buy a stuffed turtle and be on my way. Any suggestions for which shop?"

"Nancy's Nook. Right on Main Street."

Connie's overactive reflexes twitched at the name.

"You can get a yellow jacket there, too. It's our school mascot. Nancy sells cute ones small enough for a baby to hold. You buying stuffed animals for a grandchild?"

"Great-grandchild," she lied.

"Nancy has the best collection in town. Your great-grandchild will love whatever you pick." She went back to her friends, leaving Connie to wonder why she was driving alone with a bear that didn't talk back.

Chapter 13
Finding Family

Her navigation system announced "You have reached your destination on the right." She parked on the street in front of a tree-shaded house with gray shingles and white shutters. A step led to a flagstone landing and a front door framed with more flagstones. A door painted the green of the surrounding trees welcomed them.

"We're here." She spoke to the bear and to the turtle and the yellow jacket she'd bought at Nancy's Nook. The name of the store made her hope that she'd find Nancy and Amy again. At least she hadn't named the bear Amy. None of the animals had names. She bunched them together and covered them with the blanket she kept in the back seat. If Lizzie or Hannah saw them, she'd do what writers do and make up a story.

The door to the house opened and Lizzie ran to her. "Happy Birthday, Aunt Connie."

"You remember," Connie said as they hugged.

They pulled away and studied each other. Lizzie was tall like her mother and the dad she lost when she was just three years old, but she had Connie's sturdy build. Her niece was older now than her father had been when a train drove into his truck. She always thought of it that way. The train was the actor, not George, the boy Connie had a crush on but Sarah married. She'd long ago forgiven Sarah for stealing her not-quite boyfriend. Forgiven her for more than that.

"I couldn't forget this birthday. Eighty years old. How's that feel?"

She said what Lizzie had answered when she turned thirteen and everyone was asking the same question. "No different. Just older." She omitted Lizzie's "glad to be."

"You look the same as you did five years ago when we visited."

"So do you. Except the new glasses. I love the red frames."

"My nod to fashion. Hannah's escaped our myopic vision, but she's not as sporty as us. She's been asking if we'll have to go on hikes. She couldn't keep up when we visited you after my stepdad died."

"She was only seven. Has she turned into a robust teenager?"

"Not a teenager yet. We'll celebrate her thirteenth birthday in Freedom in August. Tell me you'll stay that long. She'll need someone besides my mother to hang out with."

"I promised Sarah one month. I should have come to Freedom more often after your stepfather died, but I needed to spend as much time with Stuart as I could before he died." A familiar wave of sadness rose from her stomach to her throat.

"Don't act like two grieving widows. Mark and I can't come for another two weeks. Hannah will need more than my mom's swimming pool to keep her entertained. I'm not sure this was a good idea."

Connie opened the trunk of Last Chance to take out suitcases. "You mean leaving her with two old women? I don't know about your mother, but I can keep up with her."

Lizzie grabbed the heavier suitcase. "I'm sure you can. Come inside out of this heat."

"I've forgotten how hot it feels with humidity. It's knocked the wind out of me. I wish you could blow some into Ashland."

"Maybe if the wind didn't blow west to east. Maybe in another decade we'll pump water instead of oil through all the pipelines people are fighting over." Lizzie pulled up the handle to the suitcase and started to the door. "Mark will be home soon. Dinner's simple. Salads and burgers on the grill. Tell me you haven't turned vegetarian."

"Vegan."

Lizzie stopped before opening the door. "You should have told me. I'll call Mark and ask him to pick up some veggie burgers on his way home. You can skip the potato salad. It has mayonnaise."

"Relax, Lizzie. That's a joke. I'm neither vegan nor vegetarian, though I've been eating too much on this trip. My stomach feels bloated."

"Don't start dieting until you leave St. Paul. A little weight has always looked good on you."

Connie would only mind the weight when she saw tall, slender Sarah. A glamorous sister. At seventy-eight, she'd probably look majestic instead of matronly.

Lizzie opened the door into a foyer that led to a living room furnished with an upholstered sofa and a matching loveseat and chair that faced a fireplace with a stone hearth. Books in shelves on either side of the fireplace were arranged neatly, all hardcover and most from the Library of America series. Lizzie was an English professor. These were books for show, not the marked up ones she would use in her classes.

"I'll show you your room if you want to freshen up." She pushed down the handle to the suitcase and carried it through the living room to a stairway on the right. Connie noticed the muscles on her arms. Lizzie was more like her than her mother, whose idea of exercise was to lift a wine glass.

The stairway ended on a landing with a window that looked out on a cement patio with a stone wall and a built-in stone fireplace for barbecuing.

"Hannah is in there." Lizzie gestured to a closed door on the left. "She's probably listening to music through earphones. She'll come out as soon as I tell her you're here. Mark and I are at the end of that hallway. Bathroom's here." Its open door was to the right, opposite Hannah's room. "We all share it, but Mark showers downstairs."

She started down the short hallway on the same side as the bathroom. The guest room was small, but big enough for a queen sized bed, a bureau, and a dressing table with a mirror.

"Closet's full with my winter clothes," said Lizzie. "Even if I hadn't blocked it with a towel rack for you to use, there'd be no room for your clothes. At least the rack gives you a place to hang wet towels. The top drawers in the bureau are empty. Make yourself comfortable. Come down when you're ready."

"This is perfect, Lizzie. A welcome change from the hotels I've been staying in."

"You can tell us all about your trip at dinner."

Lizzie left Connie to find a spot where she could open her suitcase. She set it in front of a low door next to the bed and at a right angle to the closet. She opened the door. It was dark, but she could see that it was a storage area under the roofline. She guessed that the other hallway had no storage area so that side of the house was bigger. Lizzie and Mark's room was probably large and Hannah wasn't sleeping in one the size of a bathroom.

She set her larger suitcase in front of the door to the storage area and put the smaller one on the bed where she could take out her ditty bag. There was nothing in the suitcase now except her dirty clothes. She pushed it into the narrow space next to the bureau. She'd rearrange things later and ask Lizzie if she could do some laundry.

She picked up her ditty bag and a towel and face cloth and went into the bathroom. When she used the toilet, she saw that the toilet paper rolled under instead of over and remembered the picture in the bathroom at The Fisherman's Bar. She'd have to give Lizzie a lesson on the science of toilet paper and why rolling it under increases the spread of bacteria.

She finished in the bathroom, her face and her teeth feeling clean and presentable. She exchanged her glasses that darkened for her clear ones. In the dressing table mirror, she saw that the gray frames highlighted her gray in a way that complemented instead of hid her age. Maybe Hannah wouldn't think of her as an old lady. When she went into the hallway, she heard the door to Hannah's room open.

Hannah was standing at the doorway, waiting for her. Connie could see inside that the room was small with a bed built under the angle of the roof. The walls were knotty pine stained a warm golden color. A laptop and earphones lay on the bed. Lizzie was right. Hannah had been listening to music.

Connie stepped toward her grandniece to give her a hug, then decided not to. Hannah would barely remember her from five years ago. Instead of a curious seven-year-old, she was now an awkward preteen going through puberty. Her developing breasts were just visible under a T-shirt that displayed the logo of some band Connie had never heard of. When she was grown, she'd be tall and thin like her grandmother. Already she looked like she was as tall as Connie. The blue of her eyes shown brighter because she'd colored her shoulder length hair the shiny blue popular with teenagers.

"You've grown." Connie used the kind of cliché she hated.

"Of course I have. I am almost thirteen." Hannah sounded flippant.

"That was a silly thing to say. You were only seven when I saw you last. That's too long. Now that Stuart's gone, I'm going to stay in better touch with my family."

"Who's Stuart?"

The question hurt, reminding Connie that she'd cut out her family for nearly forty years. Not intentionally. Distance let it happen. "A man I knew who died. You met him when you visited me in Ashland."

"That was a long time ago. All I remember is that we did lots of walking. We went to some lake that was super blue."

"Crater Lake. It's as blue as your hair." A door opened downstairs. "There's your dad. Let's go see him. When we're all together, I promised your mother I'd tell you about my trip."

Hannah shrugged and went ahead of Connie down the stairs. Mark was waiting in the landing below. "Aunt Connie," he said, opening his arms to embrace her. His hug welcomed her with the open arms of a Midwesterner. Connie returned it, feeling more comfortable than she'd felt with Hannah.

He shook his head as he watched Hannah go outside. "Hannah escapes all adults. What is it your generation used to say? Never trust anyone over fifty?"

"Thirty, actually."

"Ouch. Lizzie and I just turned fifty-five. Hannah came along late in our marriage."

Lizzie heard them as she came through the kitchen. "I call her my miracle baby. How about we open a bottle of wine to celebrate Aunt Connie. We'll have a glass before dinner."

"I brought wine from Oregon. My tenant gave me a case when I left. Let me get my car key and one of you can help me carry some in." Connie climbed slowly up the stairs for her keys. When she came back down, she figured out the floor plan of the downstairs. It was laid out in a circle. Kitchen connecting to dining room connecting to living room connecting to the landing below the stairs. Bathroom beside the landing and another hallway that she assumed led to a room they used as a study.

She found Lizzie and Mark in the dining room taking glasses from one of two cabinets that were built into the opposite corners of the wall. Whoever designed this house knew how to use the space. A present lay conspicuously on the dining room table next to an arrangement of zinnias and snapdragons.

"The present's for later," said Lizzie. "Mark will help you with the wine and I'll meet you outside." Lizzie went through the door that connected the dining room to the kitchen while Connie and Mark went into the living room and out the front door. Last Chance was on the street so it wouldn't block the driveway and the garage. She opened the trunk, handed Mark three bottles of red, and took two of the white to carry herself. "I'd give you the whole case, but I need to save some Oregon wine for my sister."

"Sarah will judge it."

"I know. Ever since she took Lizzie to Europe, she's been a wine snob. Does Lizzie ever talk about that time?"

"She only remembers bits and pieces. Lucky for me. I'm not a rich guy like the father figures she had."

"I don't rub it in, but I have more money now than Sarah has."

"You earned yours. Sarah had a husband who left her rich and a second husband who was just as rich."

"It doesn't matter. We're different, but Sarah's still my sister. How is she coping as a widow? I assume you've seen her."

"Every year. Sarah's a survivor. I wouldn't worry about her."

He was right. Whatever happened to Sarah, she always came out on top. Connie cradled two wine bottles in her arm, closed the trunk, and followed Mark inside. He found space in the refrigerator to chill the white wine, then led her through a porch that held a washer and dryer and down a couple of steps onto the patio. Lizzie was sitting at a patio table and Hannah was lying on a lounge texting on her phone. Connie feared their three-day drive to Freedom meant three days of a sullen teenager conversing in cyberspace instead of with her. No worse than conversing with stuffed animals, she told herself.

They'd lingered over dinner. Lizzie told her about Hamline University and how smart the students were in the literature classes she taught. Mark talked about his job overseeing the Como Zoo. He loved the job and promised that they'd visit in the morning.

Connie intermingled Lizzie and Mark's stories with a description of her journey. She told them about the Bluegrass Festival in Fossil and the Old-Time Gospel Singers, about the falls at Kootenai, the Going-to-the-Sun Road, and the turtle races in Perhem. Hannah wanted to go to the turtle races until Mark lectured her on cruelty to animals. Connie omitted The Fisherman's Bar and Nancy and Amy. They'd stay safe, a secret she only revealed in her journal.

At dusk, the mosquitoes found them. "Let's go inside." Lizzie directed them into the dining room. "It's time for your birthday celebration."

Connie sat with Hannah at the table while Lizzie and Mark went into the kitchen. Hannah's phone dinged and she checked a text.

Connie waited for her to finish texting back. "Do you spend a lot of time on your phone?"

"My parents limit me. This was important. My friend Robin is coming tomorrow. They'll stay overnight with me while you go to the play. They'll be here to say goodbye in the morning. I'll miss them when I'm in Freedom. A month's a long time."

Hannah's pronouns told Connie that Robin had adopted "they" instead of "she." She also gave out information that was likely the birthday surprise. Tickets to a play while she had a sleepover with a friend.

Lizzie and Mark came into the kitchen. Lizzie carried a cake with two lit candles that announced 80 and Mark carried a bottle of champagne and a can of fizzy water for Hannah. "Happy Birthday, Aunt Connie," said Lizzie as she started them singing "Happy Birthday" in the slightly off-tune key that seemed to be the family heritage.

Mark popped the champagne cork and poured the escaping first bubbles into Connie's glass. "In celebration of eighty. May we all be as healthy as you when we get there."

Connie wiped a tear that found its way into the corner of her eye. This was family. They cared about her.

"I don't even remember my real dad," said Lizzie. "I remember Grandpa Sam a little bit. How old was he when he died?"

Connie thought of the little girl chasing a robin in the cemetery when she and Sarah and Lizzie visited the family graves. She thought about how the image opened her novel *Twenty Years a Wanderer* and helped to make her famous. "Not old. Just sixty. Your grandmother was only sixty-six. You must remember her."

"Not well. I remember being in Florida playing a game of *Clue* with you. She couldn't keep anything straight."

"She had Alzheimer's."

"I never knew that," said Lizzie. "It must have been early onset."

"It was, but not real early. There wasn't yet a standard name for it. Her doctor called it "hardening of the arteries." Connie had never told Lizzie how little Sarah helped as she watched their mother descend into the disease. Another thing she had forgiven Sarah for.

"If you hardly remember her, why did you give me her name?" said Hannah. "It's so old-fashioned."

"It's a pretty name," said Lizzie. "It's nice that it's unusual now and it's a way of remembering the grandmother I didn't see often enough. I remember her saying something about her brother. What happened to him?"

"His name was Charlie. I never knew him but I found out he ended up in Oregon. I know his daughter. Named Molly after your great-grandmother. She's old, Hannah, so you don't have to worry about bad genetics." Except for a genetic line of mental illness and depression that Connie kept at bay by writing. Lizzie and Hannah didn't need to know this part of their family history. They both had escaped. At least so far. Hannah was too young to know if she'd be okay.

"Enough talk about ancestors," said Mark. "Hannah, run into the kitchen for the ice cream. It's time to eat cake and celebrate."

"She reminds me of you when you were twelve," said Connie when Hannah was in the kitchen.

"Except I didn't have a cell phone. These teenagers drive me crazy with their texting and their TikTok and Snapchat. My students are just as bad. If I see them on a phone during class, I take the phone away. The minute they leave class, they all have their phones out."

"Hannah says you limit her time."

"Try to," said Mark.

"Try to what?" said Hannah as she came into the dining room with a half-gallon of ice cream.

"Limit your cell phone time," said Mark.

Hannah put the ice cream on the table next to the cake. "No one else's parents are so strict."

Connie cut off the complaint by saying, "Vanilla ice cream. I'm glad it's not huckleberry."

"Who ever heard of huckleberry ice cream? It sounds like that book I'll have to read in high school class. All the older kids say it's awful."

"*Huckleberry Finn*. It will probably be banned as racist by the time you get to high school. It is, but it's a valuable way to teach the controversies. Teach students to face racism instead of deny it." Lizzie pushed the cake to Connie. "You get to cut the slices. Hannah, you can scoop the ice cream."

"You didn't answer me," said Hannah. "Whoever heard of huckleberry ice cream?"

"It seems to be really popular in Montana." Connie cut the first slice of cake. "Chocolate. My favorite." She passed the plate to Hannah to add a scoop of ice cream. She couldn't help but notice the black and white. Lizzie was right. It was good to teach the controversies.

While they ate, the conversation drifted to memories of birthdays. Lizzie narrated a story about the only one she remembered during her two years in Europe. She'd gotten a doll that she carried around until Sarah dropped it accidentally into a Venice canal. "I knew it wasn't an accident. She told me not to cry, the doll was getting too dirty to keep. A strange man saw what happened and took my hand. Mom went crazy and gave me the lecture on stranger danger. I think he was just being kind."

"What about you, Mark?" Connie finished her cake and washed it down with a sip of champagne.

"I grew up in Northfield. Every year on my birthday, we'd drive into St. Paul and to the Como Zoo, then explore one of the parks. I think that's why I fell in love with the city." He reached to the middle of the table and pushed the present to Connie. "Happy Birthday from all of us."

Connie pulled off the ribbon and carefully unwrapped the paper that was designed with colorful birds. Inside was a silk scarf, hand dyed with images of ferns. It reminded her of the paperweight with a fern inside that David had given her. She'd long ago forgotten her jazz musician lover, but she still liked using the paperweight to hold down whatever manuscript she was working on.

"Someone from the conservatory at the zoo makes these." Sarah explained how the woman would tape a frond or a leaf onto the white silk, hammer it until the color and shape came through, then dye the scarf in a lighter color than the imprint. "You can wear this tomorrow night if you want. We're going to the Guthrie. Which play will be a surprise when we get there."

Connie stood up and draped the scarf around her shoulders. "It's beautiful and you're all too good to me." She hugged each of them, then sat down again.

They lingered for another half hour. Even Hannah stayed off her cell phone. When Connie felt her eyes begin to droop, she announced that she needed to go to bed. She thanked everyone again and climbed the stairs to a room that promised a dreamless night in the comfort of home.

Chapter 14
Wandering the Como Zoo

A chorus from songbirds floated through the open window, mingling with a lingering dream of clouds and ferns and water-colored scarfs. As she woke, she realized how comfortable her sleep had been. It was good to be with family.

Her journal lay unopened on the dressing table on top of her computer. She'd write in it later, maybe before the play because she suspected that afterwards she'd be as tired as she'd been last night. Too tired even to scratch a pen along the pages. She checked her phone. No text from Austin or Gregory or anybody. They had her email address, so she got out of bed and turned on her computer. Ads from L.L.Bean and REI and Staples and The Warming Store where she once bought an herbal pack to ease the tension in her neck. Links to the latest issue of *The Fictional Café* and *Mystery Writers of America* and *Sisters in Crime* even though her novels weren't always classified as mysteries.

Cyberspace left nothing to privacy, especially if you were marketing yourself as a writer. It wouldn't take much for Nancy to find a way to contact her. She typed a quick email addressed to The Fisherman's Bar asking for news, then closed her laptop, vowing to forget about Nancy and Amy and enjoy the day.

She gathered clothes and her ditty bag and walked down the hall to the bathroom. Lizzie was going inside holding a four-pack of toilet paper. "I just used the last of it," she said.

Connie watched her take one of the rolls out of the pack and put the rest under the sink. She took the empty cardboard roll off the holder and put on a new one. It unwound from the bottom. "Wrong way," Connie said.

"Wrong way what?"

"Toilet paper should roll from the top. I saw a cartoon about it in one of the many restrooms where I stopped." She omitted that she saw the cartoon at The Fishman's Bar. "'No' for the under way, 'Yes' for the over way, question mark for leaving it on top of the holder. It made me wonder about it, so I looked it up. Apparently there's more chance of germs if you roll from under. Your fingers can touch the wall and exchange germs with whoever was there before you. Not that it matters here. I just thought it was amusing."

"Over it is then." Lizzie took the roll off the holder and put it back on so it would roll over. "I always put it on any which way."

"I did, too, but ever since I saw that cartoon, I keep noticing. There's more to life to worry about than how to roll toilet paper."

"Like what to do when you don't even have a bathroom. We're so privileged. I worry about Hannah. For her birthday, she wants a digital camera. She researched them and she wants one that costs almost a thousand dollars. I won't spend that much, but I want to get her a good one. She has talent I want to encourage. We're trying to teach her about money, but I don't know how much it sticks."

"You could insist that she pay for part of it."

"Then it won't be a surprise. She paid for some of your scarf, though. When she gets money, a third goes into a savings account, a third is to buy gifts or give to charity, and a third is her own to spend. My mother sends her too much money for Christmas and birthdays. Easier than buying her a present."

"I like your idea. And I promise that when we drive together, I won't shower her with gifts. Maybe I'll make her pay for the gas."

"She has money from her babysitting job and I gave her more. I trust you won't spoil her. Not like my mother. She uses money to buy affection."

"Are things okay between you?"

"They are. I long ago accepted that she's not a mother woman."

"She loves you."

"I know that. Love and mothering aren't the same thing." She picked up the empty toilet paper roll and started for the door. "Take your shower and I'll meet you downstairs."

As she showered, Connie thought of her relationship with Sarah. While Sarah put her own well-being first, she'd martyred herself to the needs of their mother. She resented Sarah's freedom and Sarah was jealous of her success. They were New Englanders. Nothing ever got said. Feelings weren't to be talked about. That's how it would be in Freedom again. It would be okay.

She finished showering, dressed in capris and a T-shirt for a warm day at the zoo, and went downstairs where she found Mark in the kitchen. "Good morning," he said. "Ready for breakfast?"

"I am. But first some coffee."

He pointed her to a fancy coffee machine.

"How do I work this?"

He handed her a mug. "Just put it under the spigot and press the button. I have it set for this size mug and strong coffee. Want it weaker?"

"Strong is good." She pressed the button and the grinder turned on. While her mug filled, she said, "This is quite a machine."

"Our biggest extravagance. It's better for the environment than those machines that use a little plastic container for each cup of coffee. Coffee's better, too, and Lizzie can make the cappuccino she likes. She'll be down in a minute. She's waking Hannah."

"Is Hannah a don't-drag-me-out-of-bed teenager?"

"Not too bad yet." He peeled bacon onto a griddle. "Bacon, celery, and cheese omelets. That okay?"

"Sounds wonderful, especially since I see that you're using white, not yellow cheese."

"Just like Lizzie. She wants New England white. You can be in charge of toast. As soon as I put the omelet on, put in four pieces. You have to slice the bread."

She saw a loaf on a breadboard, a knife beside it. "Looks homemade."

"It is. Lizzie's nod to domesticity. She uses a bread machine for the kneading then shapes the loaf, lets it rise again, and bakes it. This one's oatmeal, I think."

"Do you always cook breakfast?"

"We mostly have toast and peanut butter in the morning. But I like to cook omelets if there's a free weekend day. Keeps us a family. Hannah's growing up too fast."

"She's a lovely child."

"She is. We're working to keep her that way. She's worried about driving to Freedom with you."

"So am I. I haven't been around a girl her age since I was playing aunt to Lizzie."

"You and Hannah will be fine. Lizzie always tells me how wonderful you are. You kept her grounded when she was growing up. You're her role model. She wanted to be a writer like you, but she thinks she doesn't have your talent so she chose a PhD in literature instead."

"I'll bet she's a great teacher. People like her keep literature alive."

"Speaking of alive, I hear them on the stairs. We don't have to rush, but the sooner we eat, the sooner we get to the zoo. It's too nice a day to waste."

"Do I have time to start a laundry before we leave?'

"Go do it now. I'll wait until you come back to put on the omelet. Laundry soap's in a cardboard packet. Sheets that dissolve. Saves all those detergent jugs."

"A great idea. I'll be fast."

"No rush. We'll have plenty of time."

For a small zoo, the Como had a surprisingly large number of exhibits. They'd looked outside at hoofed animals and giant and not so giant cats, inside at aquatic animals, and birds in an aviary. Mark had paused at several of the exhibits and told them stories about animals that he treated as friends. The story about Skeeter the giraffe's foot surgery was fascinating. Skeeter was shot with drugs via a dart gun. The drugs were so strong that if any escaped into the air, the people attending him could have been affected. He'd needed an army of veterinary surgeons and anesthesiologists. A group of researchers and specialists in the care of giraffes also watched. Connie learned that giraffes were in danger if they fell to the ground because they had evolved only to be upright. They often had problems with their feet in captivity because zoos weren't able to replicate the ground in their wild habitats.

They were now at the primate exhibit, a favorite with kids. Hannah must have heard her father's commentary dozens of times. She ignored his comments and snapped photos with her cell phone. Other children were watching gorillas wander through the forest the zoo had created for them. Two of the young gorillas were wrestling together. The zoo had created a habitat that was almost convincing even though it wasn't Dian

Fossey's *Gorillas in the Mist.* Connie understood the fascination with gorillas. They were the largest of the primates and among humankind's closest relatives. Unfortunately, their communal social behavior hadn't been handed down. Humans were more closely aligned with the territorialism of the more aggressive chimpanzees.

She stopped watching the gorillas and studied a primate called a Saki Monkey. It was a fraction the size of even the smallest gorilla and covered in thick hair. "I like his mustache," she said. "He looks like Agatha Christie's Inspector Poirot."

"Actually, he's a she," said Mark. "We get lots of questions about Sakis. 'Why's their tail so long?' When I tell kids they're for balance and not prehensile, they ask what prehensile means. They ask if they can pet them and I tell them only if they want to get bitten. They're pretty shy, so I don't think a child could get near one. I love this part of my job. Lizzie likes the conservatory best. How about we go there now?"

"You betcha." Connie adopted the expression she'd been hearing since she hit Minnesota. "Funny. Any zoo I've ever gone to, I've spent more time admiring the flowers than the animals."

When they entered the conservatory, the warmth and humidity overwhelmed them. It was tropical. A huge palm formed a dome that reached to the top of the glass. Beneath it, displays of palms and cycads and orchids thrived. They walked through the area into a room labeled The Fern Room. Hundreds of ferns in variations Connie had never seen laced the area.

"Ferns are among the oldest plants. We've got over a hundred varieties." Mark took Lizzie's hand. "This is Lizzie's favorite room. It's why she chose a fern scarf for your birthday."

"I think I like them because they were so popular in the nineteenth century." Lizzie let go of Mark's hand and put hers underneath one of the fronds to feel its moisture without touching it. "Back then there were fern designs in clothing and furniture. Constance Fenimore Woolson was a collector and sent specimens she found to a botanist at Yale."

"I know her work." Connie thought of the copy of *East Angels* Everett had given her and that was accompanying her on her journey. She no longer felt the sensuality Woolson had conveyed about the Florida swamps or the feeling she'd had when she canoed in them with Everett. Forty years ago that kind of lushness had frightened her. Now it was only a pleasant memory, one she didn't want to share in the confines of a manufactured conservatory. "Why were they so popular?"

"Women loved botany," Lizzie explained. "They could talk about reproduction, both sexual and asexual, in a safe way."

Hannah stopped looking at her phone long enough to say, "How can reproduction be asexual?"

"It's complicated," said Mark. "Some ferns are male, some are female, some are both. Their spores reproduce. No pollination needed. You can look it up, try to figure out the botany. But not now. I see you're not taking photos. Put your phone away."

"I was just checking when Robin is coming."

Mark led them from the fern room to a room with fruit trees that had to be pollinated manually because there were no bees in the conservatory. Maybe life would be simpler if all reproduction happened this way. No Everett or Stuart to have sex with. No Jackson Armstrong to fend off.

When they finished in the conservatory, they walked through the zoo's outdoor displays, the garden overlooking a frog pond, the lily pond, the bonsai garden, the formal landscape and water gardens near the Visitor Center. They ate fish and chips at the outdoor café called Pier 56. Lake fish, like the fish and chips at The Fisherman's Bar. She wondered if Gregory and Austin had any news. She'd check as soon as she had a chance.

On the drive back, Mark took them on a tour of the cluster of college campuses near the zoo. Bethel, Concordia, Macalester, St. Thomas, Hamline where Lizzie taught. They were all green and beautiful, not like many city campuses.

"Is there a lot of rivalry among the campuses?" Connie said.

"We all have our niche. Hamline is the oldest college in Minnesota. Our students like to tell the students from Macalester that when they're touting their SATs. I'm lucky to have found this job. I love it here."

"I can see why."

"Wait until you see the Mississippi. Do you have enough energy to walk a bit before we go home to eat and get ready for the play or did we wear you out at the zoo?"

"No problem. I could walk all day. As long as it's not too fast, I never tire."

"Can I go home? Robin wants to come at five and it's already after three."

"As long as you pledge that you won't upload videos on TikTok."

"Whatever. You're such a Luddite."

"Glad we taught you that word. I'm a bit of one myself," said Lizzie.

When Hannah slumped in the seat, Connie said, "Don't worry. We'll work out phone rules on our drive." She wasn't so sure.

Chapter 15

Changes

The path along the Mississippi River was filled with people escaping the heat of the city on a Saturday afternoon. Joggers, skateboarders, parents pushing strollers, groups of the young and the middle-aged, old couples holding hands. Even the solitary walkers felt companionable.

"If I lived here, I'd take this walk every day," said Connie, who was enjoying time alone with Lizzie.

"Mark and I jog here. We've just started to let Hannah come with her friends. It's safe in the daytime."

"Not at night?"

"It's lighted and unless it's really late, there are plenty of people around. I worry too much."

"You take after me. I'm a worrier."

"I wouldn't have guessed that. I've always thought that worry starts with motherhood." Lizzie slowed her pace. "Except my mother doesn't worry."

"She never did. Even when we were kids. But she's more fearful than I am."

"What's the difference?" Lizzie said as they stepped to the side so a jogger could pass.

"Fear is physical. An adrenalin rush. It's only happened to me a couple of times. Worry's more like a steady anxiety. What if I miss my flight? What if the plane crashes? It can be irrational like how I worried about pumping my own gas on this trip. Are you going to worry about me driving alone with Hannah?"

"Probably. But not as much as I'd worry about leaving her alone with my mother. She'd give her some money, drop her at a mall, and forget to pick her up. Something like that happened all the time when I was a kid. And we didn't have cell phones to call."

They passed a girl about Hannah's age who was looking around as if she was lost. Connie wanted to go over to her, ask her if she needed help. In the midst of so many people, she felt the loneliness of the girl, the loneliness of Lizzie waiting for a mother who had forgotten her, the loneliness of her own future without Stuart in a place where she had no family to forget to pick her up. "Your mother might have been late, but she always remembered."

"And she always apologized. I won't worry about you watching out for Hannah. You would have been a good mother."

"I don't know. I'd have left my kids stranded while I was buried in the world of the characters I was creating. My books are my children."

Lizzie hesitated before she said, "I wasn't sure if I should tell you. I taught one of your novels last year. *Twenty Years a Wanderer* in a class on contemporary quests. I didn't tell the students that you're my aunt until we finished our discussion."

"I'm flattered. Unless you tell me they hated it."

"On the contrary. You held your own beside Marilynne Robinson's *Housekeeping*, Cormac McCarthy's *The Road*, and Joyce Carol Oates's *Solstice*."

"Eccentric, apocalyptic, obsessive. Where does *Twenty Years a Wanderer* fit?"

They moved aside for another jogger. When they began walking again, Lizzie explained her choice. "Attuned. That image of the little girl chasing a robin plays through the whole book. All those different settings she wanders through. Which one is her home? Did you find yours in Oregon?"

"I did, but I feel like I'm wandering again. I vowed I'd never go back to Freedom, but I miss New England."

"Well wander to Hamline next year and into our lecture hall. Maybe on your way to Freedom again. I miss it, too."

Connie stopped to look at the river. "At least you have water. I hate that Ashland is so far from lakes. Even the Rogue River isn't close enough for someone who grew up in Massachusetts.

"I know what you mean. The Mississippi dwarfs the Merrimack and St. Paul is a wonderful city. What I miss the most is New England's history. When I go back, I take Hannah to places like Plymouth and Salem and Concord. She wants to know why I'm so interested in dead people. You can't repeat the past."

"My tenant said the same thing to me when I started this journey. I'm not like Gatsby. I'm not trying to repeat it."

"Hannah's never read *The Great Gatsby*. Maybe it's a universal feeling among the young. They live in the present. Like those teenagers," said Connie, pointing to a group throwing a frisbee.

"I read somewhere that an interest in history doesn't develop until almost age twenty."

"That's why it's so hard to teach history in high school. Teaching kids about their own ancestry is supposed to help, but I don't like to talk much about our past with Hannah. Too much illness."

"You know about that?"

"After Hannah was born, my mother told me. I catch myself watching her to see if she's inherited the family curse."

Connie hoped that Sarah had shared only part of the family

history. "Your grandmother battled depression, but she lived a full life until she got Alzheimer's. I wonder why you named your daughter Hannah if you worry about genetics."

"I didn't know about my grandmother then. All I remember is that I liked her. What about you? Have you had to battle depression?"

"My worst time was when your grandmother died and a man I loved left me. That's sorrow, not depression. Writing helped me through it."

"Is this trip helping you heal after Stuart's death?"

"It is," said Connie. "I'm looking forward to getting to know Hannah. She reminds me of you at her age."

"I should warn you that she doesn't want to go on this trip. The young want to be with the young. I hope she'll grow to love you the way I do."

Connie put her arm around Lizzie, touched by her statement of love. "Let's go back. I'll work on Hannah. Show her that an old woman can be a good companion."

"The best," said Lizzie.

As they walked back, Connie noticed the little girl still standing alone. She started toward her at the same time that a woman appeared who must be the girl's mother. The woman turned the girl around and directed her over the grass to a parking area. Connie thought about constructing a story out of that image. Self-absorbed mother. Lonely, frightened child. Maybe *Travels with Connie* wouldn't be her last book.

Away from the river, the heat had settled in despite the shade trees. When they reached the house, a teenager was getting out of a car.

"That's Robin," said Lizzie.

Connie wondered how to refer to a pre-teen who went by "they." A girl? A sister? A daughter? She'd have to be careful.

Lizzie stopped at the car and through the open window introduced Robin's mother, Julia. "Connie's my favorite aunt," she said, no matter that she was her only aunt.

"Lizzie's told me so much about you. I'm not much of a reader, but I promised her I'll read one of your novels." Julia didn't realize how hollow the promise felt.

"Connie and Hannah have to leave by eight-thirty tomorrow," said Lizzie. "They're taking a two o'clock ferry across Lake Michigan."

"Avoiding Chicago traffic? It wouldn't be bad on a Sunday," said Julia.

"It's always bad around Chicago," said Lizzie. "Besides, Hannah will enjoy a ferry ride."

"Okay. I'll be here by eight." Julia started to raise her window.

"Mark and I will be home if they want to sleep late." It took Connie a second to realize "they" meant Robin.

"Robin will want to get up to say goodbye to Hannah. I'll be here. I made them leave their cell phone at home. No all-nighter watching TikTok videos."

"We won't be here to monitor, but I'll threaten to take Hannah's phone away until Mark and I join her in Freedom. I'll set up a movie and popcorn for them. They should be in bed asleep before we get home. Thanks for letting them stay alone."

"They're growing up. One small step to independence. I'll see you tomorrow. Nice to meet you," Julia said to Connie.

She pulled away from the curb, leaving Connie dizzy trying to follow a conversation with a singular they and a plural they. She reminded herself to be careful as she and Lizzie went inside.

Hannah looked up from the dining room table where she was showing Robin something on her computer. "Hi, Mom. Aunt Connie, this is Robin. I'm showing them a photo I took at the zoo."

"You took lots of photos," said Lizzie. "It's a good thing cameras are digital so I don't have to keep you in film."

"What's film?" Robin's question was surprising.

"You're joking," said Hannah.

"I'm not." said Robin. "Films are what grownups see when they don't want to say they're going to a movie."

Robin might not know about camera film, but Connie liked her—their—wit. "My friend Stuart and I used to argue about whether we were going to a film or a movie. Old cameras used film that came in small rolls. You could take twenty-four or thirty-six shots with each roll and have them developed at a camera shop. Usually only a quarter of them were any good."

"That sucks." Robin used the phrase common to teenagers that Connie hated.

"It wouldn't happen if I were taking the photos. I only deleted a couple of the ones I took at the zoo." Hannah moved the computer away from Robin. "This one's the best. I only edited a bit."

Connie sat down and Robin stood so Lizzie could take the other chair beside Hannah. Lizzie was right when she said that Hannah had talent. The photo showed the backs of Connie and Lizzie. They were looking at the giraffe who'd had the foot operation. Their heads were tilted upward and a shaft of sunlight seemed to be reaching down to them. The giraffe's head was cocked at the same angle toward a tree branch dappled by the sun. Hannah had manipulated the colors. The ground behind the giraffe was a stone pattern of golds and tans that mimicked the giraffe's skin. Connie and Lizzie wore tan shorts and cream-colored T-shirts. Their bare arms and legs were a lighter tan than the shorts.

"I wanted it to look like a statement on how nature and animals and people connect," said Hannah. "I'm deciding what to call it. 'Mother and Daughter and Giraffe' or 'Mother and

Daughter and Baby.' Robin likes 'Unity.' What do you think?"

Lizzie stood up, then bent down to kiss Connie's cheek. "I like 'Mother and Daughter and Giraffe.' I often feel like Aunt Connie is my mother."

"We used to make jokes about maiden aunts," said Connie.

"Why?" said Hannah.

Lizzie moved away from Connie. "People felt sorry for women who never married. You two are lucky. You can choose marriage or career or both."

"And I can be 'they.'" Robin seemed to be challenging Connie.

Hannah closed her computer. "No one cares, Susie."

"Robin."

"Oops." Hannah said as she stood up. "Robin was Susie until six months ago. Sometimes I slip, but we're still the best of friends." She picked up her computer and they walked together to the stairway.

"They make transgender seem easy," said Connie. "Is everyone so accepting?"

"Robin's dad had some trouble but he's coming around. As far as I can tell most of the kids at school are fine. Robin and Hannah have the same circle of friends they've had since kindergarten."

Connie remembered Engla in the Perhem Museum and her story about Flippy Rochen. She suspected there was more than one Flippy in Hannah's school. But there was progress. This wasn't the segregated world The Old-Time Gospel Singers had faced. Wherever Nancy found a place for herself and Amy, Connie hoped it would be among friends like Hannah and Robin. "I'm going upstairs for an hour. I want to write in the journal I'm keeping because I'll be too tired after the play."

"Can I read your journal? Hear more about your trip?"

"Not even if you were my daughter. It will all come out in *Travels with Connie*."

"You're writing another book? I thought you announced that there'll be no more."

"No more fiction, though I've seen plenty on this trip to spin into another novel or two. This is a travel narrative. I'll dedicate it to Hannah and Robin and our brave new world." She gave Lizzie a quick kiss on the cheek and went upstairs.

Before she picked up her journal, she checked her email. Two messages labeled FishBarPend jumped out at her. She opened the first one. It was short and direct.

> Mason's truck has been found, but he's still missing. Now Nancy can keep defrauding others.

It was signed simply Gregory.

She felt the physical response she'd described as fear, not worry. It was irrational. She opened the second email.

> Mason's truck was in the parking lot of a motel in Glendive. After several days, the motel owners called the police. They've been asking us more about Nancy. They believe she was in the truck because they found a pacifier in it. I didn't tell them you saw her. She needs to find a safe place to start over with Amy. She's not as callous as Gregory thinks. You helped her when she needed help. Now forget her.
>
> I look at your dollar bill on the ceiling every morning. You're a good woman. Austin.

Worry replaced her fear. Austin's message was softer. The two messages captured a difference between Austin and Gregory Connie hadn't noticed during their brief meeting. Gregory was quick to feel wounded the way he'd so easily given up writing after a few rejections. Austin was too ready to believe in Nancy's goodness. She was more convinced than before that he was Amy's father. She speculated. Nancy lied to her about staying with a cook named Ronnie. She had keys to Mason's truck from when they worked the marijuana scheme. She used his truck to find her motel and left the truck at Mason's before she found Last Chance. She wanted to know where Nancy was, to know she was safe. She opened her journal to try to capture what she'd been feeling since yesterday.

> *Ever since I reached St. Paul, my thoughts have been racing. Maybe that's why my stomach feels weird. Bloated with anxiety. First there's Nancy and Amy. I'm more than worried. I'm afraid for them. Should I be like Gregory? Stop being fearful and blame her? Contact the police to let them know I left her at Detroit Lakes? But I want to believe Austin, let her find a new life. She's like me. Opening a new chapter.*

She stopped writing and forced herself to continue with something she could use for *Travels with Connie*.

> *I'm feeling closer to Lizzie than I ever have. Hannah's photo that could label us as mother and daughter makes me think of The Wizard of Oz. What's the line? "There's no place like home."*
>
> *Hannah and her friend Robin give me hope for this new generation. I won't be alive when language catches up to Robin's identity. They/them will feel natural and "they is" or "they are" will evolve the way language always evolves. These are brave*

teenagers who declare their identity. Eventually society will catch up to them the way it caught up to women voting and a Black man being president.

She stopped writing before she sounded like she was preaching to herself. Had she done enough in her lifetime? What did her novels matter when she could have been being doing more for the Civil Rights movement that she left after her early marches? She could have used her writing to expose all kinds of prejudice. She could have lobbied on behalf of the environment instead of just creating pleasant scenery that people like Engla enjoyed.

Could have, should have. *Travels with Connie* would be her last exit. There'd be no story about a lonely girl waiting for her mother. She vowed to make her journey show the challenge and promise of the America she'd been seeing.

She was glad she hadn't spoiled Lizzie and Mark's surprise by checking what play they were seeing. *All the Way.* The title came from Lyndon Johnson's campaign slogan, "All the way with LBJ." She'd seen the play with Stuart at the Oregon Shakespeare Festival and it had changed her mind about Johnson. She always remembered him as the president who kept the country mired in Vietnam. All those years ago, she'd marched and chanted, "Hey, hey, LBJ, How many kids did you kill today?" The play showed her that despite all his flaws, Johnson had enacted Civil Rights legislation. She should have known that because she'd joined the 1963 March on Washington when she was an undergraduate. Plays like *All the Way* made her understand that art mattered.

They exited the theater into the cocoon of a warm Minnesota evening. She thanked Lizzie and Mark and said, "The play was wonderful."

"You must remember those times," said Mark.

"Every time I despair about the present, I remember how bad things were during the Civil Rights Movement and the Vietnam War." Connie captured what she'd been feeling all through the performance.

"My mother never talks about my dad." Lizzie sounded wistful. "I don't remember him, but I remember the picture of him in his army uniform."

"The war changed him." Connie thought of all the young men who came back from Vietnam traumatized. She wouldn't add to whatever Sarah had told Lizzie about her father.

"My dad never talks about it," said Mark as they walked. "Even now he won't watch a war movie or celebrate Veteran's Day. He's not proud of his service."

"He saw horrors we only had images of on the three television networks," said Connie. "You must see some of the positive legacy now. Doesn't Minnesota have one of the largest populations of Vietnamese?"

Lizzie answered while Mark stayed quiet, as if he was thinking of his father. "I don't know, but I see Vietnamese, and Laotian Hmong in my classes. They know nothing of war, but they share their parents' stories, especially when we read *The Things They Carried*."

Connie remembered that book well, though she hadn't read it since it first came out in 1990. "Tim O'Brien captures what it must have been like for so many young men like your fathers. They came from small towns and knew nothing of cultures other than their own." Like Engla in Perhem, she thought. Another thread to weave into *Travels with Connie*.

"That book creates an interesting dynamic in my classes," said Lizzie as they reached the car. "Kids with grandparents who fought in a country torn apart by war. Others whose families were torn apart by the anti-war protests."

"And kids with families like mine who fought in a country they'd never heard of." Mark unlocked the car.

"I like that a play like *All the Way* makes us think," Connie said as she got into the back seat. "I wish I had written books like O'Brien's. His matter."

"What are you talking about?" said Lizzie. "Yours matter. The characters are always on a journey that shows how complex the world is. If there's a crime solved or an ending that's happy, that doesn't make the book less true. And you're not done yet. Keep your pencil sharpened, Aunt Connie."

"Ideas are percolating." said Connie from the back seat. "Thank you both for a wonderful evening."

"It's not over yet, said Lizzie. "We've got leftover cake and ice cream waiting for us."

Connie forced herself to eat a small piece of cake while Hannah and Robin talked about how they'd stay connected when Hannah was in Massachusetts. They'd spent the evening coloring Robin's short hair the same blue as Hannah's. Blue-blood sisters. Connie corrected herself. Not sisters, friends. When she excused herself for bed, Robin and Hannah also claimed they were going to sleep. She imagined they'd stay up most of the night talking the way she had when she was their age.

In her bedroom, she checked her email one more time. Nothing from The Fisherman's Bar. She went into the bathroom to brush her teeth. When she came out, she could hear Hannah from behind her door complaining to Robin. "You'll have all the fun while I spend the next two weeks with my old lady aunt and my old lady grandmother."

The comment surprised Connie. Hannah had been disguising

her feelings well. She got into bed and pulled the covers over her head, ignoring the knot that had formed in her stomach.

Chapter 16

On the Road with Hannah

Through the front window of the guest room, Connie watched Hannah and Robin on the sidewalk waiting for Robin's mother. They were engaged in some kind of conversation vital to teenage girls. Teenagers, Connie reminded herself, wondering if she'd live long enough to sort out the gender references.

She looked through her email messages one more time. A note from her publisher telling her that *Forty Years Found* would be published in Dutch. One from Sarah asking her to let her know when she and Hannah would arrive. Another from Tim saying that he was monitoring the raccoon poop on her roof and asking how her trip was going. She'd answer him from the hotel she'd reserved in Ludington. Nothing from Gregory or Austin. Nothing from Nancy about Amy.

She closed her laptop, zipped it into her smaller suitcase, and went downstairs. "You all packed?" Mark asked from the kitchen where he was cleaning up from the pancakes he'd insisted they eat before they started out. She would have preferred a piece of toast, but she'd managed a small pancake and two slices of bacon.

"I am. I'll leave this suitcase outside with Hannah and come back for my bigger one and to say goodbye."

153

Mark came into the hallway. "I'll get your suitcase. Lizzie's outside with Hannah and Robin. I don't know how those two gir—teenagers—will survive the next month." He was struggling like her to get used to a new vocabulary.

She went outside just as Robin was getting into the car. "Goodbye, Robin," she said. "I'll make sure that Hannah emails you every day."

"We text, Aunt Connie. Email is what old people do."

Connie wanted to say that she'd transitioned from typewriter to word processing to the internet. She was perfectly capable of sending a text message. She could even attach an emoji.

"That's rude," said Lizzie. "Apologize."

"I'm sorry." Hannah made things worse when she said, "I forgot that you're old." She held onto Robin's hand through the car window and said, "I'll text. Maybe I'll teach Aunt Connie how to do it."

Connie resisted the line Stuart used to say about their communications. Texting was like the grunts of teenagers. At least in email, they could converse.

When Robin and her—their—mother drove away Hannah rolled her suitcase to Connie's car and went into the house for something else.

"I kept worrying that I'd slip with the pronouns," Connie said to Lizzie.

"You slip at first, but they understand. They have bigger things to worry about than a pronoun."

Connie wondered if "they" meant Robin or Robin's family. Mark was coming out of the house with her suitcase. How would Mark react if Hannah became a "they"? The fathers she'd known always seemed more protective of their daughters than their sons.

She opened the back door of Last Chance and put her suitcase in the backseat. Mark carried her heavier suitcase down the walk. She opened the trunk and he put it and Hannah's suitcase next to the half-full case of wine. "You might need a bottle after eight hours in the car with Hannah," he joked.

"We'll be fine and it's more like four and a half hours to the ferry in Manitowac. We can play Titanic on the boat."

"No hanging over the railing," said Lizzie. "I should tell you that Hannah hasn't had her first period yet. I gave her everything she needs with instructions in case it happens before I get to Freedom."

"Please don't let that happen." She raised her hands in a mock prayer as Hannah banged out the front door. She carried a backpack in one hand and a book in the other.

Connie looked at the title when Hannah reached the car. "*Secrets*. That's the first novel I published." She was flattered that Hannah wanted to read it. It would give them something to talk about.

"Are the secrets good ones?" said Hannah as she put her backpack on top of the suitcases.

"I wrote it a long time ago, but I remember enjoying uncovering them." She also remembered Will and how she'd been attracted to him until he told her the secret he was keeping about his homosexuality. How much healthier the world was now when teenagers like Hannah and Robin could decide whether to be she or he or they. "I had a friend who helped me through the first draft. Will Baldwin. He was a professor in the English Department at Bayview College. That's in Florida. He's still my best first reader. You'll meet him. He'll be in New Hampshire with his family and is going to visit me in Freedom." Will was the only one she could confide in about Nancy and Amy. She remembered her Uncle Charlie. Secrets seemed to have followed her all her life.

Hannah closed the trunk and opened the passenger side door. "What should I do with these?" The copy of *East Angels* and the photo of Connie and Stuart were on the front seat.

"I'll put them in the back." She opened the back door and rested them on the seat next to the stuffed animals that lay hidden under the blanket like another secret. "They've been keeping me company. I'll tell you about them while we drive."

"Whatever." Hannah hugged each of her parents, lingering in her mother's embrace before she got into the car and closed the door.

Lizzie hugged Connie even longer than she'd hugged Hannah.

"I'll take good care of her," said Connie. "I'll see that she texts every day. I'll send emails. They'll be more detailed than what you'll get on a text."

"You mean more than a grunt?" Mark opened the driver's side door for her.

"Just the word I was thinking of." She got into the car and lowered the window when she turned on the ignition. "Seatbelt on?" she said to Hannah.

"Of course."

She clicked in her own seatbelt, put Last Chance in gear, and gave a final wave to Lizzie and Mark. After she powered up her window, she glanced at the rearview mirror and watched them recede into the distance.

As soon as they reached Route 94, Hannah opened *Secrets* and began to read. Connie wondered if she was interested in the book or if she was simply avoiding conversation.

An hour into the drive, Hannah closed the book. "I'm at a scary part."

"What part is that? I don't remember anything frightening."

"Maura's in the woods alone looking for clues that might connect her brother to the murder. She just picked up a mushroom. I'm afraid she's going to eat it and die."

"She's just curious. She's a botanist and the mushroom is a rare one."

"How do you know so much about botany?"

"Research. After the novel was published, I met a real botanist. He helped me with my second novel. *The Orange Grove* is set in Florida. He gave me that book that's in the back seat. *East Angels*. It's also set in Florida."

"Would I like it?"

"I don't think so. It was written in the nineteenth century and it's pretty dense. Lots of descriptions." Connie remembered its scenes in the Florida swamps and how sensual they were. She was as in love with the landscape as she'd been with Everett.

"Is that why you left Florida? A broken heart?" Hannah was letting her imagination run free.

"No. I was doing a book tour. When I got to Ashland, I liked it so I stayed."

"I hope I can do something like that. I'll publish a collection of my photographs. Robin can come with me. Unless I have a boyfriend."

Hannah stopped talking and began to fiddle with her phone.

"Do you have a boyfriend?" Connie wanted to learn more about this grandniece of hers who was approaching puberty. When did girls her age awaken to their sexuality?

"There's this one boy I like. He's going into ninth grade next year so he won't be at my school. Robin's just my friend if that's what you're asking. They're not interested in boys or girls."

"I liked them."

"We made a playlist for you while we were working on the photograph of you and my mother and the giraffe."

"Plug it in. I won't need my navigation system until we get near Appleton, Wisconsin. Then there are lots of turns." Connie let Hannah figure out the technology. The most she'd mastered was changing the radio stations as she drove through the country.

"The playlist isn't that long." Hannah unplugged Connie's phone and plugged in her own. "Gospel music," she said. "I know you like it."

The playlist opened with The Old-Time Gospel Singers blending their voices to "Oh Happy Day." She reached for Hannah's hand. "You remembered my story."

"Just listen to it." Hannah was finished talking. Their moment of connection was over.

Connie listened to a selection of classic gospel singers. Mahalia Jackson, Aretha Franklin, Elvis Presley, Sam Cook. Either Hannah and Robin had good taste or they'd found a YouTube site that they could easily download. When Elvis's version of "Peace in the Valley" came on, she watched the flat, unvaried Wisconsin farmland, imagined that life in the scattered towns was peaceful, and remembered when Elvis's gyrations were considered obscene. The last song was another one by The Old-Time Gospel Singers, the one she'd listened to when she left them outside of Lake Pend Oreille. "You're Home to Stay." Wherever her last home would be, it would be different from the world she grew up in.

"Thank you, Hannah. This is a perfect playlist." She pointed to the lavender hand sanitizer in the cup holder at the front of the console. "Cedric, one of the gospel singers, gave me this after he taught me how to pump gas."

"Can we stop for gas soon? I need to use the bathroom."

"Is it urgent? We should go a bit further."

"It's urgent. My stomach's feeling funny."

Connie saw a sign for Abbortsford. "Maybe there's a quick

stop of sorts in this town." She took the exit and found a shop called Hawkeye Dairy Store on the main street. "There should be a restroom in here."

The choice was a good one. Hannah went into the restroom first while Connie looked at the array of cheeses and meats in a display counter. Gift baskets of various sizes and possibilities lined the top of the counter. When Hannah came out of the bathroom, she said, "Can I have the car keys? I need my backpack."

"Let's pick out something for your grandmother first."

"When I get back. The keys."

Connie wondered what was so urgent. She needed to use the bathroom herself, so she gave her the keys and went into the restroom. When she came out, Hannah was waiting at the door. She handed Connie the keys and bumped her with the backpack as she went into the restroom for the second time.

Connie went to the counter where the salesperson had been watching them. She was a big woman, almost six feet tall. Her hands looked as if they'd been made strong from cutting meat and cheese. The apron wrapped around her torso read Hawkeye Dairy. Her dark eyes made Connie think of the hawk of the dairy's name.

"Your granddaughter's in a mighty hurry," the woman said. "What'd she need that backpack for?" The woman seemed to imply that Hannah was going to steal something.

"She's my grandniece. Just needs some toilet supplies." When she said it, she knew what Hannah needed.

She took a basket from the counter and looked at what was displayed beneath the cellophane. Three kinds of cheese—cheddar, Colby, and Monterey Jack—two sausage rolls, an oblong box of crackers, and a jar of pepper jam. Hannah came out of the restroom and set her backpack on the floor. "Should we get this for your grandmother?"

"Sure. She can eat something when she drinks that wine you brought."

Sarah always drank a lot, but Connie worried that she was drinking even more since she became a widow. "How much is the basket?" she asked the woman, who was still eyeing them like the hawk on her apron. "Fifty-two dollars. It's written on the bottom."

"We'll take it." She looked at a freezer at the end of the counter. "It's early, Hannah, but if you're hungry, I'll buy you an ice cream cone."

Hannah touched her stomach. "I'm not hungry."

Connie wasn't hungry either. Her stomach still felt bloated from breakfast. She took out her credit card and paid for the basket. Outside, she opened the back door to Last Chance and set the basket on the floor. Hannah put her backpack on top of the blanket that was hiding the stuffed animals.

When they got into the car and started to drive again, Connie risked a question. "Did you just start your period? Is that why you needed your backpack?"

Hannah rested her head against the side window. "My mother told you."

She only said you hadn't had one yet, but that she gave you supplies. Everything okay?"

"I'm fine. My stomach's just a little crampy and I have a headache."

"I have some ibuprofen if you need it." She reached into the storage place between the seats and took out a pill box she always kept in it. "It will go away soon. If you need to stop again, let me know."

Hannah took out two pills and swallowed them with the water she'd put in the slot on her door. "Thank you." She closed her eyes.

Connie hoped she hadn't inherited the kind of response she'd had to her first periods. Headaches, cramps, dizziness that sent her staggering down the school corridor every month. After a few years, the cramps and dizziness disappeared, but the headaches plagued her until menopause. Some things were good about aging.

Hannah woke when they stopped at a gas station outside of Green Bay. She went into the restroom while Connie pumped gas. "Feeling better?" Connie asked when she came back to the car.

"Some. I could have pumped the gas. I know how."

"There'll be plenty of time for that."

Hannah put her backpack into the car. She nudged the blanket that was covering the stuffed animals, then pulled it aside. "Why do you have these animals?"

"Let's start driving and I'll explain." When she turned on the ignition, she said, "Will you plug in my phone? We'll need the navigation system now." Maybe Hannah would forget about the animals and she wouldn't have to lie about buying them. A disembodied voice said, "Start out going southeast on Route 29."

Hannah overtalked the voice. "A book from an old boyfriend. A photo of you and another boyfriend. A novel titled *Secrets*. Do you have a secret grandchild somewhere?"

The question surprised Connie. "Of course not. Even if I did, she'd be too old for stuffed animals."

"Or he."

"Or they."

"Very funny, Aunt Connie. Who are these animals for?"

"You'll meet my friend Will in Massachusetts. His brother has a great-grandchild." That didn't explain the animals, but it wasn't a lie.

"You told me about him. Your best first reader. Is he an old boyfriend, too?"

"No. He's gay." If Hannah could so easily talk about transgender teenagers, she could hear about eighty-year-olds who'd had to hide their homosexuality.

"Why a bear, a turtle, and a yellow jacket?" Hannah was more interested in the animals than in Will's sexual identity.

"Merge onto 41 south toward Appleton." The navigation voice gave Connie a minute to compose her answer. "When I was in North Dakota, I stopped at the Theodore Roosevelt National Park. I went into the cabin Roosevelt stayed in when he was exploring the West."

"Roosevelt?" Hannah needed a lesson in history more than a lesson in teddy bears.

"Theodore Roosevelt. A president of the United States at the beginning of the twentieth century. He's known as the conservation president because he preserved so many federal lands."

"What's that have to do with a stuffed bear?"

"He was a hunter, but he respected the animals he killed. Once in Mississippi he refused to kill a bear that was tied to a tree. That's where he earned the name 'Teddy.' After that, stuffed bears—they're called teddy bears—became all the rage."

"I get it. What about the turtle and the yellow jacket. That's a lot of stuffed animals for a baby." Hannah wasn't any more interested in a long dead president than she was in Will's homosexuality.

"I told you about the turtle races in Perhem. The high school mascot there is a yellowjacket, not a turtle. I almost got attacked by a swarm when I had a picnic in a park."

"Attacked by a swarm of turtles or of yellowjackets?" Hannah was trying to be clever.

"Yellowjackets. They were nesting in a tree."

"That doesn't explain why you bought stuffed animals."

The navigation voice told Connie to exit onto 172 East.

"Well?" Hannah was waiting for an explanation.

"An impulse buy," she said, hiding the hope that she'd find Nancy and Amy. "They've been keeping me company."

"Too bad you didn't buy a stuffed giraffe at the zoo."

She returned Hannah's quips with her own. "Maybe we'll find a stuffed fish at the ferry landing. Have our own zoo in the back seat."

"They can have a tea party. Talk about the olden days. It must have been scary when you were my age."

"Why?"

"People were like the character in your book. They could meet an animal in the woods and have no cell phone to call for help." Hannah opened *Secrets*. "I'm going to read a few more chapters."

Their conversation was over, but they were making progress.

The *S.S. Badger* billed itself as the last coal-fired ship in the country. Connie wondered how long before its coal would be phased out. Coal or not, the ship would cut their travel time from Wisconsin to Michigan and keep them off the highway around Chicago. She parked Last Chance in a hold that would be filled with almost two hundred cars, vans, and motorcycles. The ship felt as big as an ocean liner.

She and Hannah found lounge chairs on the front deck. As soon as they pulled into the open water of Lake Michigan her stomach began to roil. It was going to be a rough crossing. She hoped she wouldn't be as seasick as she'd been when she was Hannah's age and a friend talked her into helping him empty his lobster traps. *The Hilltop*. She still remembered the name of the boat and the turbulent ocean. She'd spent the morning throwing up over the boat's railing. At least the *Badger* was big. It could have fit twenty *Hilltops* in its hold.

"I'm cold," said Hannah who looked as green as Connie felt.

"It was so hot on shore, I'm surprised it's this cold. We can go inside." She led Hannah into a room where people were sitting at a bar snacking on popcorn and drinking whatever bar concoctions they ordered. The thought of even a beer made Connie gag. A few children were at tables with their parents playing something billed as Badger Bingo. As far as Connie could see, it was just a standard Bingo game, designed to help kids pass time on the four-hour ride. A few other children were at windows watching the waves roll by.

"It's worse in here," said Hannah.

"I'll go to the car. Do you have a sweatshirt in your suitcase?"

"In my backpack."

"Go back to where we were on deck and I'll find you." She went to the stairway that led to the hold where the cars were parked. It was blocked off. No entry to cars allowed while on board. She found the ship's gift shop and bought a hooded sweatshirt that announced S.S. Badger A Legacy on the Lake, along with a picture of the ship. She bought one without a hood for herself. They might not want to remember this crossing, but at least the sweatshirts would be warm.

When she went back onto the deck, she nearly collided with a young man who was handing out buckets to people who were seasick. He seemed to be enjoying himself. The turbulence of Lake Michigan felt as bad as that day she went lobstering. She gave Hannah the sweatshirt and picked up the bucket that was lying at Hannah's feet. She threw up into it, her own vomit landing on top of Hannah's. They should have driven around Chicago. It was going to be a long four hours.

As soon as the *S.S. Badger* left the open water and reached the dock in Ludington, Connie's stomach settled.

"Wow," said Hannah. A healthy pink had replaced the green in her face. "I'm glad we skipped lunch."

"How are your cramps?"

"Puked into the bucket. But my head still aches."

"I can give you more ibuprofen."

"I'll be okay when I get off this boat."

"You don't need to come into the hold. It will be claustrophobic down there. Go onto the shore and find the spot where the cars are coming out." Connie watched Hannah walk onto the dock and disappear around the front of the boat. She joined a line of passengers descending to their cars. Last Chance was at the back of the hold, the penalty of being early. First on, last off. She took off the sweatshirt that was too warm for the bowels of the ship. While she waited inside her car, she talked out loud to Stuart, Everett, her stuffed menagerie. "Poor Hannah. First she gets her period, then she gets seasick. Her travels with Aunt Connie won't leave her with good memories."

When she finally drove out of the boat, she expected to see Hannah waiting. She parked Last Chance, got out, and walked through groups of people who'd just gotten off. No Hannah. Her stomach cramped and the nausea she'd felt on the boat threatened to explode onto the sidewalk. She choked it down and began to ask if anyone had seen a twelve-year-old girl with blue hair. A woman taking a photo of twin girls with blond hair moved between them as if to protect them. "I'll call the police."

"Don't call," said one of the twins. "I saw her. She went into that store."

The other twin pointed to a convenience store across the street. "Mom, can we color our hair blue? Hers was really pretty."

Connie didn't wait to hear the mother's answer. She started

across the street just as Hannah came out of the store. A man was walking beside her. He wore a navy T-shirt with white letters that spelled out Boston. When she got closer, she heard Hannah say, "I'm going to Freedom, Massachusetts. It's near Boston."

"Where in Freedom? I know people who live there."

"Sha—"

Connie stopped her before she blurted out an address. "Hannah, you were supposed to wait for me."

The man touched a strand of Hannah's hair. "If I drive through Freedom, I'll watch for someone with blue hair." He fixed his dark eyes on Connie, then covered them with sunglasses and walked away.

Connie put her arm on Hannah's back and directed her onto the crosswalk. "What were you thinking of giving a stranger your grandmother's address?"

"He was nice. We started talking in the store because I said something about his Boston T-shirt."

"That's fine. But it's not fine to tell him where you live."

"It's not where I live. It's not even where I want to be going."

"Home or not, it's where we're going. Why weren't you waiting for me?" She knew she sounded hostile.

"My mouth tastes like a garbage pit. Want some?" Hannah held out a tin of breath mints.

"Thank you." She took a mint from the tin, then unlocked the car door. "When we find our hotel, we can brush our teeth, wash our faces, then find some dinner. Food will help you feel better." And maybe improve our moods, Connie thought.

The hotel was another nondescript chain. Serviceable if not fancy. Dinner had relaxed both of them. As soon as they returned to the hotel, Hannah texted Robin then fell quickly asleep. Connie looked at her blue hair against the white pillow. She didn't like it, but she knew that she'd have followed the trend when she was twelve. She'd had her Elvis Presley Duck's Ass that she always abbreviated to D.A. In the years she'd marched for Civil Rights, she'd let her hair grow enough to get it permed into an Afro. By the time she'd taken her mother to Florida, she'd cut her hair short. It had moved from brown to salt and almost pepper to full gray, a measure of the passage of time. She found her journal and began to write.

> *I should retitle my book, 'Travels with Hannah'. I'm getting an education. At first she avoided talking to me by reading Secrets and then putting on a playlist of Gospel music she'd made with her friend Robin. Eventually she warmed up and became curious about my life. She got her first period and didn't want advice from me on what to expect. Not so different from when I was her age. To talk about it was embarrassing. The boat trip across Lake Michigan didn't help. We were seasick and grumpy.*
>
> *Teenagers know so much more than I did growing up. But they're still naïve. Hannah was supposed to wait for me when she got off the S.S. Badger. Instead, she went to a convenience store and talked with a man who was wearing a Boston T-shirt. I wonder what she would have done if the T-shirt had a Q on it. This man was clean-cut, but his eyes bore into me when I stopped Hannah from giving him her grandmother's address. Those eyes felt as threatening as Mason's.*
>
> *Austin emailed me again. Mason is still missing. If he knows where Nancy and Amy are, he's not saying.*

She stopped writing and turned out the light. As she drifted into sleep, she saw the TikTok videos that Hannah showed her at dinner. A barber shaving someone, a hairdresser cutting hair into a 1920s bob, a gazillion cats and dogs, an obstacle course that looked deadly. Some of the art videos were interesting. A carving out of a watermelon of faces on Mt. Rushmore with Donald Trump added and devoured by imitation rats. Monster faces carved from pumpkins on Halloween. Hannah showed her one she and Robin had made while she was at *All the Way*. It was the most clever of all. A collage of photos Hannah had taken of animals at the zoo. One by one, she overlaid a snake on a turtle then added a lion and a gorilla and giraffe. At the end, she moved all the animal photos so they formed the petals of a daisy. Lizzie was right. Hannah was talented. Her taste would mature beyond TikTok. If she didn't become too trusting of strange men wearing Boston T-shirts.

Chapter 17

The Education of a
Maiden Aunt

The teddy bear had come alive and was urging her to go faster. When the car crunched over a turtle, a swarm of yellow jackets flew through an open window. She was pushing them away when she jolted awake. Hannah stood above her.

"You were dreaming, Aunt Connie. You kept saying 'Nancy, don't.'"

She breathed deeply to slow her heart rate before she answered. That part of her dream surfaced. Nancy had jumped out of the car and handed Amy to Mason who was beckoning her into a cornfield.

"I was dreaming about the stuffed animals in my car. I was driving through a cornfield and the stuffed animals had come alive. Except for the turtle. I ran over it."

"Poor turtle. Who's Nancy? You sounded terrified."

"My friend and I used to play with stuffed animals in her backyard. It's interesting how memories get integrated into dreams." What she said was true, though her friend's name was Roberta. "What time is it?"

Hannah picked up her phone from the nightstand between the two beds. "Six-thirteen."

Thirteen. A bad omen. She started to shiver from the sweat her dream had produced. "Let's get an early start. We can have a big breakfast. Maybe for lunch get that ice cream cone we skipped in Abbotsford. Then an early dinner in Niagara Falls. We'll have plenty of time to tour the Falls. They're all lit up at night."

"Whatever." Hannah used the sullen tone she'd had for part of yesterday.

"Do you need the bathroom before I shower?"

"I'm fine." Another phrase from yesterday. Hannah might be fine, but their relationship still had a ways to go.

Connie pulled clothes out of her suitcase to take into the bathroom. An almost teenager didn't need to see the chicken-skin body of an eighty-year-old. She went into the bathroom and let the shower rinse off the sweat her dream had produced.

When she came out of the bathroom, she expected to find Hannah hidden under the covers. Instead, she was sitting up in bed holding her cell phone. "Are you texting Robin?"

"Obviously not. We crossed a time zone on that awful boat ride. It's only five-thirty in St. Paul." Hannah got out of bed. Still holding her phone, she pulled clothes out of her suitcase and went into the bathroom leaving Connie to wonder what she'd been looking at on her phone. She remembered how Hannah had talked with the man at the ferry landing. As much as kids had been exposed to through social media, they were still kids. They might know the danger of the world, but they didn't recognize the danger on their doorstep.

She folded her pajamas into her suitcase and took out her laptop. She ignored Gmail's social and promotion tabs and looked only at the primary box. Two new messages, one from FishBarPend and one from her tenant. She opened FishBar's first.

It was from Austin.

> Gregory doesn't know it, but I heard from Nancy.
> She's safe. Forget about her now. Austin.

She hit Reply and typed in "Where is she?" She hit send before she realized that Gregory might see the return message.

Hannah came out of the bathroom and stood over her. "You old people are as bad with email as we are with text messages."

"I need to send a message to your mother." She typed in Lizzie's email address and wrote:

> We're off early, all recovered from seasickness.
> Hannah is delightful.

"You lie," said Hannah, who was looking at the messages.

"Only a little." She pointed to her screen. "One unread message. It's from my tenant. Tim." She opened the message. Hannah continued to read over her shoulder.

> Peas are harvested. Tomatoes are blossoming.
> Raccoon under control. How's the teenager? Is she
> under control? You must be getting an education.
> Bad TikTok videos. Bad music. No words, just
> grunts. You should call your book *The Education of
> a Maiden Aunt*. Write when you can.

"He sounds mean. Why do you adults hate us?"

Connie stood up from the desk where she'd been looking at her messages. "He's joking. Adults don't hate teenagers. They worry about them."

"You don't need to worry about me."

171

"I'm more interested than worried. I've been away from young people for too long. Truce. We've got a long ride today. You can listen to any music you want as long as it's not too loud. Have your passport handy. We'll be crossing through Canada."

"Passport? I need a passport?"

Connie's stomach clenched in the way it had been doing for days. "You don't have one? I told your mother you needed one."

"I'm joking. Teenagers like to tease adults." She pulled her passport out of the front pocket of her backpack.

"Maybe we can forge passports for our traveling animals. You can take the passport photos."

"I wish we thought of this in St. Paul."

"When you hadn't found my traveling companions. Too late. Time to go to Canada. With no live animals in the back seat."

They stopped in Port Huron just before the border crossing into Canada. After Connie pumped gas, they went inside to ask where they might find good ice cream. The cashier directed them to an ice cream truck near the St. Clair River. Connie must have looked dismissive because he said, "It's not one of those traveling Good Humor trucks. It's Guernsey ice cream, the best in Michigan. You can get a cone and walk along the river."

The cashier had been right. They were now walking along the St. Clair River, admiring the view and, even more, the ice cream. Connie's chocolate was dark and creamy with a hint of bitterness beneath the sweetness. Hannah bit into chunks of strawberries that dotted her choice.

A woman jogged by pushing the kind of stroller athletic mothers favored. Mothers with money and time. It was one-thirty on a Monday. Wherever Nancy was with Amy, she'd be looking for work and a place to live. Unless she had taken enough money from where she hid it at The Five Trouts. But why then had she stolen her money at the motel in Detroit Lakes? Maybe she needed more. After all, she'd sacrificed her investment in The Five Trouts when she escaped Mason and the police.

"We'd better turn around." Connie wanted to get through customs into Canada and back into the United States at Niagara Falls. She wanted to call Austin. Find out what he knew. As good as the ice cream was, it was sitting like a clump in her stomach. When they got to the car, she dropped what was left into a trash can. She needed a real meal.

When they reached the Canadian side of the Blue Water Bridge, their joke about animal passports almost became a reality. The Border Services officer motioned them to the side where another officer told them to get out of the car. He was big, the navy uniform shirt he wore pulled tight on his shoulders. He took the animals out of the backseat and poked around them as if he were an oncologist checking for cancer lumps. He carried the animals to another officer who was tending to a dog on a leash. He let the dog sniff the bear, the turtle, the yellow jacket. The dog wasn't interested.

He returned, put the animals into the car, and asked for the passports they'd already shown to the first crossing officer. "Sorry for the delay. Smugglers like to hide drugs in kids' toys. You're free to go. Have a good trip."

When they got into the car, Hannah leaned over the seat to look at the animals. "I hope he didn't hurt you. All that poking around."

Connie laughed. "You're as bad as me. Talking to the animals."

Hannah settled in the seat. "If I had friends around, I wouldn't have to talk to animals." Hannah's good mood had melted away like the ice cream Connie had only half eaten.

The drive through Canada surprised Connie. As far north as they were, the temperature had risen to a hundred degrees and as much as she cranked up the air conditioner, she could still feel hot, humid air in the car. As they passed the town of Strathroy, she started to comment on the billboard that declared it the turkey capital of Canada, but Hannah was asleep. She wondered if Canada's poultry farmers used something more humane than the packed-in cages in the United States. The fields looked much the same as they had in Wisconsin and Michigan. Industrial farming of corn and soybeans that mesmerized her for several hours. As they got closer to Niagara Falls, the towns became larger and signs pointed to exits that led to suburbs. This part of Canada was a United States' clone.

Hannah woke just a few miles before the Rainbow Bridge that they'd take to cross into the United States. "You had a good sleep," said Connie. "We're almost there."

"Almost there? Did I sleep all the way through Canada? I might never get to see it again."

"You didn't miss much." Connie had lost the idealistic notion about her friends who had moved to Canada to escape the Vietnam War. But it had been different in the 1960s. "We'll stop at the Canadian side of the Falls. When I saw that side forty years ago it was more spectacular than the American side."

She followed signs that led to a parking area, then drove through it for several minutes before a car pulled out. Kootenai Falls and Glacier National Park were crowded. Niagara Falls was insane. They got out of the car and followed signs toward a viewing area where they wedged themselves between people so they could see the panorama of the Horseshoe Falls. The mist cooled them and the roar of millions of gallons of water plunging to the pool below mitigated the noise of tourists.

"What's the boat down there?" Hannah pointed to a boat that

looked like a toy in the whirling water below the Falls.

"It's called *The Maid of the Mist*. It gets you right up to the edge of the waterfall."

"I can barely see the people. It looks like they're all in blue."

"Rain slickers. We have to get to the American side if we want to take a ride. It might be too late today, but we could skip Buffalo and get tickets for the first ride in the morning."

"No thanks. I've had enough of boats. Let's go to the American side. Maybe it's less crowded there."

As they walked back to Last Chance, two men passed them. Connie sucked in her breath when she saw a Q on their shirts. She thought the conspiracy crazies had infiltrated even into Canada until she saw that the T-shirts said Quebec and she heard them speaking French. Before they reached the car the taller one bumped into Connie. "Excuse me. Did I hurt you?" While he apologized, the shorter man walked ahead of him, passed Hannah, then stopped to wait.

"I'm fine," said Connie. She pressed the key to unlock the car.

As they were getting in, Hannah said, "I'm hungry. What's the name of that restaurant we're going to?"

"The Anchor Bar."

When they were both buckled in, Connie backed out of the parking space. The two men who had passed them were getting into a black SUV that had two bicycles in a rack on the back and a canoe on top. The men flashed them a peace sing as they drove away and toward the signs that pointed to the Rainbow Bridge.

The crossing into the United States was easier than the crossing into Canada had been. The border patrol woman simply glanced at their passports and, recognizing them as American said, "Welcome home." No poking or sniffing at stuffed animals. Being Americans coming into their home country must have helped.

Hannah looked for her phone to turn on the navigation. "My phone's not here." She fumbled around in the seat.

"Use mine. It's in my purse. Yours has to be somewhere in the car." Connie opened the center console to show Hannah where her purse was.

"Can't we look now?" She sounded panicked, her voice rising an octave.

"It's not going anywhere and there's traffic pouring off the bridge."

Hannah stopped hunting long enough to find the address for the Niagara Bed and Breakfast on Connie's phone. A voice directed them to stay on Rainbow Boulevard. She set the phone on the floor between them and wiggled around her seat to keep looking for hers. She unbuckled her seatbelt and climbed into the back of the car.

"Buckle in, Hannah. We're almost there and I'll help you look."

Hannah buckled in but continued to rummage through the back of the car. She began talking to the animals. "Where is it, Teddy?"

Through the rearview mirror, Connie could see her pressing on the animals the way the border inspector in Canada had done. "Do you think you lost it when we crossed into Canada? You were asleep after that so you wouldn't have noticed."

"You saw me. I took photos at the Falls even though most of them had people's heads showing."

The navigation system said, "Turn right onto Sixth Street." Connie obeyed the quick directions the voice spit out. Right onto Buffalo Road, left again. "You have reached your destination on your right," the voice said.

As soon as she stopped in the parking lot of the Niagara Bed and Breakfast, Hannah jumped out of the car and opened the trunk. She grabbed her backpack and started to look through it.

Connie picked up her purse and her phone and got out of the car to join her. "Relax. I'll call your phone and we'll hear the ring." She pressed Hannah's number. No ring anywhere. No voice mail.

Hannah rocked back and forth and clenched her fists. "It's gone, isn't it."

"There's no ring and no voice mail. It must be out of service range."

"I was taking photos at the Falls. There's plenty of service there." She started to cry.

Connie slipped her phone into her purse and hugged her niece, which made her cry even harder. Between sobs, Hannah choked out, "My friends. I'll be stuck in Massachusetts with no one to talk to."

Connie tried to calm her. "Let's go inside. We'll figure out something."

The walkway to the front of what had once been a Victorian mansion was lined with varieties of blooming daisies, blending whites and yellows with the pink of echinacea. Hannah put her backpack on and picked up her suitcase. Connie followed with just the small suitcase she'd been using for overnight stops. They climbed to a porch that ran the length of the building. A sign on the door read, "Please ring bell."

Hannah set her suitcase on the porch floor and bent to run her hand into the outer pocket. She stood up when a woman with hair in the coiled bun of a nineteenth-century hostess opened the door and said, "Come in."

When they stood in the entryway, the woman stared at Connie. "I recognized the name when you booked, but I never thought you'd be *the* Constance Lewis. I have copies of all your books in the parlor." She pointed to a door that led to a sitting room. "Our guests always want to leave with ones they haven't finished reading. I direct them to the Book Corner on Main Street." She looked at Hannah. "Hello, sweetheart. Is this your grandmother? You must be proud of her."

Hannah managed to say, "My aunt."

"Of course. Constance never married." The woman pointed to a table beside the doorway. "You can sign the register. Maybe later you'll sign the books I have. We have four other guests, two couples. You have the only room with two beds. If you don't see the others before breakfast, they'll be thrilled to meet you then. I serve at eight o'clock."

Hannah picked up the one set of keys on the table. "Are these to our room?"

"They are, sweetheart. The smaller one is to your room. The larger one opens the front door. I have to keep it locked. There are a lot of thieves around here. Tourists attract them. Not like it used to be."

"Where's our room?" Hannah must have realized she sounded impolite because she added, "I really need to use the bathroom."

"Up the stairs. Yours is the one at the end of the hall. You have a view of the Niagara River. Why I call this the Niagara Bed and Breakfast. I'm Lillian, by the way." Her name was as old-fashioned as her hairstyle.

Hannah carried her suitcase up a wide staircase that was fashionable in the houses of the well-to-do in the nineteenth century.

"She's in a hurry," said Lillian. "Probably needs to get on her phone. Kids these days. That's all they want to do. I have books for them in the parlor, but they never get read."

"She's upset. She lost her phone on the Canadian side of the Falls."

"Probably stolen. Canadian side's no safer than the American side." For someone who opened her home to strangers, Lillian didn't trust people.

"I'll sign those books later." Connie lifted her suitcase and climbed the stairs. She needed to figure out what to do about Hannah's phone.

Hannah had left the door to the room ajar. She was standing at the window looking at the view of the Niagara River. "That woman's awful. I'm not a sweetheart."

"Sometimes older people don't realize that it's insulting to call anyone over five 'sweetheart.'"

"You're old and you know better. I need my phone."

Connie scored one for herself. She was making lots of mistakes with Hannah, but calling her "sweetheart" wasn't one of them. "You can use mine if you want to take photos." She took her phone out of her back pocket and gave it to Hannah, thinking that she was lucky she'd left it and her purse in the car when they were at the Falls. She'd only carried her keys and forty dollars in her pockets. She checked the back pocket where she'd put her money. It was gone.

She waited for her body to relax before she spoke. "My money's not in my pocket. Someone pickpocketed us."

"I had my phone in my hand until we got close to the car. I bet it was those two guys with the bikes and canoe. Call the police. They can find them." She held the phone to Connie.

"Will you tell the phone to call the Niagara Falls New York Police Department. It never recognizes my voice."

Hannah held down the phone button and spoke clearly to the machine voice. She gave the phone to Connie when a real voice answered. "Niagara Falls Police Department. How can I help you?"

"I need to report a theft."

"One moment and I'll connect you to the right department."

A male voice answered. He listened while Connie told him about the stolen phone and the money.

"You said this happened on the Canadian side?"

"Yes. My niece had her phone until we were walking to our car. Two men passed us. One bumped into me."

"Can you describe them?"

"One tall and thin. The other one was small. Young, maybe thirty. They were driving a black SUV."

"Make?"

Connie moved her mouth away from the phone. "Hannah, do you know what make of car they were in?"

Hannah shrugged and shook her head no.

Connie spoke into the phone. "We didn't notice. They had two bicycles on the back of their car and a canoe on top."

"Not much I can do from here. The Falls are crowded. Anyone could have taken the phone and your money," the man said. "Leave me your name and number and I'll call the Canadian police. Try a Find My Phone app. Best thing to do is to call your phone carrier. If that doesn't work, cancel your number, then call your credit card company about any fraudulent charges."

"I told you. It's my niece's phone. She's twelve years old. She doesn't have a credit card."

"At least that part's lucky. Kids that age are lost without their phones." He hung up.

"Let's call your mother. Does she have one of those Find My Phone apps?"

"She'll be mad."

"I doubt it. It isn't like you lost it. We both had something stolen."

Connie took her phone from Hannah. "I'm calling."

Lizzie answered right away. "How's Niagara Falls?" She knew their itinerary.

"Crowded." Connie paused. "We had a small problem."

"What's the matter? Is Hannah okay?" She sounded panicked.

"We're fine. Her phone was stolen." When Connie finished explaining, Lizzie said, "Wait. I'll see if I can locate it." When she came back on the line, she said the last location was Crystal Beach in Canada an hour ago. "There's no ring or voice mail. Whoever stole it probably threw it into Lake Erie. How upset is she? Her phone's her lifeline."

"Here. You can talk to her." She handed the phone to Hannah, who started to cry. Connie could hear only one side of the conversation.

"It wasn't my fault. It was in my pocket. ...Will you call my friends? ...Well call their parents. Robin's anyway. They can tell Robin to tell everyone else. ...Thank you. ...I'm sorry."

She hung up and gave the phone back to Connie, who found the contact number for AT&T. After three machine voices, she managed to get a person. She struggled to understand the woman's accent, but finally managed to cancel Hannah's phone number.

Hannah was at the window, her back turned to Connie. Instead of looking at the view, she had her head down in the posture of the bereaved.

Connie brought her phone to her. "AT&T is canceling it. Was there anything important on it?"

Hannah let her know that she'd said the wrong thing. "Just my whole life. My friends will think I'm dead."

Connie handed her the phone. "Call one of them."

"Only old people know telephone numbers."

Hannah was right. Connie could still recite her parents' phone number, Sarah's, Everett's, Stuart's. She only relied on her phone for new ones.

"You could email them."

181

"No one checks email. I've been posting photos on Snapchat every day. They'll wonder when I don't put one up from today."

"Will you lose all your photos?" She knew how much they mattered to Hannah.

"They're on the cloud."

Connie never used the cloud. She preferred keeping her manuscripts on her computer and on a thumb drive. "I'll call your number. See if it got disconnected." She found Hannah's number and pressed the call button. A machine answered instantly. "The person you are trying to reach is not accepting calls at this time."

"It's disconnected," said Connie. "Even if those two guys have a dead phone, it won't do them any good. They'd need a passcode or your thumbprint to get into it. Like your mother said, they probably threw it into Lake Erie."

"It's like they threw away my life." Hannah grabbed her backpack and went into the bathroom, closing the door behind her. Connie understood how her world was collapsing. She'd started her period and had a headache and seasickness along with it. She'd lost her phone and was traveling with an old woman. It was going to be a long day tomorrow.

Chapter 18
Buffalo Memories

The Buffalo wings at The Anchor Bar were spicy and tender, but too much food after a long day of driving. They were walking now along the lighted pathway around Goat Island. A few people passed them, but the island was blessedly quiet after the daytime crowds. The Niagara River split on either side of the island. They could hear the rapids and smell the mist that kept the plants on the island lush.

"My dad would like this," said Hannah. "Except he'd complain that the path is paved."

They completed the loop around the island and headed back toward Prospect Pointe. "He's a purist," said Connie. "The Falls and this island must have been spectacular before development started. Even in the nineteenth century, there was no shortage of tourists. People would read about the Falls in travel narratives, then visit and see what the writers told them to see. We're supposed to be awed by the beauty."

They reached Prospect Pointe and joined twenty-first century tourists mesmerized by the spectacle of the Falls at night. They were lit up like a neon sign in blues, greens, purples, yellows. Behind them, the skyline of the city looked more like

Las Vegas than a natural wonder.

"I wish we could see the Falls without all these lights and all these people," said Hannah.

"We could get up at dawn and walk here before breakfast."

"Served at eight o'clock. Sweets for the sweetheart." Hannah had stopped worrying about her phone enough to make a joke.

"Want to?"

"I do. Let's go back. I'll read a few pages of *Secrets*. It will put me to sleep."

"It's that interesting?"

"I didn't mean it that way. I like the book. It's a little creepy right now. The character is alone in the woods. It made me glad there were a few people on Goat Island."

When they reached the bed and breakfast, Connie inserted the key into the lock. She resisted the urge to look behind her, remembering what Lillian had said about robberies. She was glad when the door locked behind her.

A couple in the parlor were playing some kind of board game. "Want to play something?" she asked Hannah.

"I'll just think about my phone. I want to read a few pages and fall asleep."

Connie unlocked the door to their room. She dropped her keys next to her laptop on the dressing table. "I need the bathroom. Can you wait for it?"

"Yes." Hannah flopped on the bed.

Connie went into the bathroom to use the toilet. She reached for the toilet paper and thought the direction of the roll had been changed. It rolled under instead of over. When she washed her hands, she remembered thinking about that earlier. The roll hadn't changed and she was becoming paranoid.

Hannah took her place in the bathroom and Connie quickly changed into pajamas. She took her laptop and journal to the bed and found a comfortable position with her back against the headboard. She opened the laptop, then remembered that she should use the WiFi network. The connection said 'Niagara Bed and Breakfast,' but she needed a password.

She asked Hannah, who was coming out of the bathroom, "Is the password on the dressing table?"

Hannah looked there and on the nightstand between their beds. "Not here."

"Do you mind going downstairs to ask for it so I don't have to get dressed again?"

"Can't you skip email tonight?"

"I'd rather not. It will just take you a minute. If Lillian isn't available, the couple in the parlor probably know it."

Hannah didn't reply. She closed the door hard when she left the room. Connie closed her laptop and opened her journal.

> It's been a day to forget except for excellent ice cream in Port Huron. Hannah slept through half of the drive. The Canadian border control spent a long time checking the stuffed animals for drugs as if an eighty-year-old and a teenager were likely smugglers. The Canadian side of Niagara Falls was a carnival. We didn't stay long. Just as we were leaving, someone pickpocketed us. I lost only a couple of twenty dollar bills, but Hannah's phone was stolen. Now I get to spend a last day in the car with a teenager disconnected to social media.

She heard Hannah try to open the door. It was locked. She got out of bed and let her in. "The password's 'americanfalls.' No capitals and not very original."

"Thank you. Get comfortable now and into bed." She repeated

the password to herself and went into the bathroom.

When she came out, Hannah was in her oversized T-shirt that passed for pajamas and sitting up in bed reading. "You okay, Aunt Connie? You already went to the bathroom."

"I'm fine, but I must confess I ate too many Buffalo wings. Goodnight."

She got into bed with her laptop and opened her email. Magazine and book sites. Ads for products she had once bought online and no longer needed. Nothing from Tim or anyone else in Ashland. Nothing from The Fisherman's Bar. One message from her editor, who wanted to know how the trip was going and if she was seeing enough to turn into a book. She typed a quick reply.

> I'm seeing the good and bad of America, thinking I'd like to live in a simpler past. But I know it wasn't that simple. I'm in Niagara Falls. I'll do a little research and write a chapter on how the Falls have been degraded ever since the railroad opened them to tourism. I'll figure something out so I don't sound like a bitter old woman. Actually, I'm enjoying my adventure. Most of it anyway.

She pressed send, then looked at the subject line of the unfamiliar email address to decide if it was a scam. It read, "We're OK." The address was obscure—woodpeckertree. It reminded her of the year she watched a woodpecker drilling holes into the Ponderosa Pine in front of her house in Ashland. Finally she called a tree company. The tree was dying and they had to cut it down. The memory and the subject line told her she should at least look at the email.

The message was short and unsigned.

I'm sorry I stole your money. You were good to us.
Leave us alone now. We'll be okay.

She typed a reply.

I would have given you the money. Won't you please
tell me where you are? I want to help.

She pressed send. The message bounced back as undeliverable.
She closed her laptop and closed her eyes, trying to figure out
how to trace Nancy and Amy. The email address must have been
from a public place. Nancy wouldn't risk having her own address.
It referred to a woodpecker tree. That didn't narrow it much.

She fell asleep to the memory of the woodpecker tapping
rhythmically into her Ponderosa Pine.

Her sleep was restless, disturbed by images of mothers dropping
babies over the Falls and teenagers stepping into the froth of the
Niagara River. She woke when the sky was beginning to turn
pink and shut off her alarm before it sounded. They'd miss
sunrise over the Falls, but they could walk there in the early
morning light. Hannah could sleep a few more minutes.

She showered, woke Hannah, and they walked to a viewpoint
of the Falls. The park wasn't empty, but it was less crowded. The
light flickering through the mist of the Falls and the water below
was prettier than the colored lights of the night. They stood
quietly together, listening only to the roar of a natural wonder
until the sound of a lawnmower broke the mood, a reminder of
industrial power.

They walked back to the bed and breakfast. Lillian greeted
them the moment they came inside. "Coffee's on the sideboard.

You look cold, sweetheart. Want hot chocolate?"

"I'm not a kid. Coffee's fine." Hannah wasn't a coffee drinker but at least she hadn't said she wasn't a sweetheart.

Connie was ready for coffee, but first she wanted to call The Fisherman's Bar. "I need to go upstairs for a minute. I'll meet you in the dining room." Before Hannah could protest about being left alone, she went to the stairs.

The Fisherman's Bar's phone rang for nearly a minute before Austin answered. "Fisherman's Bar. Can I help you?"

"Austin. It's Connie. Nancy emailed me yesterday from some site called woodpeckertree. Do you know where she is? Did you give her my email address?"

"Leave her be. She's taking good care of ou—her baby. They deserve a new life."

Connie used a statement, not a question. "You've been in contact."

"It doesn't matter. I don't know where she is. I just know she's okay and that Mason will never find her. I have to go. We've got customers. Put The Fisherman's Bar into that book of yours, but leave Nancy out of it." He hung up. If she had any more contact with him or Gregory, it wouldn't happen until she was writing about Lake Pend Oreille and the dollar bills on the ceiling of the bar.

They parked near the Albright-Knox Museum at the edge of Delaware Park. "This is a big park," said Connie as they got out of the car. "Let's walk a bit before we go into the gallery."

"Do you know your way?"

"I don't. We'll just follow this path and see where it takes us."

"If I had my phone, I could find a map. Can I use yours?"

Connie gave Hannah her phone. "Don't find a map. It will be fun to feel lost. But you can take photos with my camera."

They started along a path at the right side of a small lake. Hannah stopped at a rose garden and said, "This is much nicer than Niagara Falls. I can smell the roses and hear a few birds. Nature unspoiled." She began snapping pictures.

She wondered if Hannah would always manipulate her photos into art instead of wildness. "Unspoiled, but highly designed. Frederick Law Olmsted helped design Delaware Park."

"Who's he?"

"He was a famous landscape architect. Your dad will know more about him than I do. I only know that he designed many parks, including this one, Central Park in New York, and the Emerald Necklace in Boston. That one winds along the Charles River for seven miles. I used to walk there when I lived in Boston."

"You lived in Boston?"

"I did. Before I went to Florida with your great-grandmother."

"Maybe I'll go to college in Boston. Why'd this Omster guy design so many parks?"

"Parks were supposed to provide green spaces for everyone. Look at that family ahead of us. They could be rich or poor or in the middle. Any color or ethnicity. Parks are the great equalizer."

"Elliot, stay on the pathway." A mother called to a boy who looked about three years old. He was running on the grass toward a statue. "Edward, go catch him."

The father was tall, over six feet. He took a couple of long steps, picked up the boy, and put him on his shoulders. The boy was as high as the statue.

Connie and Hannah stopped to look at it. They could hear the mother. "Put Elliot down so he can see better. This is the statue I told you about. Michelangelo's David, one of only a few cast from the original."

The father lifted Elliot off his shoulders and set him down in front of the statue. "What's wrong with his wiener?" Elliot pointed to a fig leaf that hid the penis.

"You explain, Mandy," said the father.

Mandy took the boy's hand away from the fig leaf he was touching. "The statue is called David. A man name Michelangelo made it over five hundred years ago. He gave David a penis. This is a copy and the people who brought it to the park didn't want everyone to have to look at a naked body, so they covered it with this leaf. It's called a fig leaf."

"That's silly," said Elliot.

"It is," said Mandy. "But you wouldn't want to run through the park naked, would you?"

"I like to get all nakedy."

"You can do that this afternoon," said Edward. He took hold of one of Elliot's hands and Mandy took the other. They swung the boy along the path.

"Is she right?" said Hannah. "They hid David's penis with a fig leaf."

"They did. Even with the fig leaf, he's beautiful."

"Worth a photo." Hannah used Connie's phone to take some from every angle. When she finished, she said," I wish I'd gotten one of that boy on his father's shoulders. And one when he touched the fig leaf. I like little kids. Do you ever wish you had children?"

"My books are my children." Connie said what she'd said to Lizzie yesterday. She looked at Hannah and realized that she'd need to live into her nineties if another child came into the family for her to watch grow. The sight of little Elliot had triggered a sense of what she'd missed. It was too late. As long as she could walk in beautiful spaces on beautiful mornings, there'd be more joy in her life.

They crossed a bridge to the other side of the park's small lake. The path landed them in a Japanese garden with overhanging branches, dwarf maple trees, and stone paths that led through gently flowing water. Connie sat on a bench and watched Hannah take photos. She preferred wilder spaces like the ones she'd hiked with Stuart, but she could be seduced by a garden like this one. The forest was a place to live. The garden was a place to rest, to grow old, to die.

Hannah took one last picture of her sitting on the bench. She showed Connie the image she'd captured and said, "I'll call it 'Woman Remembering.'" The title was more accurate than Hannah knew.

They left the garden and walked passed the Buffalo History Museum where they could see a statue of Abraham Lincoln above the stairway on the landing in front. If they'd had time, Connie would have stopped to look more closely. She always connected Lincoln with the idea of freedom. On this, the last day of her journey to Freedom, memories rose like the title of the novel she read from in the Albright-Knox auditorium so many years ago. *Homeward Bound.* Did the title mean bound for home or bounded by home? Was she driving toward Freedom or would she return to the freedom she'd found in Ashland? She only knew that she was finding her way.

They finished the walk to the Albright-Knox. Too many memories, she told herself as she caught her breath at the top of the steps. They went inside, first into the gallery of impressionist paintings. The memory of the evening she'd read there was more vivid than the brush strokes of a Cézanne or a Monet. The red-haired woman in the audience, her little boy who pushed up the seats of the auditorium chairs when the reading was over. Everett's sister. She'd asked her to autograph a copy of *Homeward Bound* for him. She remembered the exact words she'd written, "To Everett Eaton. With fond memories. Constance Lewis." Colder even than what he'd written in the copy of *East Angels* she'd been traveling with. "Fondly, Everett Eaton."

SHARON L. DEAN

Hannah only glanced at the paintings. She wanted to look at the special exhibit of photographs done by area high school students. That gallery was small, but the photographs well-lit. They ranged from multi-colored close-ups of autumn leaves to sepia-toned pebbles to profiles in black and white. A display of digital art showed manipulated images of a girl reading a book, a cartoon of Donald Duck and Mickey Mouse, a neon rain shower.

Hannah studied a picture that looked almost like a pencil drawing of an elderly couple dancing. "My 'Woman Remembering' would fit there."

"It would. One old woman alive and dancing, the other alone and remembering."

"You sound sad."

"Just a little nostalgic. I was here forty years ago when I was driving in the other direction. Away from Massachusetts." Hannah's empathy threatened to turn nostalgia into sorrow. She tamped that down by saying, "Speaking of Massachusetts, we need to get on the road soon. Let's find a restaurant on the river front. I'll introduce you to beef on weck."

Hannah took a photo of the lunch plate they'd decided to split. A sandwich with enough roast beef for two sandwiches, a mound of potato salad, and two long slices of pickles. "What's weck mean?"

Connie put half the sandwich, most of the potato salad, and one of the pickles onto Hannah's plate. "It's a Kimmelweck roll. Basically a crusty white roll baked with salt and caraway seeds on it."

Hannah bit into the sandwich. "It's good. And enormous."

Connie finished chewing her first bite. "Even this half is too much for me after the breakfast we had."

Her stomach resisted the beef on weck, but it seemed to ignite

192

Hannah's curiosity. "What was it like driving across the country fifty years ago?"

"Forty years ago. My friend Eva was with me. It was quieter. Niagara Falls wasn't quite as overrun with tourists, there was less traffic, and if we got into any trouble, we had no cell phones to call for help."

"Was it scary?"

"Not until we got to Oregon. Eva was worried when we were on narrow roads with lots of curves. I was driving a Volkswagen we called The Yellow Submarine."

"Like the Beatles song. I like that one."

"We named my car for the color. In Oregon, the wind nearly blew us over the edge of some cliffs. It's still pretty unpopulated in that part of our country. We needed to be sure we carried water so we wouldn't get dehydrated if the car broke down. But The Yellow Sub was reliable."

Hannah finished her sandwich. "Tell me about your stops."

"I'll tell you about the interesting ones, then we need to get on the road. Want the rest of my sandwich and potato salad? I'm overfull."

Hannah accepted the food while Connie told her stories of the past. About her reading in Boise and how they'd gotten up at four o'clock to watch the wedding of Prince Charles and Lady Diana. She explained who they were and omitted what she now knew, that Gregory had attended her reading of *Homeward Bound*. She described the three fossil sites in Oregon and told her about Kam Wah Chung, the herbalist in John Day. She omitted the part about her Uncle Charlie's connection to the herbalist. When she got to Antelope and Rajneeshpuram, she omitted the temptation she'd felt to join the cult.

Hannah listened, pausing between bites of sandwich. She was as attentive as the audiences were when Connie had done her readings from *Homeward Bound*. When the waitress came with the bill, Connie said, "Enough stories. I need to start driving before I fall asleep over our empty plates."

As they walked back to the car, Connie said a silent goodbye to the Niagara River. If she drove alone back to Ashland, she'd take a different route through Pennsylvania. There was more to discover. She didn't need to repeat the past again after this trip.

The New York Thruway was long and flat. They could have been in North Dakota except for the traffic. It became more hilly as they neared the Massachusetts border. When they reached a tollbooth, Connie lowered her window to pay at the one entrance open to cars without E-Z Passes. The attendant took her money and the highway entry card she'd gotten in Buffalo. He handed her a new one for the Mass Pike and said, "You live out of the E-Z Pass zone?"

"I've been living in Oregon."

"Oregone." He mispronounced it the way she used to. "Long way from home."

"I was." She raised her window and eased Last Chance into the line of traffic. The trees she saw in the distance welcomed her.

Hannah watched out the window. "This looks like Minnesota."

"A bit. Lots of maple and oak trees, lots of lakes and rivers."

"It's not like Oregon. At least what I remember of it."

"Most of Oregon is much drier. But its trees are taller and its mountains are higher." Connie defended the state she'd learned to think of as home.

"Are you going back?"

"My roots are here. I don't know yet how deep they go." She turned her attention to the road ahead as if Last Chance could show her the way.

Chapter 19

Sarah's Freedom

The exit into Freedom led them onto a roundabout that had been constructed when Connie was sixteen and learning to drive. It was more complicated now with lights that controlled the traffic. She took the first turn-off and followed the road past the mill complex where Sarah used to live.

She pointed to the mills that had once spun cotton into cloth. "Your mother and grandmother used to live in one of those condos. There was a restaurant there the last time I visited. Cotton to Cocktails."

"It's still there." Hannah's resentment at visiting Freedom crept into her voice. "Every time we visit, Gram takes us there. She acts like she owns the place."

"She owns the buildings. Your grandfather's family owned them and your grandfather renovated them into condos and shops and a restaurant."

"Is that why Gram's rich?"

"That and the money Andy left her." Connie gripped the steering wheel as she thought about how Sarah craved luxury. Money brought her status and status brought her happiness.

They drove past the high school that was now a middle school and onto Brookside Drive where Sarah had lived for over forty years. She parked in the driveway of a ranch house surrounded with grass and trees. Everything green and manicured. Even the roses in front of the house had been dead-headed.

Sarah must have been watching at the window. As soon as they got out of the car, she walked toward them. She was still blond and thin. The V-neck on her shirt showed a touch of the cleavage Connie had one envied. Sarah hugged Hannah before she turned to Connie. "Welcome home." Her hug was tentative.

Connie hugged her harder, then pulled away and held her hand as she studied her face. It was more wrinkled than five years ago, but still beautiful. Her eyes were the same blue and even at seventy-eight she had taken care to highlight them with a touch of blue eyeshadow. Connie felt ancient next to her. Ten days of traveling had worn her out.

Sarah released Connie's hand. "Come inside. Hannah, help us with the luggage."

They unloaded the suitcases, backpacks, and cooler and set them on the ground. "Oregon wine for you," said Connie as she lifted the half case from the back. There's a charcuterie basket in the cooler from a shop in a little town in Wisconsin."

"We'll use it with the salad I made when you called to tell me you weren't arriving until eight o'clock. I'd planned for us to go to Cotton to Cocktails, but it's too late. I don't cook much." Already Connie felt like she was an inconvenience.

"We're not very hungry. Too big a lunch in Buffalo." Connie would rather eat nothing than face another restaurant meal.

"I ate most of the lunch and I'm starving." Hannah looked in the back seat. "What about bear, turtle, bee?"

Connie explained to Sarah. "Three stuffed animals. A teddy bear from Theodore Roosevelt National Park and a turtle and yellowjacket from a town in Minnesota famous for its turtle races."

"Turtle races? Weird," said Sarah. "Why'd you buy stuffed animals? Did you need company that badly?"

"I bought them for my friend Will's grandnephew." Connie reminded herself to give the animals to Will. It wouldn't be a lie.

"You can set them on the bed to keep you company. You're in the guest room. Hannah's in Lizzie's old room. When Lizzie and Mark arrive, Hannah gets to share your room. There's a pull-out ottoman we bought when Andy's family used to descend on us."

"Do you still see his family?" Connie remembered that Andy had two younger brothers. They hadn't reached high school when she and Sarah and Andy graduated.

"Not since Andy died, thank God. One brother lives in Connecticut and the other one's in the Winnipesaukee house. Andy signed over his share before he died. Said I wouldn't be going there alone."

Hannah opened the front door and went inside. Before they followed, Connie asked Sarah, "Would you have?"

"Have what?"

"Gone to Winnipesaukee alone."

"I'd never have it to myself. His brothers and their kids and now their grandkids infest the place. I'm glad I have only one child. Anyway, Andy's brother paid him his share. I have plenty of money to keep me until I die."

Connie let Sarah go into the house first. "No talk of dying. We're both healthy."

Inside, Connie noticed right away that Sarah had redecorated. Gone was anything related to Andy. His recliner, his pile of boating magazines on the coffee table, all the photos of him on the bookshelves. Even the one of Andy with Sarah in her blue wedding dress was gone. The flowered upholstery on a sofa and chairs had been replaced with the sleek lines of loveseats upholstered in a pale yellow. The bookshelves were filled with vases and statues and miniatures that Sarah had bought in Europe, but the walls were sterile, a large television screen on one, a few black and white prints framed in metal scattered on the others. Connie recognized each one as an image of Freedom, the mill that became Cotton to Cocktails, the high school they'd graduated from, Zach's where Sarah had flirted so much with George that he married her. A room that should have felt familiar and welcoming felt as cold as the air conditioning that blew through it. For the second time, Sarah seemed to have embraced widowhood, to have freed herself of anything connected to the men she'd married.

"Is it really your last one?" Sarah pointed to *Forty Years Found*, the only book on the coffee table.

"I'm working on a book about this trip. *Travels with Connie*. Something to show that an eighty-year-old woman can still have adventures." She vowed that this wouldn't be her last chance at an interesting life.

"Did you?"

"Did I what?"

"Have adventures."

"More than I can write about." Nancy and Amy would stay as hidden as their real names.

"Put your suitcases in the guest room and come outside. I'll get the wine and you can tell me about your trip."

Connie rolled her suitcases to the guest room and lifted them onto the bed. She unzipped the smaller one, took out her laptop, and checked her mail. Nothing from The Fisherman's Bar or woodpeckertree. She found a plug behind the ottoman to keep the laptop charged, then went into the bedroom where Hannah was unpacking. "Will you help me bring in the rest of the things from the car?"

Hannah pulled a bathing suit out of her suitcase. "Then can I swim? Gram has a pool."

Connie remembered Lizzie at Hannah's age. The day Sarah married Andy she was swimming and flirting while the adults ate and drank and congratulated the bride and groom. "You can ask your grandmother. She's in charge now."

"You're nicer."

"Don't say that."

"It's true."

"Never mind. Let's get everything out of the car so we can eat and you can swim."

They went outside into the humid air of a Massachusetts evening. Hannah took the cooler out of Last Chance and Connie picked up the stuffed animals, her copy of *East Angels,* and the photo of her and Stuart. Hannah carried the cooler to the kitchen while she went into the guest room. She arranged the animals on the bed and the photo and book on the dressing table. The paintings Sarah had hung on the walls were all of places in Europe she'd visited half a century ago. She spoke to the book and the photo. "Sarah had Europe, but I had both of you."

"She reminds me of Lizzie at that age." Connie was watching Hannah in the pool.

"Lizzie spent more time roughhousing with friends than swimming laps."

"You must miss her."

"I do, but I don't miss kids. You would have been a better mother than I was."

Connie was surprised at Sarah's self-awareness. "You still are a mother. Lizzie will be here for you when you need her."

"Truth is, I like being a widow with no family hovering around to check on me. I get to decide when and what I eat, what TV to watch, when to leave Zach's or Cotton to Cocktails."

"You go out alone?"

"Sometimes alone, sometimes with friends. I see a lot of Rick Reagan."

Connie remembered the name and remembered Lizzie flirting with his son the day Sarah married Andy. "I used to have a crush on him."

"Before you had a crush on George. Don't worry. I won't steal another boyfriend from you."

"Are you telling me he's your boyfriend?"

"Just someone to go out with. Like I said, I prefer living alone. How about you? How is it without Stuart?"

"Lonely even though we never lived together. This trip is helping. Except for eating and drinking too much." Connie sipped the wine she'd been nursing while Sarah poured what was left into her glass.

"I guess you don't have my metabolism."

"I don't. I was always jealous that you stayed thin. You still look great. A sophisticated older woman."

"It takes work."

Connie wanted to say that she had better things to do than dye her hair, put on make-up, and paint her nails. She watched Hannah get out of the pool, her body slim and glistening under the stars showing in the clear night sky. "I think Hannah inherited your metabolism. She ate half my meals this whole trip."

"Better my genes than yours. Do you still fight depression the way our mother did?"

"Grief, not depression. They're different. Mum had to battle depression even when there was nothing to grieve about. It's why she took Valium."

"Let's not go there." Sarah finished her wine. "I'll open another bottle."

"Please don't. I'm going to say goodnight. It's been a long day."

Connie forced down her last swallow of wine and stood up. She went over to Hannah to say goodnight.

"I'm going to bed, too," said Hannah as she got out of the pool to dry off. "At least Gram has a pool. Can we go buy a new phone tomorrow?"

"You and your grandmother can talk to your parents about it. If they say okay, I'll take you to pick one out." Connie kissed her on the cheek. "Goodnight now."

She stopped at the table to touch her cheek to Sarah's, then went into the house and her room.

She changed into pajamas and went into the bathroom, glad that the guest room had a private one. As she brushed her teeth, she studied her face in the mirror. Gray hair, gray glasses, face pale without make-up. She took off her glasses and washed her face so she didn't have to compare herself to Sarah the way she had all her life.

She found a place for her suitcases in the bedroom under the window that looked out on the front yard. She unplugged her laptop that had fully charged. With the laptop and journal next to her, she settled herself against the pillows propped against the headboard.

She opened the laptop first, hoping there'd be an email from Austin or Nancy. Nothing. She emailed her editor to tell her that she'd arrived and was ready to start writing *Travels with Connie*. She opened her journal to try to make a plan for what would be the arc of the story.

I've arrived, but where have I been? Landscapes littered with tourists and trash and industrial farms. People like Jackson Armstrong who seduce women and Mason who stalk them. Men who ask teenagers for their addresses and others who steal cell phones.

Maybe I can use this to show how the world has changed–more congestion, more people so more bad ones. But everything hasn't changed. There is still beauty in the landscape and the people. Gospel singers and bar owners who befriend strangers and ask them to tack dollar bills on the ceiling. Women in visitor centers directing people to a land they're proud of and women at historical societies proud of their communities, teenagers who die but also one who's teaching me about her world. Huckleberry ice cream, Guernsey ice cream, turtle races, buttes and rivers and lakes and waterfalls. There is still beauty in where I've been. Where am I going? I don't know yet. Right now to sleep.

She stopped writing, shut down her computer, and turned out the light.

Chapter 20

Reconnecting

They arrived at the computer store in downtown Lowell when it opened at ten o'clock. Connie remembered how she and Sarah and their mother would take a bus to Lowell and the stores would open at eight. She could still name them. Bon Marché, Pollard's, Cherry and Webb's. They'd driven passed The Acre that had been filled with Irish and French Canadians like Jack Kerouac and that now was home to immigrants from Southeast Asia, passed what had been Lowell Teachers College and was now part of the University of Massachusetts system, and entered the city where many of the working mills were now renovated into restaurants and condos.

When they reached Merrimack Street, Connie searched for a parking space. She found one behind what had been The Union National Bank and was now a restaurant closed until four o'clock. They found the computer store in the building that had housed Prince's Bookstore. She could still see the books that had lined the walls, could still sense the smell of them.

Hannah went immediately to the display of Apple phones. She'd done her homework and picked up the one she wanted. She looked at the price and put it back down.

Connie had done her homework, too. She handed the demo phone back to Hannah. "This is your birthday present. The camera in the phone will be better than in the one you lost."

"You mean the one that someone stole." Hannah began scrolling through the camera features. "Wow. This is even better than the camera I asked for. It's a little complicated but I've got two weeks to master it."

"Why just two weeks?"

"To get better before I go back to Minnesota. Look at these images." Hannah gave the phone to Connie. "Just scroll through. They're examples of what the phone can do."

Connie took the phone and scrolled. Raindrops sharply focused on flowers. Faces with different skin tones against backgrounds faded so the faces looked sharper. A panorama of a mountain with its shadow clearly visible in a lake. A figure jumping and clicking heels together above a rocky ledge, the action stopped so there was no blurring. She finished scrolling. "Let's get this bought so you can start practicing."

Hannah picked up a box packaged with a new phone inside. "They're really expensive."

"We're going to split the cost. Me, your parents, your grandmother. Don't be disappointed when you have no present to open in a couple of weeks on your birthday."

Hannah held the camera box and wrapped her arms around Connie. "Thank you, thank you, thank you."

Connie unwrapped Hannah's arms and took the box from her. "There's one condition."

"Anything."

"I need a new author photo. Something that will show me traveling."

"We can go to Gram's right now and sit you on the hood of your car."

"I might fall off."

"There's more room on the roof. Maybe you could sit there with your legs dangling over the edge."

"How about just leaning on the door? I'll wear purple to contrast with the white of the car." Connie remembered some kind of line about "When I am an old woman I shall wear purple."

"We'll buy you an outfit. Something sporty."

"Promise you'll air brush the wrinkles out."

"Wrinkles are good. They show that you've lived."

Hannah's maturity surprised Connie. She liked it, liked this grandniece of hers. "We have plenty of time. I haven't started to write the book yet. Before we go back to Gram's, we need to visit some graves."

"My grandfather's?"

Connie had to think a moment to remember that George was Lizzie's father and Hannah's grandfather. "Yes. We'll also stop at your great-grandparents' graves. Two different cemeteries. I put a trowel in the car before we left and I saw some geraniums in the store next to this one. Your grandmother probably put flowers on the graves the way we used to on Memorial Day. But we'll buy some anyway. Just from us. A team."

Sarah hadn't put flowers on George's grave. It was one of the largest gravestones in the cemetery and was positioned among some of his ancestors. Only his name was carved on it. George James Bainbridge, March 9, 1943–February 13, 1971.

"This cemetery looks like a park," said Hannah.

"It does." Connie glanced around at the oaks and maples scattered among the graves on the perfectly mowed grass. Most of the graves had flowers and many had flags that marked the deceased as a veteran. George's had neither even though he'd served in Vietnam. "Do you want to dig or shall I?"

"I'll dig while you tell me about my grandfather."

Connie gave Hannah the trowel and set a pot of red geraniums that were in full flower on top of the gravestone. "We were in school together. Mostly I remember working with him on the school newspaper. When he married your grandmother, I thought it would be forever."

Hannah read the dates on the gravestone. "1943 to 1971. He was only twenty-eight when he died."

"Not quite twenty-eight." Connie ran her finger over his name, remembering the way they'd piece together articles for the school newspaper in the years before war exploded and the world changed. "George married your grandmother before he was sent to Vietnam. When he came back, he took over the mill his family owned and renovated it into condos and a restaurant."

"The restaurant's nice. All those big windows and the brick still on the walls. Here's a flower for you, Grandpa." Hannah took the geranium out of the pot and set it into the hole she'd dug. "How did he die?"

"His truck got caught on some train tracks. It must have stalled." Connie put the responsibility on the truck, not on George.

Hannah stood up. "The flower will die if we don't water it."

Connie took the pot it had come in and found a water spigot. She set it on the ground, filled it, then picked it up and ran to the grave before all the water dripped out. "My bucket's got a hole in it," she said to Hannah. They laughed, though Connie felt the holes in her life left by George and her parents and Stuart. The longer she lived, the more people she watched die.

They started back to the car. "Can we stay longer?" said Hannah. "I want to take a photo."

"Of course. Your first photos can commemorate your ancestors." Connie watched Hannah manipulate the phone. She waited in the shade under a maple tree while Hannah took several shots.

"Come over here, Aunt Connie. Stand behind the stone and I'll take one of you."

Connie walked to the grave. She put her hands on the stone that was warming in the sun. She breathed her love into her hands and imagined it reaching George in the earth below. "Now you," she said when Hannah was satisfied with the photo.

Hannah took her place. When Connie focused the camera, she could see George's face imprinted on his granddaughter. She felt her holes filling up with a new generation.

They walked back to the car. While they drove to the cemetery where Connie's and Sarah's parents were buried, Hannah explored the camera functions on her phone and Connie watched the familiar landscape of Freedom pass by. The mill that had become Cotton to Cocktails, the stop where'd she board a bus, the school that had been new and was now the Freedom Senior Center. She could have put her car on autopilot and it would have found the graves of her parents. She parked Last Chance on the dirt road in front of the graves.

Hannah took the trowel and two geraniums from the car. "Why do we have two?"

"I'll show you." Connie stood in front of a grave that belonged to her great-grandmother. Molly Davis Anderson, 1879–1939.

"Did you know her?" Hannah set the geraniums in front of the stone.

"No. She died before I was born."

"Did you know her husband?"

"He left, my mother told us. Molly raised her and her brother Charlie alone."

"What happened to Charlie?"

"He died in Oregon. He has a daughter named Molly. She's a friend of mine." Connie thought of Oregon and how she had left Molly alone in Green Springs. They'd both be cremated, so there would be no graves like these to mark the passing of generations for girls like Hannah and the generations that would come after.

Hannah stood up and brushed off her knees. "I remember now. You told us about him when we had your birthday in Minnesota." She carried the trowel and the last geranium to a stone marked Samuel Mattson Lewis, March 4, 1912–January 24, 1973 and Hannah Anderson Lewis, January 20, 1914–May 16, 1980.

"Hannah and Sam were my parents."

"I know." Hannah set down the last geranium. "So my great-grandparents."

Connie looked at a maple tree she remembered as a sapling when she was a child putting flowers on the graves of her ancestors. It had grown to its first maturity and would have years left to grow into old age.

"Sam owned a hardware store and when he sold it, he and Hannah started to spend time in Florida." She used first names to keep from getting lost in relationships. "Your mother doesn't remember Sam, but she remembers visiting me and Hannah in Florida."

"She told me about Florida," said Hannah. "She said that's when you learned to be a writer."

"My mother and I were together in Florida for seven years. It's where I wrote my first two novels."

"*Secrets*. Is that because there's a secret about my family? Did someone get murdered?"

"Oh, no. My plot's all made up." What Connie said was true. She suspected that what she left unsaid even Lizzie didn't know.

She stood behind the grave and fingered a stone. She remembered how she'd carried it from Oregon and set it in the heart-shaped indentation on top of the granite. How familiar everything felt. This cemetery with its lichen-covered gravestones, some dating back to the seventeenth century.

Despite forty years away, the pull of family invaded her. She shook off the feeling. She wasn't ready to make a decision yet.

Hannah finished planting the last geranium. "Another photo. Actually two. One behind my great-grandparents, one in front of Molly—I guess she's my great-great grandmother. Can you kneel?"

"Of course." Connie followed Hannah's instructions. When she got up from where she knelt, she felt the kind of head rush she only got when she was sick. She held onto Molly's stone until it passed.

She laid out the clothes on the ottoman in the guest room she was learning to call home. Hannah had helped her choose them in one of the chain department stores that made her miss the old Lowell one-of-a-kind stores. Hannah recommended a long-sleeved Henley in a silky fabric with shades of purple and light gray slacks with a comfortable drawstring instead of a zipper. When she tried them on, she still felt bloated from erratic eating habits. Sarah had served them a late lunch of chicken salad from a local delicatessen. It was good, but she only managed a few bites. A dinner later at Cotton to Cocktails wouldn't help with the weight she must have gained and that always made her feel fat next to Sarah.

She propped herself against the bed's headboard and turned on her laptop. An email message from FishBarPend jumped out at her. She opened it and read.

Nancy's Five Trouts Resort will be put up for sale by the state of Oregon to recover losses from shutting down the marijuana grow. The process is complicated, but I'm buying it. If I ever find Amy when she's grown, I'll give it to her. Gregory doesn't like the idea, but he agreed when I convinced him that Amy's innocent. It has nothing to do with Nancy. Wherever they are, the police haven't found them.

If you give me your address I'll send you a photo of Nancy and Amy. I took it the first day Nancy brought the baby to the bar. She's holding a dollar bill in Amy's hand. They pinned it to the ceiling for good luck. Maybe you can use it for your book. Not the photo. Just the idea. Keep Nancy and Amy out of it.

She typed a return message.

Buying The Five Trouts is a wonderful idea. You and Gregory will be as successful running it as you are at running The Fisherman's Bar. I'd love to have the photo. Nancy showed me that people can change. Whatever kind of woman she was when she stole the money and ran instead of reporting the marijuana operation, she turned into a good mother. You can send it as an attachment, but if you want to mail it, my address here is…

After typing in Sarah's address, she pressed send. She closed her computer and closed her eyes to an image of Nancy cradling Amy against her chest. Nancy had exchanged marijuana for motherhood and grown into her better self.

She gave into a nap and woke an hour later, groggy from having slept too long. She forced herself out of bed and into the bathroom where she used the toilet, brushed her teeth, and ran a comb through her hair. Hannah could decide which glasses she should wear for the photo shoot. The ones that darkened might make her look exotic, but their tortoise shell frames might be too much.

As she dressed in the clothes Hannah had helped her choose, she scanned the room. Sarah had thought of everything for the room. Paintings of Europe on the walls, a dark blue comforter dotted with tiny flowers, matching curtains, and the ottoman with a slipcover in the same fabric. Andy had been a contractor and had designed the interior with a closet big enough to hold a suitcase, with space to hang clothes and drawers for more clothes. It saved on space so even with a queen-sized bed and a dressing table the bedroom didn't feel cramped.

The full-length mirror attached to the closet door told her that she looked better than she felt. Despite the July heat, she was glad for the long sleeves and long pants that would cover what she affectionately called her chicken skin.

She found Hannah in the back yard playing with her phone and sat on the empty chair next to her. "Have you discovered lots of things about your camera?"

"Some. I've been loading in my friends' numbers."

"I thought you didn't know them."

"I talked to my mom and told her my number. She gave me Robin's number and Robin texted my new number to all our friends. They've been texting their numbers and I've been saving them in my contacts."

"I guess you have a lot of friends."

"Only about twenty whose numbers I want. I've already heard from fourteen of them."

Hannah made Connie realize how few friends she had left in Ashland. Some had moved away to be closer to their children, others had so many health issues they could no longer hike with her. Too many, like Stuart, had died. She thought again of the holes in the flower bucket, then shook away her melancholy. She had a book to write and a photo to have taken. "Let's get the photos done," she said.

Hannah got out of the chair and put on a shirt over the bathing suit she was wearing. They walked around the house to the front where Connie had parked Last Chance in the driveway.

"Should I move the car? Park it on the road under that maple tree?"

"It's better here," said Hannah. "I'll just get you and the car. Later I'll insert a good background. What would you like? You must have taken some scenic photos."

"I'll look through my camera. Maybe one of a bridge over Kootenai Falls in Montana. Green suggests life at eighty. Falls suggest movement and adventure."

"And purple suggests royalty. Lean against the hood."

"Which glasses? The ones that darken or these with the gray frames?"

"The gray frames. They blend with your hair and go well with the purple."

Connie followed Hannah's directions for all the shots. Beside the car with her arm on the hood, against the side of the car, behind the open door with her face and shoulders forward. She even climbed on the roof and dangled her legs over the side. She knew she wouldn't choose this one, but Hannah had been so excited she had to agree to it. When she jumped off the roof, she landed hard on both feet. She might still be agile, but the drips of urine she felt reminded her that her bladder had become leaky with age. Worse since she started her trip, she realized.

Hannah gave her the phone. "Which one do you like?"

She scrolled through. "This one." She gave Hannah the phone open to the image of her behind the door, her body facing forward.

"My favorite, too. I think just you and the car and the purple that shows on your shoulders and arms is enough. The background can be a light color and the title and your name can be in purple."

"You're twelve years old, but I can see a future for you already."

"Almost thirteen," Hannah reminded her.

Hannah marked a new generation in the line of ancestors they'd talked about in the cemetery. Hers was a generation that gave Connie hope for the world.

Chapter 21

Sisterhood

The Tuesday before Mark and Lizzie were to arrive, Sarah and Connie dropped Hannah at one of the fancy houses on Crystal Lake. Lizzie had introduced her to a friend's granddaughter and the two had begun hanging out at Sarah's pool or on the beach that the developer had left when he turned the sandpit into a housing project.

As they drove out of the maze of houses with their manicured lawns, Sarah said, "I never told you, but it was Andy who developed this area. I wish he hadn't. I loved it here when we were kids."

"I met someone on my trip who said he lived in the one cottage on this lake that hadn't been renovated into a big house."

"That's impossible. I bought that cottage after Andy died. The man you met was lying."

"I found that out. He'll be in my book. I had a T-shirt once that said 'Careful or you'll end up in my novel.' He wasn't careful enough. I'll change his name and put him in *Travels with Connie*. If he reads the book, he won't like what I've done with him."

"Does that scare you?" Sarah turned onto a rutted road that led to the edge of the lake.

"The man? He was charming at first, but he wasn't dangerous."

"I meant using people's names. Aren't you afraid one of them will sue you for invading their privacy?"

"I'll disguise some names. But some of the places I stopped will like the business I can generate." She thought about The Fisherman's Bar and her promise to Austin and Gregory that she'd recommend it. Time enough to figure out how to do that without exposing Nancy. Real bar, fake motel. She was the writer. She could invent the truth and find the beauty beneath a changed and cluttered world.

Sarah pulled into the parking area next to a small cottage. "This is it. I bought the cottage because I wanted something to remind me of the old days on the lake. I didn't rent this summer because I want you to stay. Come inside. See what you think."

As they stepped through the door, Connie felt touched that Sarah wanted her to stay. The inside was a place she could feel at home in. The living area had a wall of windows looking out on the lake. Another wall had a fireplace and bookcases that were mostly empty. The room was furnished with a sofa and a recliner. Beyond, Connie could see an alcove with more windows and a table that would be perfect as a writing desk. To the left of the living room, a galley kitchen had cabinets painted an inviting yellow.

"The bedroom's here." Sarah led Connie into a small room furnished with a queen-sized bed and a bureau. "What do you think?"

Connie didn't know what she thought so she delayed answering. "Is the water running? I really need to pee."

"It is. Do what you need to, then tell me if you want to stay."

She went into the bathroom next to the bedroom. It had just enough room for a toilet, a sink, and a bathtub with a hand-held shower. When she finished, she found Sarah sitting outside on a deck. Only a single boat with a water skier behind it disturbed the quiet of a Tuesday afternoon.

"Well?" said Sarah.

"Give me a few days."

"I should warn you that the lake gets busy at times. But after Labor Day, it's like no one lives here."

"You really want me to live so close?"

"You're my sister. Whatever was between us in the past is over. I'm sorry I didn't help more with Mum. We should be together now in case one of us gets Alzheimer's like she did. Promise me you'll give me a pill and not send me to a nursing home. I'd do the same for you."

"Do you have some pills?"

"I'm working on it."

"Let's not talk about Florida. In the end I think Mum was glad to die."

"George was, too."

"What happened between us is buried."

"Not all of it."

When Sarah started to twist the diamond on her ring finger, Connie said, "That looks like the ring George gave you."

"I started wearing it after Andy died. It belonged to George's mother. I like it better than the one Andy gave me. You know I only started to date George because I knew you wanted to."

"It doesn't matter. If I hadn't gone to Florida with Mum, I wouldn't have become a writer."

Sarah stopped twisting the ring and started to tap her finger on the wooden arm of her chair. The tapping made Connie think of Nancy and woodpeckertree. She put her hand on Sarah's to stop the tapping. "I was jealous of you."

"For marrying George?"

"Long before that. You were always the pretty one. Even when we were little, people would say how cute you were with your blond curls. By the time we were teenagers, you were taller than me and had a perfect body. Thirty-six, twenty-four, thirty-four. You look like your measurements are still the same."

"I'm afraid these thirty-six breasts are drooping a bit." Sarah took her hand away from Connie and lifted up her breasts. "What you have has lasted better than what I have."

"What do you mean? I'm only two years older than you, but I've got twenty years more wrinkles."

"Wrinkles show wisdom. I'm still jealous of your brain. You were the smart one. Every time you got another honor, I'd buy myself a new outfit."

"Like that orange and white checked mini dress that you wore with those orange boots. I wanted that outfit."

"I can do you one better. I wanted the girl athlete award you won in high school. Highest average. And captain of the field hockey team."

"What I really wanted was to be a cheerleader like you."

"I wanted to work on the school newspaper."

"I wanted to be prom queen."

"I wanted to write novels."

"I wanted to go to Europe."

"Enough. I want you to stay here now."

Connie looked along the lake at the beach that was still there despite the housing development behind it. She remembered Sarah waterskiing, graceful in a 1960s version of a bikini.

Sarah read her mind. "I was always jealous that you could ski on one ski."

"It doesn't matter. We're too old for jealousy. I'll decide about the cottage in a few days. I'm going to stop in the bathroom again, then we can go back to your house until it's time to pick up Hannah."

"We've been here less than an hour and you have to go again. Don't think I haven't noticed all your bathroom trips. And how you sometimes wince like you have a pain. You might have a urinary tract infection."

"I'm okay. My system is still unsettled from traveling. And it's difficult making this decision about Freedom."

"If it's urinary tract infection, it's easy to treat and bad to ignore. I'm making an appointment for you tomorrow."

"Isn't it hard to get an opening?"

"My doctor is Rick Reagan's daughter. She always keeps an opening for emergencies."

"I wouldn't call this an emergency." Connie protested only half-heartedly. She was beginning to think something more than overeating and anxiety was happening.

She went into the bathroom. When she came out, she looked across the lake again. She'd run away fifty years ago, vowing never to come back. But now it was tempting to stay.

Chapter 22

Choices

"Well?" Sarah was in the backyard paging through a *Better Homes & Gardens* magazine when Connie sat next to her.

"It's not a UT infection." Connie settled in her chair and watched Hannah in the pool. "She's getting strong."

"She wants to swim across Crystal Lake on Saturday with Tara."

"It's nice that she made that friend. It's helped her get through these two weeks with just us."

"Unfortunately, Tara's leaving Monday for Paris. I loved Paris when I was there. Do you ever regret that you never got to Europe?"

"I was jealous of you at first, but I found a good life for myself. This trip has made me appreciate the vastness of the United States."

"I hope you've seen enough. You should stay here."

"Give me another week. Will's coming on Tuesday. He'll try to talk me into going back to Florida."

"That would be a bad choice."

Connie thought of the tests Alyson Reagan had ordered. Dr.

Reagan. How odd to meet the daughter of a high school friend who was older than she had been when she moved to Oregon. "Right now there are no bad choices. No good ones either."

"What's that mean? What did Alyson tell you?"

"It's not a UTI. More likely a response to traveling or maybe anxiety."

"Why anxiety? You've never been the anxious type."

Sarah was right. Anxiety was different than depression. "I'll be okay. Older women often have trouble, I'm not ready for bladder control medicine yet. Alyson lectured me about not having a physical for the last three years. I'm scheduled for blood tests and a mammogram on Thursday. Everything routine." The CT scan Reagan had ordered told her it was more than routine. She'd been hiding her bloated stomach and she'd seen the scale that told her she'd lost ten pounds despite the bloating. But she wasn't ready to talk or listen to Sarah's arm-chair diagnosis.

"They're here," Hannah called from the edge of the pool. She'd finished her laps and was toweling off. She dropped the towel and ran around the side yard to the front. Mark and Lizzie had arrived just in time.

She ignored her symptoms over the weekend by enjoying the added company of Mark and Lizzie. They'd driven to Kimball's where the ice cream cones were a little smaller and the crowds were bigger than they'd been when Connie and Sarah were kids. Lizzie reminded Connie of the day they'd gone there when she was about seven years old and she'd bought her a stuffed cow. On Friday Sarah had arranged a barbecue with Rick Reagan and his son who'd once been Lizzie's crush the way Rick had been Connie's. When Rick bragged about his daughter the doctor, Connie didn't mention the appointment she'd had with her.

Nostalgia turned to sadness on Saturday when they all watched Hannah swim across the lake with her friend Tara. Their goodbyes were like too many Connie remembered. Each night she'd watched Hannah asleep on the ottoman in the room they now shared. She envied the young who had so much life before them.

The days since Lizzie and Mark arrived had flown into Thursday. She waited now in a room furnished with a desk and two small upholstered chairs angled to face each other instead of waiting in a cold room on top of a paper-covered examining table. No nurse had taken her blood pressure or put her on a scale to measure her height and weight. This was going to be a consultation and she knew it wouldn't be good.

Alyson Reagan knocked, came inside, and sat on the chair facing Connie. "It's what we feared."

"Ovarian cancer." Connie said the words she'd been hiding all week from herself and her family.

"I'm sorry." Dr. Reagan became the daughter of Connie's high school crush as she reached across the gap that separated them and squeezed her hand. "I know you were friends with my father."

"Please don't tell him."

"I won't. I'm not a specialist so I won't be your doctor. We have an oncologist on-site today. Dr. Yvonne Carriel. If you like her, she'll be your doctor for future appointments."

"How much of a future will there be?"

"She'll discuss that with you. I'm sorry," she said again as she stood up to leave. She opened the door to a woman dressed in black slacks and a pink shirt that screamed breast cancer awareness. Connie would have preferred that diagnosis.

Dr. Reagan closed the door, leaving Connie alone with a doctor who carried a laptop that outlined her fate.

Dr. Carriel bent to shake Connie's hand, then sat down and opened the laptop. She looked at it for only a moment as if to collect herself before telling Connie what the records showed. "How much did Dr. Reagan discuss with you?"

"Only that it's ovarian cancer. I should have known. My stomach's been off ever since I left Oregon."

"You're from Oregon?"

"I grew up in Freedom. Dr. Reagan's father was one of my friends."

"What brings you back to Freedom?"

"The chance to drive across the country to visit my sister."

Dr. Carriel looked at her laptop. "You're eighty. Was someone with you?"

"I was alone half of the way. My sister's granddaughter has been with me since Minnesota."

"That must have been quite an adventure. How long have you lived in Oregon?"

"I've been there for forty years. I'm a writer. I'm turning this trip into a book called *Travels with Connie*."

"Will you stay here to write it?"

"It depends on what you tell me." She was finished with the game of establishing a rapport between patient and doctor.

She appreciated that Dr. Carriel was direct when she explained. "It's advanced. The tests we gave you indicate that it's metastasized. We'll need to do more tests to see what organs might be affected. We know there's fluid in your lungs, so the cancer is likely there as well as in your ovaries."

"What's my prognosis?"

"Once we know where the cancer is, we can do surgeries to remove any tumors we find."

"Surgeries? Plural?" Connie looked directly at Dr. Carriel. "Tell me the worst."

Dr. Carriel glanced down at her computer. "I'll be honest. At your age the prognosis isn't good. We'd do three rounds of chemotherapy first to shrink any tumors. Depending on how far it's spread you might need several surgeries. Ovarian cancer at this stage grows fast."

Connie studied her hands that showed the wrinkles of age. She held them together to hide their trembling. "How long do I have?"

"You've been healthy. You could be one of the eight percent who survive five years. The surgeries and the chemo will take a toll."

"If I do nothing?"

"We'd do palliative care. Regularly drain the fluid from your lungs. That will make you feel better. You'll likely have six months, maybe a little few more. At the end we can manage the pain."

Connie dug her fingernails into her palms. She felt pressure, not pain. "What do you recommend?"

"I can't answer that. You need to decide how long to fight this. And how hard." Dr. Carriel stopped a minute, then summarized the options. "More tests to locate any tumors. Depending on what we find, chemo, surgery. It won't cure the cancer. You might get a few years. Much of your time will be spent in recovery. Chemo only, you might get a year. The chemo treatments are easier than they used to be. Palliative care only, like I said, six months, maybe a little longer."

"What would you do?"

"I'm fifty-one years old. My options are different. Ask yourself what you want to do in the time you have left."

"No surgeries. I'll think about the chemo. Which choice will give me the most time feeling okay?" She unclenched her hands and shook out the fingers that she'd use to write her last book.

"Some people handle the new chemos well. You won't know unless you try. You should feel okay with weekly draining of the fluids we saw. Eventually, you'll have that done at home."

Dr. Carriel closed her laptop as if she were closing the last chapter of Connie's life. "I'll have the cancer center call you to set up an appointment. You can tell them if you want to start chemo or just come in for fluid drainage. Dr. Reagan tells me you have a good support system. That's important."

Connie imagined herself alone with Sarah who'd hover over her acting like a martyr.

Dr. Carriel stood up and touched Connie's shoulder. "Take your time before you leave. We have support groups if you want to connect with others."

Connie sat alone for a few minutes studying the area rug between the two chairs. It was a simple gray color with a few ridges that formed a geometrical pattern. Nothing too complicated for the decisions so many patients must make in this room. She knew what hers had to be. She would take six months of feeling okay and die in the town where she was born. But first she'd move to the cottage on the lake and compose the book that would capture her last journey.

Will sat with Connie outside Sarah's cottage where they watched the few boats on the lake on a Tuesday afternoon. His sandy hair had turned white, but his eyes were the same blue, their gaze sharp and unencumbered by glasses. His voice made her feel as comfortable as an old pair of jeans, well-worn and familiar. "It's a lovely cottage, but I'd rather you move back to Florida. Sid's added even more Indian dishes to his repertoire."

"How is he?" Will had visited Connie several times in Oregon, but she'd seen Will's partner only after technology had evolved to let them communicate via computer screens.

"Slower walking on the beach, but as good as ever in the kitchen. We've been together almost fifty years. Must be some kind of record for a gay couple. Monogamy helped us escape the fate of so many of our friends who died from AIDS. If you insist on staying in Freedom, at least come to Florida for a visit."

"I can't."

He put his hand on her knee. "Something's up. You didn't bring me here just to show me this cottage."

"I have ovarian cancer." It was easier to blurt the truth fast.

Without speaking, he pulled her out of her chair and into his arms. His body was as strong as she remembered it from when he'd comforted her after her mother died and her lover left. He'd helped her out of a depression so deep she couldn't even lift a pen to write. She held both his hands as they sat down again. "This is my last journey. I'm going to need you on it."

"Are you telling me it's terminal?"

"A year." She exaggerated the prognosis.

"Aren't there treatments?"

"The time they'd give me isn't worth the pain they'd put me through. I'll have a few good months. Enough to write *Travels with Connie*."

He released one of her hands and wiped his eyes. "I'll read the drafts."

"You've always been my best reader. It won't be maudlin. I want you to be sure it gets to my publisher. I also want you to be sure that I burn the journal I kept on my trip."

"I can do the first part, but why burn your journal?"

"There are things in it no one can see."

"Secrets? Did something happen to you on your trip?"

"I met someone who can't be in the book."

"Now you have me curious. One last fling?"

"God, no. I'm long past that kind of desire. I helped a woman and her baby."

"That should be a good thing to put in."

"I can't. The woman was escaping the police. She'd stolen money from one of those illegal marijuana grows that have been infesting Oregon. It was awful. Shacks with little heat. Feces all over outside. Minimum food. Wages never paid. Undocumented Central Americans afraid to come forward. To say nothing about the impact on Oregon's water supply."

She shared Nancy's details with Will. Her involvement with Mason, her baby that was probably Austin's, her escape from The Five Trouts. "I recognized her at a restaurant in Montana where Mason found her. I helped her escape again. She's safe somewhere with her baby."

"Somewhere?"

"I don't know where. She's a good mother. I want her to find a new life and raise her baby."

"If she was involved with a marijuana farm that wasn't just illegal but that kept workers prisoners in squalid conditions, why do you want to protect her?"

"I don't know her background. Why she got involved or how. But I watched her with her baby. She's a good mother." She knew she'd been repeating herself, maybe rationalizing.

"Are you mothering her? Protecting the child you never had?"

Will might be right. She hadn't examined her feelings closely, but being with Hannah made her realize what she had missed when she let books substitute for people. "You know me too well. Nancy won't be in *Travels with Connie*. Promise me that if I can't burn my journal, you will."

"We'll do it together. I'll come back here. Help you get everything in order."

"You've been more than my best reader. You've been my best

friend. We should go back to Sarah's now. Mark's barbecuing and I'm going to pretend to eat. Don't tell them about my cancer. I'm waiting until after Hannah's birthday tomorrow."

As they walked to Will's car, she stopped and took his hand. The sun was glistening on the calm lake and in the distance she could see the lone swan that had decided to live on it. "Imagine me writing in this beautiful setting. I feel like I'm coming home."

The sun was just beginning to set behind the trees that lined Sarah's back yard. The first of the mosquitoes were arriving when Will stood up and announced that he should leave. "Thank you all for welcoming me. Mark, you make a mean barbecue. Lizzie, Hannah reminds me of you when you were thirteen."

Lizzie stood up and bent to put her arms around Hannah. "I remember you when my mother married Andy."

"That was a long time ago," said Sarah as she stood up to say goodbye.

"Don't forget Teddy, Turtle, and Yellow Jacket," said Hannah. She'd spent the afternoon photographing faces to make a family collage, insisting that Will was part of the family.

"And who might those be?" said Will.

Hannah pushed her mother's hands off her shoulders and stood up. "Didn't Aunt Connie tell you? She bought stuffed animals on her trip for your great-granddaughter. Or is it grandson?"

"My brother's great-grandson. Jasper."

"There's a story behind the animals," said Hannah. "Teddy's from a national park. What is it, Aunt Connie? I forgot."

"Theodore Roosevelt National Park."

"The turtle and the yellow jacket are from a town in Minnesota where they have turtle races and so many yellow jackets they're

the high school mascot. We wanted to make passports for them."
Hannah described the crossing into Canada and the examination
of the toys.

"I'm glad the border patrol certified them as safe," said Will.
"Jasper will love them."

"Come inside and I'll give them to you." Connie led Will
into the house. She found a paper bag in Sarah's kitchen. In the
bedroom, she put just the turtle and the yellow jacket in the bag.
"I want to keep Teddy. In case I ever see Nancy again."

"You should stop worrying about her. But keep the bear. He'll
comfort you later."

She knew he meant later when the pain of cancer took over.

After they said goodbye to Will, Sarah herded them into the
screened porch where she opened another bottle of wine. She
handed Connie an envelope. "This came for you when you were
at the cottage. What's The Fishermen's Bar?"

"That's the bar I told you about with dollar bills on the ceiling."
She opened the envelope and pulled out a photo that Austin had
sent of her tacking a dollar bill to the ceiling. Behind her image
were the bar and the booth where she'd eaten. Beneath the photo
was another one of Nancy standing on a small ladder, her face
hidden. She was holding Amy toward the ceiling as if the baby
were tacking up a dollar bill. She slipped that photo back into the
envelope, understanding why Austin hadn't sent it as an email
attachment. There was something else in the envelope. It would
have to wait until she found some privacy.

Hannah looked at the photo of Connie and said, "Maybe you
can use this as a book cover. Maybe a collage of different places
you stopped." Hannah's design of the day had been collages.

"You can be my photo consultant. But right now I'm going to

excuse myself and head to bed. I want to write a few notes in my journal before I fall asleep. Thank you all for welcoming Will." She gave them each a quick hug and went to her room, hoping that she'd have a few minutes before Hannah joined her.

As soon as she got there, she looked to see what else was in the envelope. It was another envelope, thick with the single word "Connie" written on it. No return address, no postmark. She opened it and pulled out money wrapped in a piece of plain typing paper. She unfolded the paper and recognized Nancy's handwriting. The note was brief.

> *Here's the money I stole from you. I'm sorry. I need*
> *to be on my own with my baby. Don't look for us.*
> *We're okay. Thank you for helping.*
> *You're a good woman.*

The note was unsigned. She counted the money. Seven twenty dollar bills, a five, and six ones. If that was the amount Nancy had stolen, she didn't know. She found her computer and typed a quick message addressed to FishBarPend with Austin in the subject line. She phrased her message carefully in case Gregory saw the email.

> I got the photo. Unless you saw Nancy, the note
> must have reached you in another envelope. What
> was the postmark?

She pressed send. An answer came back immediately.

> It came in the mail and I destroyed the envelope. I
> don't remember the postmark. Forget this part of
> your trip. Write that book. I hope the photo helps.

Austin was probably lying about forgetting the postmark, but he was right that she should forget about Nancy and Amy. She hid the note and the photo in her suitcase so Hannah wouldn't see them, then opened her journal and began to write.

> *I want to write Dear Diary. Make this a final confession. But I have nothing to confess. My travels are over. Nancy and Amy will be erased. So will I. As soon as Lizzie and Mark and Hannah leave, I'll move to Sarah's cottage. I won't write about dying. I'll write a book about living.*

Chapter 23

In the Gold Light

Connie, Lizzie, and Hannah decided to visit Concord the day of Hannah's birthday. Hannah could photograph some of the historic sites that still looked the way they had in the nineteenth century. They stopped first at The Old Manse. Before they went inside, Hannah began photographing the vegetable garden Thoreau had planted for Hawthorne and his bride Sophia. It was flourishing with beans and summer squash and tomatoes just beginning to ripen.

When Hannah had enough garden pictures, she began to focus on the maple trees that were in full leaf in front of The Old Manse and on the river that flowed in the distance behind it. While Hannah photographed, Connie and Lizzie watched a chipmunk scurry in and out of a stone wall at the edge of the property. The wall and the chipmunk made Connie feel at home.

They went inside, paid the entrance fee, and joined the group of five just beginning the tour. When they finished with the kitchen, the parlor, and the dining room, the docent led them upstairs to the bedrooms and the room that Hawthorne had used as a study. The docent pointed to the window and said, "Sophia and Nathaniel etched these words onto the windowpane with Sophia's diamond." She read the inscription aloud.

Man's accidents are God's purposes.
Sophia A. Hawthorne 1843
Nathl Hawthorne
This is his study 1843

The smallest twig
Leans clear against the sky

Composed by my wife
and written with her diamond

Inscribed by my
husband at sunset
April 3d 1843.
In the Gold light - SAH

Hannah pointed her camera at the etching. "This is so romantic. Look outside. Grass, trees, the river. If I could go back in time, I'd live in Concord. Did they have cameras then?"

"Daguerreotypes," said the docent. "Hawthorne's novel *The House of the Seven Gables* has a character who's a daguerreotypist."

Hannah stopped photographing and asked, "Did he write it here?"

"No. He wrote stories here. They're in a book called *Mosses from an Old Manse*. He and Sophia went back to Salem when this house was no longer available for them to rent." The docent had been well-trained in the history she was expected to present, but she was ready to end the tour. "Our time's up, I'm afraid." She moved into the hallway while Connie, Lizzie, and Hannah lingered another minute in the room where the Hawthornes had begun their married life.

"Can we visit more historic places?" Hannah said as they left the room.

Thinking about more house tours exhausted Connie. "Maybe we should walk around Walden Pond instead. It's too nice a day to be inside."

"Aunt Connie looks tired," said Lizzie. "We can come back to Concord with your dad."

Hannah defended Connie. "She has more energy than I do. She likes walking."

Connie ignored her fatigue. She wanted a last walk around the pond she'd visited so many times when she was young. "I'm fine, Lizzie. And I love Walden Pond."

"What's so special about it?" said Hannah.

Connie answered before Lizzie could give the history lesson. "Henry David Thoreau wrote a book called *Walden* there. Remember when I was talking about huckleberry ice cream? Emerson called him 'the captain of a huckleberry-party.'"

"Emerson?"

"He was an essayist," said Lizzie. "You'll need to get a few years older before you like him. But you'd like *The House of the Seven Gables*."

They went to the stairway where the docent was making sure that everyone left. She looked at her watch. "Do you have any last questions before I meet the next tour group?"

"Does anyone ever see a ghost in here?" said Hannah.

"People in the nineteenth century believed in the spirit world. When they were in Europe, the Hawthornes had a governess, Ada Shepard, who was also a medium and Sophia participated in some seances with her. But no one has confessed to seeing a Hawthorne ghost." The docent led them downstairs and into the room that served as a lobby. Even the historic Old Manse hadn't escaped merchandising. But instead of trinkets, there was a generous selection of books about nineteenth century Concord and its famous inhabitants.

Hannah surveyed the shelves. "Can I buy a book about the Hawthornes?"

"I have several biographies at home," said Lizzie. "How about you just buy one of his novels to read until we go back to St. Paul?"

Hannah searched the display of books. "This one. I'll read about a daguerreotypist and learn something about nineteenth-century photography."

Connie paid for the book and said, "Happy Birthday." She was glad of the fresh air when they were back outside. She looked at the Concord River beyond them. It meandered in the same quiet direction it had when the Hawthornes etched their memories onto the window. She hoped for this kind of quiet on Crystal Lake when she wrote her own memories.

They drove the short distance to Walden Pond where they passed people sunbathing on its small beach and began their walk around the lake. Connie thought of Thoreau and the three chairs he kept in his house, "one for solitude, two for friendship, three for society." Too often she had embraced solitude. Right now she was enjoying the companionable feeling she'd had all day with Lizzie and Hannah. How many times had she and Sarah listened to their mother tell them about Thoreau and about the richness of Massachusetts history? Thoreau and the times he walked through Freedom on his sojourns, Longfellow's "one, if by land, and two, if by sea" that described the midnight ride of Paul Revere, Emerson's "rude bridge that arched the flood" in his poem about the Revolutionary War. She remembered their visits to Plimoth Plantation and how their mother talked about the faithful Indian Squanto. Now at eighty, she'd heard how much more complicated that history was, but she could still feel it in her blood.

Lizzie and Hannah had walked ahead of her and were looking in the replica of Thoreau's cabin. When she caught up to them, she pushed away the memory of Nancy and Amy in Roosevelt's cabin. Her heart was beating fast because of memory as much as from her cancer. The umbilical cord of history was pulling her back to the Massachusetts where she was born. She'd spend her last days on a lake the same size as Walden Pond, one she'd walked around hundreds of times as a kid. She'd complain about the noise of boats the way Thoreau had complained about the sound of the invading railroad. Life had changed. But the soil beneath them and the trees above still gave shelter to the birds whose songs Thoreau woke up to every morning. She'd turn her journal into *Travels with Connie* the way he'd turned his into *Walden*. In a hundred years no one would remember her name, but perhaps another Hannah would walk around Crystal Lake and learn the story of her ancestor who lived alone in a cottage and had written a book about her return home.

Lizzie came into the backyard carrying a cake with thirteen candles and a voice that started them in a chorus of Happy Birthday. When she reached the table where the others were seated, only one of the candles had lost its flame. Connie took a burning one from the cake and relit it. "No dead candle allowed." Yes, she thought, as if the candle were a symbol of her future.

Lizzie bent to hug Hannah. "Make a wish, my teenage daughter."

Hannah closed her eyes, then opened them and blew out the candles. She had to take a second breath to blow out the one that Connie had reignited. "Does that mean I don't get my wish?"

"Maybe it was already granted and is in this package." Mark moved the cake and replaced it with a present wrapped in paper designed with images of faces and cameras and the words "You're My Best Picture" scrolling among them.

Hannah untied the blue ribbon. "Where did you find paper like this?"

"I gave the paper to your mom and dad. Andy found it years ago and there was just enough paper left. He wrapped this ring in it for our thirtieth anniversary." Sarah held out her right hand to show off the gold band with a perfectly round pearl stone. "The pearl is real, not cultured."

"He had good taste," said Hannah as she carefully removed the paper. Inside was a small wooden box.

The box triggered another memory like the ones Connie had been thinking of all day. Her mother's blue box with the image of a snow-capped mountain. It had held the secret of Charlie's disappearance and led Connie to Oregon and her discovery of what happened to him.

Lizzie sat down next to Hannah. "It's to store all the photos you're going to download and print. Remember, the phone's from all of us."

Hannah picked up the phone that she'd used to take pictures of their dinner, lobsters arranged on plates before they cracked them open. "This phone is better than the camera I asked for. Now I'm glad my old phone was stolen." She aimed the camera at the cake and took another photo.

"Look in the box," said Mark.

Hannah opened the lid and took out a card. She jumped out of her chair and hugged her mother and father. "This is the best ever."

Connie reached across the table to look at a card that Mark or Lizzie must have designed. A message was bordered with images of cameras. "This entitles you to a year of lessons with Monica Mayfield." She put the card on top of the photo box and asked, "Who's Monica Mayfield?"

"Only the best photographer in St. Paul," said Hannah as she sat down.

Lizzie moved her chair closer to Mark's. "Your dad arranged it when Monica was doing a photo shoot for the zoo. He showed her some of your photos and she agreed to mentor you until you can take photography in high school."

"This is the best birthday ever." Hannah arranged her gifts on the table and stood up to photograph them and the box with the card on top.

Lizzie set two more gifts in front of Hannah. "Enough photos for now. Open these so we can have some of this cake."

Hannah sat down and opened the one from her grandmother first. A necklace with a silver chain and a small green stone.

"It's a peridot," said Sarah. "They get formed from volcanic rock and are rare. Your birthstone." She made sure Hannah knew its value. "Here, I'll put it on you."

Hannah let her grandmother fasten it and said thank you, then opened Connie's present. She beamed when she saw the leather photograph album and the postcard of Crater Lake. Connie had written on the back of the card, "An album to keep a record of your travels. I hope that one day you'll get to Crater Lake." She suspected Hannah would put photos in the album more than she'd ever wear the peridot necklace.

"I'll visit next summer. Will you take me?"

"Wherever you travel." Connie avoided saying that she would never see Crater Lake again.

"Time for dessert," said Sarah as she moved the cake in front of Hannah. "You get to cut it."

"Just let me text Robin one photograph." Hannah moved her

fingers around the phone. When she finished, she looked for a knife to cut the cake. "Something's missing."

"Plates, forks, knife, ice cream. I'll get them." Connie stood up and went into the kitchen. Before she gathered what they needed, she ran into the bathroom. As much as she loved lobster, her stomach was rebelling. She finished on the toilet and studied her face in the mirror as she washed her hands. The transition lenses in her glasses had turned clear. Behind them, her eyes looked tired. She told herself she'd be okay. She wouldn't spoil Hannah's birthday by going to bed too early.

She went into the kitchen, took the ice cream out of the freezer, and found the plates and forks and a knife. "Time to eat cake," she said as she stepped into the last of the evening sun.

Chapter 24
Embracing Moments

Connie and Lizzie were drinking coffee on the back porch, screened from the early morning mosquitoes. A hummingbird drank from a delphinium that had opened to a brilliant purple. Lizzie sipped her coffee then said, "Until I was a teenager, I used to love getting up early to watch the birds. I suppose now that Hannah's thirteen, I'll have to drag her out of bed. Why do teenagers sleep so late?"

"Biology, I'm afraid. We gave her a nice party yesterday."

"We did, but you seemed a little distracted. A little less perk in your step when we were in Concord. Are you okay?"

"I'm okay now that I've made a decision."

"About staying in my mother's cottage?"

"That and something else. I'll explain when your mother gets up." Connie watched the hummingbird move from the delphinium to a lupine hybridized to a delicate pink.

Lizzie set down her coffee mug. It showed the town seal of Freedom. "I hope you'll stay here. I'll come twice a year instead of just once. It was a good place to grow up."

"It's so much bigger than when I was a kid. We had no housing developments like this one, no mini-malls, only one

239

high school. Cotton to Cocktails was still a working mill and the only hangout place for teenagers was Zach's."

"I remember Zach's. After my dad died my mother liked to go to Zach's and flirt with Andy."

"Did you resent him?"

Lizzie picked up her mug and sipped again before she said, "No. He was a good stepfather. I think I needed his stability after the way my mother dragged me around Europe. Freedom may be different now, but it's still Freedom. Things change. Life goes on."

For some of us, thought Connie.

"You both look serious," said Sarah, who came onto the porch cradling a steaming mug of coffee.

Lizzie answered first. "We were just talking about how Freedom has changed, but is still the same. Aunt Connie's about to tell us her decision. I've been telling her to stay. That way I'll be able to see her when I visit."

Sarah sat on the wicker loveseat across from the matching chairs Connie and Lizzie were in. "Have you decided?"

Connie sat straighter in her chair. "I'll stay. Maybe Hannah will enjoy helping me decorate the cottage before you go back to Minnesota."

"I'm glad, Connie. We're sisters. We should be together now."

"There's something else." Connie picked up the coffee mug she'd set on the table and sipped. The coffee was as cold as she felt.

"You're sick," said Lizzie. "I could see that yesterday."

"What—"

Before Sarah could finish her sentence, Connie said, "I have ovarian cancer."

Sarah set her mug on the table so hard it almost shattered. "Is that what Alyson Reagan told you? She's not a cancer specialist."

"I had more than a mammogram on Thursday. I got the diagnosis Monday, from a cancer specialist."

"And you kept it hidden all this time?" Lizzie put her mug next to Sarah's. Gently, though. "No wonder you seemed tired yesterday. You should have told me. Keeping this kind of secret makes it worse."

"I didn't want to spoil Hannah's birthday. I told Will. He's going to see that I write *Travels with Connie* and that it gets to my publisher."

Sarah got out of the loveseat and stood in front of Connie. She took both her hands. "Are you telling us it's terminal?"

"It is." While Sarah continued to hold her hands, Connie explained the treatments she refused and the palliative care she accepted. She extended the prognosis to a year, enough time to finish her book. "Will you tell Mark and Hannah? I can't say this all over again."

Lizzie jumped from her chair and bent to put her cheek next to Connie's. "I'll tell them now. They'll want to get out of bed to be with you."

"Give them some time before they see me. Right now, I'd like to be alone, maybe drive around Freedom a little, remind myself that this will feel like home again."

"You shouldn't be driving," said Sarah. "I'll come with you."

"Please don't. It will be months before I can't drive." She stood up to go inside behind Lizzie, wobbly from the strain of talking about her cancer.

Lizzie hugged her tightly. "I love you, Aunt Connie."

Connie unwrapped her arms. "I love you too," she said, then went into the room where Hannah was peacefully sleeping. The teddy bear she'd brought inside lay in the closet next to *East Angels* and the photograph of her and Stuart that she'd moved when Hannah began sharing the room with her. "You'll be my traveling companions," she whispered as she found her purse and her keys. Hannah opened her eyes, said "Good morning," and rolled over onto her stomach.

She went out the front door and into Last Chance. The only drive through Freedom she wanted was to the cemetery. She found her way there and stood in front of her parents' grave. She touched the indentation where she'd placed a stone from Lithia Park so many years ago. "I'm home," she whispered. As if in answer, a child near a maple tree beyond her began chasing a robin. The image would carry her through *Travels with Connie* the way it had helped her begin *Twenty Years a Wanderer*.

Sarah, Lizzie, Hannah, and Mark had all arranged chairs outside in a circle. Mark stood up and led Connie to an empty chair. Before she sat down, Hannah jumped from her chair and hugged her tight enough she could have expelled the fluid Dr. Carriel said was in her lungs.

She sat and stopped the questions that were coming at her. "Please. Let's just enjoy the week we have left before you go back to Minnesota. Sarah, maybe you can take me to the hospital tomorrow and the rest of you can tour Salem. Find a witch to perform a voodoo ceremony and exorcize this cancer."

"Hospital?" Sarah ignored Connie's gallows humor. "I thought you were refusing treatment."

"Palliative care." She hated the words. "They're draining the fluid from my lungs and putting in a catheter so they can do it easily every week. I'll feel better after that and I'll feel better if you enjoy yourselves. Maybe another day. I'll even visit the Alcott house with you. If I hadn't been told I have cancer, I'd just think age was catching up to me. What should we do today? I don't want to mope around here while you treat me like I'm dying."

"You are dying," said Sarah.

"Pretend I'm not. It's a beautiful day. Let's drive to the coast, sit in the sand, play in the waves."

"You've lived in Oregon too long," said Sarah. "Here we say the beach, not the coast."

Mark got out of his chair. "Beach, coast, whatever. It's a good idea. Can I drive your car, Sarah? We'll all fit."

"Better Sarah's SUV than Last Chance." Connie felt the gallows humor rising again. It was going to be a long week before she could move into the cottage and away from family who had her dead and buried. A long week and a short one, too. Embrace the moment, she told herself. The moments. There were too few left.

The week proved easier than she expected. With the fluid drained from her lungs, she felt better. She'd made the trip to Concord and enjoyed the tour of the Alcott house and Hawthorne's Wayside next to it. She'd called Tim and asked him to pack up a few things that she wanted with her—clothes, books, her desktop computer and printer, her favorite blanket. The blue box that had belonged to her mother and led her to Oregon. The fern paperweight that the first of her three lovers had given her. Everything else he could sell. She asked that he drive to Green Springs and tell Molly that she was dying. She made an appointment with a lawyer to update her will so Tim could inherit the Oregon house. Sarah had enough money and Molly would have found it more a burden than a blessing. Everything else she'd will to Lizzie and, in trust, to Hannah. Except for her royalties that would continue after her death. They'd go to Will.

Though she hadn't moved in, the cottage was starting to feel like home. The refrigerator was stocked, house plants promised to thrive in every room, the bedroom closet held new clothes that Sarah had insisted she buy. They were all sitting outside the cottage now at full dark, past the sunset mosquito invasion. The calm water sparkled under the quarter moon and a star-lit sky.

"You're sure you want to stay here tonight?" said Lizzie. "I don't like to leave you alone."

"I've lived alone for forty years. I'll be fine. I'd rather say goodbye here than at Sarah's. When you get back to Minnesota, imagine me swimming laps until the weather turns to fall."

"No swimming across the lake." Mark held his wine glass toward the water in a mock toast.

"Just laps. Hannah's the long-distance swimmer. How many times did you swim across?" She ruffled Hannah's hair whose blue dye was giving way to brown roots.

"Every day since we started to fix up the cottage. Plus the time I swam across with Tara. So five." Hannah fiddled for a moment with her phone, then passed it to Connie. "Your book cover. I'll get it fixed better when I'm back home and can use my dad's computer. The background will be faint green trees. The title will go above the photo of you and Last Chance and your name will go at the bottom. Both in purple like we said."

Connie studied the image of herself leaning over the open car door. She looked happy, energized even. "It's perfect. I've loved having you with me. I have faith in your generation."

Hannah took her phone back. "I thought this vacation would be awful. But it's been good. Do we really have to leave tomorrow?" She directed her question at her parents.

"Leaving at 4:30 a.m. Time to go back and to bed." Lizzie got out of her chair and picked up the platter of cheese and the empty wine bottle. "Everyone carry something inside. We don't need to leave Aunt Connie with a mess on her first night."

They followed Lizzie's instructions. Sarah and Mark started washing the dishes while Connie went outside with Lizzie and Hannah.

"We'll call every day," said Lizzie.

"Please don't. I'll be writing. Call once a week. Sarah will keep you updated. I feel okay right now. This is my last chance to share my ideas about this country of ours."

Sarah and Mark came outside. When they'd finished with the hugs and the goodbyes, she watched them drive away. She touched the front of Last Chance, said "It's been a good run," and went inside to the place where she'd complete her journey.

Chapter 25

Travels with Connie

She watched the lake from the window in the dining alcove where she'd set up her desktop computer that had arrived. Her mother's blue box held the fine-point pens she wrote with and the fern paperweight sat on top of her stack of yellow legal pads. This would be a good work space, a good time of day. The lake was quiet and she was sheltered from the sunrise mosquitoes. She vowed to write every day until mid-morning when she'd swim, paddle the kayak that was stored at the side of the cottage. Too many afternoons would be filled with doctor appointments, visits with Sarah, trips to her parents' and George's graves that she planned to visit once a week. She'd swim again before dinner and after dinner look over what she'd written. A routine after a routineless month traveling. A routine for as long as her energy lasted.

She opened her journal and picked up her pen to take a few notes before she began *Travels with Connie*.

> *- First stop. Antelope. Barbara and Harshad. The past haunts the present.*
> *- No. Start earlier. A final walk through Lithia Park.*

Tim's promise to care for the house and shovel raccoon poop off the roof. When I finish have a section on finding Freedom. Nothing about dying.
- Fossil. Callie's choice to stay rooted to the place she calls home.
- The Old-Time Gospel Quartet. The legacy of music. It rose out of a past stained by slavery and segregation. Nostalgia selects what to remember, what to forget.
- The drive to Lake Pend Oreille. The extraordinary trees of northern Idaho.
- The power of water. Nature gets manipulated but she survives.

She stopped writing notes and avoided thinking about Nancy by typing in a dedication.

For home, wherever we find it.

She entered a page break and typed the epigraph she'd chosen.

We were born not to survive
Only to live.
—W. S. Merwin, "The River of Bees"

She entered another page break and began not in Lithia Park as she'd planned, but in the green burial plot that was Stuart's.

A field studded with the large yellow blossoms of balsam root. Mountains rising in the distance that hold onto spring's green. A grove of pines where a woodpecker taps its rhythmic notes.

"Death leaves Us homesick," wrote Emily Dickinson. I said goodbye to my partner Stuart. We'd given him a green burial in this spot months ago. It was time to move on, pack up the car I affectionately named Last Chance, and go for one more road trip, this time to the town where I was born. Freedom, Massachusetts. I was turning eighty. I needed to decide. I might have another two decades of life. Would I spend them in Ashland or in Freedom? It didn't matter. This would be an adventure, a way not to survive but to live, a way to rediscover the vast landscape we call America.

She crossed out "America," typed in "The United States," and put aside her writing. The quiet of the lake beckoned. She wanted to have her first swim before Sarah decided she had to come check on her. There was time to write the book. At least for now.

She swam back and forth the length of the cottage's shoreline, feeling strong for the first few laps. By the time she reached a tenth, she was exhausted. She knew she wouldn't improve, but she set a goal to maintain what was a quarter mile distance for the next month. When September weather turned too cool, she'd find another routine. Maybe morning hikes in the wildlife sanctuary behind the far end of the lake.

She climbed the granite step that bordered the deck, took a second step onto the deck, and picked up the towel she'd left on the picnic table. Her phone lay underneath the towel, showing a missed call. She recognized the number from The Fisherman's Bar. She dried only her hands and tapped the message. Gregory. He didn't identify himself, but she knew the voice. "Call. I have news." "I," not "we." She pressed the call-back button, afraid he was going to tell her that Austin had left, was going to find Nancy and the baby she suspected was his.

"Connie. Hang on. I'm going to take this outside where no one can hear."

She waited until the background noise of the restaurant disappeared. When he came back on the phone with a "That's better," she said, "What's wrong? Is it Austin? You said 'I' have news, not 'we.'"

"I did?"

"You did. What news?"

"It's about Nancy."

"Have you found her? Are she and Amy okay?"

"I said that wrong. It's more about Mason."

She exhaled in time with a loon that flew low over the lake near the cottage. "Did the police find him? Arrest him?"

"No need to arrest him. He's dead."

"So Nancy's free. She doesn't have to worry anymore. He can't get her or her baby."

"Stop defending her. She's more than a thief. She's a murderer."

"What are you talking about? No one was murdered at the marijuana grow."

"Just living in conditions that could have killed them. The place has been shut down and the owners are in jail."

"Mason wasn't an owner."

"He was Nancy's partner in theft. That much the Feds know." Gregory must have been standing in the alley behind the restaurant where they kept the trash barrels because his voice was drowned out by the noise of a garbage truck.

When the truck moved away, she said, "I couldn't hear what you said. How do they know Mason and Nancy planned to steal the money together?"

"One of the workers confirmed what Mason told the police before he jumped bail. The worker heard them planning. He wanted to go with them, so he kept watching the room where they kept the safe. It was only Nancy who broke in. When he approached her, she threatened him with a gun. Probably the gun she used to kill Mason."

"Wait a minute. Back up. Mason was shot? When? Where?"

"In Glendive. Some kids found his body washed up under the Bell Street Bridge on the Yellowstone River. He'd been dead for at least a month. Right around that time you gave Nancy a ride. You need to tell the police or the FBI."

She stepped off the deck and sat so she could calm herself by cooling her feet in the water. The Nancy she knew wasn't a murderer. "There must be a mistake. Why assume Nancy murdered Mason?"

"The pacifier they found in his truck. Here's Austin. He'll tell you the same thing."

Austin's voice replaced Gregory's. "It's true, Connie."

"You think she's a murderer?"

"I'm afraid I do."

"She must have been desperate."

"I'm sure she was. But what might she do with Amy if she's desperate enough? Gregory's right. You need to tell the police or the FBI."

Another heron flew across the lake. It made her think that there must be a rookery nearby. A nest. A home. "All Nancy wants is a safe home for her and her baby."

"As long as Nancy's running, Amy will never be safe. She can plead self-defense. Post-traumatic stress. She's not evil. If Mason hadn't found her here in Pend Oreille, she would have built a new life. Safe and embraced by our town."

"And by you? Are you Amy's father?"

"Why do you say that?"

"Why else would you buy a motel you don't need and put it in trust for Amy?"

"Don't speculate. If Nancy gets caught, Amy will be placed in foster care until her mother gets out of prison. She won't get sent to Nancy's abusive family. Gregory's motioning me inside. Call someone. Report where you last saw her. It's not much of a clue, though. Nancy's clever. She might be okay." He hung up.

She took her feet out of the water. They felt as numb as her heart. She pulled her knees to her chest and studied the sand under the water as she debated with herself. If she called anyone, it would be the Glendive police, not the FBI. They'd have fewer resources to find Nancy. If she didn't report Nancy's drive with her, Gregory would.

She climbed onto the deck and went into the house. Before she searched her computer for the Glendive police, she took her time getting out of her wet bathing suit. When she finally made the call, she convinced herself that she was doing the right thing. If Nancy was found, she could plead self-defense. Amy could go into foster care while Nancy served a reduced prison sentence. She used her refrain. Whatever else she was, Nancy was a good mother.

Chapter 26
Home

The days turned into weeks and into the stretch of holidays that spread from Thanksgiving into a new year. Weight fell off Connie as if in tune with the leaves falling from the trees. By the time of the first snow, she was draping a blanket over her shoulders and wearing fingerless gloves to help her stay warm while she wrote. She spent Christmas with Sarah and Rick Reagan. They gave her comfortable leisure suits in the smaller size she needed. She opened packages that Lizzie and Hannah and Mark had sent. A book filled with Minnesota jokes and a copy of *Dearly*, Margaret Atwood's collection of poetry from Mark. A hand-knit shawl from Lizzie. A manipulated photograph from Hannah that showed the two of them eating ice cream cones beside the St. Clair River. A balloon caption over Hannah read "Huckleberry?" and one over Connie read "Not if I can have chocolate." She'd given each of them a poem she'd written and had printed out on heavy stock paper. She was convinced there'd been telepathy with Hannah when she titled the one to her "Huckleberry Hannah."

On New Year's Day, she sent the last pages of *Travels with Connie* as an email attachment to Will. The message she wrote with it used the gallows humor she'd begun to practice as a way of coping.

> Attached is my Last Chance for writing, your Last Chance for critiquing. I've given up driving. Happy New Year.

Will called as soon as he received the message. "What do you mean that you've given up driving? Are you worse?"

"It's a metaphor. Driving to get this book finished. When I'm too weak to actually drive, I want you to have my car."

"I'm coming. As soon as I can book a flight."

"Not yet. Read my last chapter. Send me feedback. Come after I send the manuscript to my editor. Be honest. I still have the stamina to finish."

"I'll read it now."

"Take your time. Celebrate the new year. 'Ever the best of friends.'" She said goodbye in the way she'd been doing since August, quoting Joe to Pip in *Great Expectations*.

Will's response to the end of *Travels with Connie* came on January third. He recommended only a change to the ending. "Make it a beginning, not an ending," he'd advised. He was right. People shouldn't read this as a death knell. She thought of the epigraph, "only to live," then composed a new ending on the last page of the legal pad she'd been using.

> *Last Chance took me away from the city of Ashland that I still love. I miss walking ten minutes to see a play or driving ten minutes to hear a piano concert or walking for ten minutes to arrive at a trail that*

would take me to the Pacific Crest Trail. I miss Green Springs and Stuart, Tim and the raccoon on my roof. But it's been a good journey.

I embraced everything I saw. Eastern Oregon where a group of believers once created a community in the high desert. Last Chance led me to Fossil and bluegrass festivals, Pend Oreille and dollar bills on the ceiling of a bar, Kootenai Falls and the power of the river, Kalispell and mansions that announced the opening of the West, Glacier and Roosevelt National Parks, sunflowers in North Dakota, turtle races in Minnesota, the mighty Mississippi and the mightier Niagara Falls. I discovered a country as beautiful as it is vast.

I wasn't alone. There were gospel singers who taught me to pump gas, women in welcome centers and historical museums who shared their pride in community, young men who recommended ice cream, an older man who pretended to like me, a teenager who called themselves "they," a niece and a grandniece and a sister who welcomed me with the warm embrace of family.

This is America. These are its people. Flawed but beautiful. Home.

Will helped her out of Last Chance and she watched while he dug a hole in the February snow in front of a gravestone that announced Samuel Mattson Lewis and Hannah Anderson Lewis. They birthed her. They nurtured her. In the spring Sarah would fill a hole with her ashes and a flower that would mark her life.

"The cover won't burn," he said as he began to remove papers from her journal. "Are you sure? You really want to burn these?"

"Everything I want people to know is in *Travels with Connie.*"

"You could burn only the parts where you write about Nancy and her baby."

"I haven't the energy to find them."

"To find the pages or to find them wherever they're hiding?"

"The pages. Wherever they are, they're safe. I can feel it. Nancy will read my book. She'll recognize the dollar bill next to the one I tacked up on the Fisherman's Bar."

"Did you make that up? A bill that says trout and teddy bears?"

"The bar and the dollar bills are real. But not that one. It's a clue to tell her that I kept her secret."

"Here." Will handed her a book of matches. She struck one and lit the first page. She handed the burning paper to Will, who lit the next page. Back and forth until all the pages had been reduced to ash.

While Will shoveled snow over the ashes, she picked up the stone from Lithia Park that she always touched when she visited the grave. She kissed it, whispered "goodbye" and placed it back on the granite. Will took her arm and helped her to the car that she'd never drive again. She was ready to leave. There'd be no more Last Chances.

The end came in April in the cottage she'd learned to call home. Hannah held a book to her. A green cover with the hint of trees. A photo of a smiling woman dressed in purple and looking over the open door of a white car. Above her in purple the title *Travels with Connie.* Below her in purple the name Constance Lewis. "Do you think she sees it?"

Lizzie pulled Hannah into her arms. "She does. She opened

her eyes. She's listening to the music now." "Last Train to Glory" by the Old-Time Gospel Quartet played quietly in the room.

"You should go back to the house now. I'll stay with her." Sarah was sitting next to the bed holding her sister's hand.

They each bent to kiss Connie. Mark, Lizzie, Hannah. When she was alone with her sister, Sarah placed the teddy bear in the crook of one arm while she still held the other hand. "I'm glad you came back. I wasn't always the best sister. But I love you. I hope you've forgiven me."

Connie opened her eyes once more. She closed them. A vision of words from an Emily Dickinson poem floated through what was left of her consciousness, "…and then I could not see to see." She breathed a last breath and traveled into an empty page.

Acknowledgments

Finding Freedom begins in Ashland, Oregon, where I have found a new home. The most thanks go to my son Michael, who has allowed me to live in a house he owns, and to my daughter Emily, who has allowed me to use some of her property to plant my garden. Both of them and their families have gone beyond welcoming me to making me feel at home. Thank you as well to my family and friends who still live in New England and have seen that I keep my connections to the place I called home for so many years.

I couldn't have written this novel with the encouragement and advice of my Monday Mayhem critique group, novelists all: Carole Beers, Clive Rosengren, Jenn Ashton, and Michael Niemann. Encircle Publications has welcomed me into the fold: Eddie Vincent, Cynthia Brackett-Vincent, and Deirdre Wait. Special thanks to BJ Magnani, PhD, MD, FCAP for the medical knowledge she offered. Thank you as well to my new friend Mireya who taught me a few things about the lives of thirteen-year-olds.

Finally, thank you to the people who answered my questions about the various places where my character Connie travels and to the websites that gave me a wealth of information to work with. I've not been to all of these places. I've fictionalized some of the details and all of the characters. Writing about them helped me appreciate the diversity of places we call home.

About the Author

Sharon L. Dean grew up in Massachusetts where she was immersed in the literature of New England. She earned undergraduate and graduate degrees at the University of New Hampshire, a state she lived and taught in before moving to Oregon. Although she has given up writing scholarly books that require footnotes, she incorporates much of her academic research as background in her mysteries, and continues to write and research in the landscape she's still discovering in the Northwest.

She is also the author of the prequel to *Finding Freedom* which is entitled *Leaving Freedom*, reissued by Encircle Publications in June 2023. Sharon's mystery series featuring librarian and reluctant sleuth Deborah Strong includes *The Barn* (Encircle, 2020), *The Wicked Bible* (Encircle, 2021), and *Calderwood Cove* (Encircle, 2022). Her highly-acclaimed collection, *Six Old Women and Other Stories*, was published by Encircle in December of 2022. You can learn more at sharonldean.com, and follow Sharon L. Dean, Author, on Facebook, and @ sharonldean3 on Instagram.